The Art Of Accidents

Steve Beed

COPYRIGHT 2025©STEVE BEED

ALL RIGHTS RESERVED

ISBN:9798289661326

TO ANNIE, CAROLYN AND ALAN AND EVERYONE ELSE WHO HAS ENCOURAGED AND HELPED ME. THANK YOU.

ACKNOWLEDGEMENTS.

All characters and events in this book are fictitious; any similarity to persons living or dead is coincidental.

CHAPTER ONE

Sometimes, it felt like everything was stacked against Joe, every bit of bad luck and each misfortune was just another item to place in the evidence locker, proving that the cards of life were being dealt by a crooked dealer. He sometimes complained, quietly and to himself, that it wasn't fair, and there was a truth to this. There was another truth that he occasionally acknowledged, even more quietly, that some of his problems were his fault. He would alternate between being sanguine and angry about this, but ultimately fatalistic – it was what it was.

He was slumped on the concrete walkway outside Mike's flat. The rain, which had been stopping and starting all day, seemed to be setting in as the afternoon light faded towards evening, the wind blowing splashes over the third-floor balcony and onto the path in front of his soggy trainers. The accumulated droplets created a dark, damp patch that had begun to merge with the one his dripping clothes had created. The wetness was bisected by a set of wheel marks and footprints from where Mike's neighbour had come back earlier. Joe had moved himself and his bag out of her way and asked if she knew what time Mike might get back. She didn't. Joe shivered and wished he'd asked if he could use her loo, but only after she had disappeared inside with her pushchair and grizzly toddler. He was pretty sure she would have said yes, but it would have been awkward and made her uncomfortable, so it was probably for the best.

The jangle of keys being pulled from a pocket roused Joe from the semi-doze that he had, surprisingly, fallen into. He looked out from under his hood as Mike approached the door, rain dripping from his unruly tangle of floppy hair.

"Wakey-wakey, sleepyhead. Sorry, I kept you waiting, mate. I got held up at work."

"It's not a problem." Joe scrambled stiffly to his feet and grabbed his bag.

"Let us in, though; I'm bursting for a pee."

"It's that door on the left", Mike told him, pointing as he held the front door open for him. Joe hurried in towards the small bathroom.

Inside, the flat was not much warmer than it had been outdoors. Mike put on a small electric fan heater that gave out a thin stream of hot air that they attempted to share. Joe knew that Mike had been in the flat for several weeks now, although it was the first time Joe had visited. If he hadn't known this, he would have assumed that Mike had only just got the keys. There was minimal furniture, no curtains, and a sparse collection of belongings, mostly still in moving boxes. A worn sofa faced a TV that was hooked up to a games console, surrounded by a sea of controllers and game cases. There were stacks of DVDs taking up the floor space that wasn't already occupied. In the opposite corner was a bright red surfboard, although they lived nowhere near the sea and, to the best of Joe's knowledge, Mike had never been surfing. There were some mismatched bowls and plates piled in the kitchen sink next to two open cereal packets, a couple of still unpacked boxes, and a small pile of unopened mail addressed to the previous tenant. It wasn't much, but at least it was somewhere dry to sleep tonight.

"I hope that settee's going to be alright for you. I'll make a cup of tea. It'll have to be black, though."

The settee looked kind of small, but Joe thought he could probably pull the cushions onto the floor if he needed to. He wasn't hopeful about the possibility of bed linen, but he had a blanket stuffed into one of his bags, which would have to be enough.

"It'll be fine, thanks for letting me stay."

"No problem, it's what mates are for. You'd do the same for me."

"Course I would, but still, I appreciate it."

"Yeah, hey, can you pop out and get some milk? I hate black tea."

"No problem, shall I grab a couple of pizzas while I'm at the shop?"

"Yeah, that'd be brilliant, I'm starving."

Joe went back out, checking he still had enough money for the pizzas as he walked through the drizzle to the corner shop. When he returned, he was surprised and pleased to see that Mike had found a pile of sheets and an old sleeping bag from somewhere; they were now folded next to the end of the settee. The pizzas went into the oven, and the milk was poured into two mugs of tea, then they sat on the settee together.

"Call of Duty?" asked Mike.

"Only if you want to get beaten."

"As if," Mike replied, picking up a controller.

They spent the rest of the evening creeping through war-torn landscapes as they hunted down pixelated enemies, shooting on sight while trying to stay alive. The gaming session went on for several hours, while they were playing, Mike talked about his job at the removal company; it was paying well enough for him to afford the flat by himself, and he didn't mind the long hours. Also, they were paying for his driving lessons. Finally, he stood up, yawning and stretching.

"I'm going to turn in, busy day tomorrow. We've got two vanloads to pick up and deliver. It's furniture, all bulky, heavy, and awkward to carry. Did you want me to ask again if they need anybody else?"

"You make it sound really good. But yeah, if they need another pair of hands, let me know."

"Sure, goodnight."

Joe waited for Mike to finish in the bathroom, then turned the volume down low and carried on running, hiding, and shooting until his eyes started to droop in the early hours. He regretted this when Mike woke him in the morning, standing by the kitchen counter, he told Joe,

"I'm off to work, help yourself to anything. I've only got one door key at the moment. I'll get a spare cut today. If you do go out, I'll be back about five, okay?"

It didn't matter if it wasn't okay; he left, pulling the front door shut behind him. Now Joe was left with a dilemma: if he went out too early, he would be stuck out for the rest of the day; if he went out too late, he wouldn't get to ask around as many places as he could about jobs. He went back to sleep while he thought about it, which neatly resolved the issue for him as he didn't wake up again until after midday.

CHAPTER TWO

"I've put the chilled stuff in the fridge. Is there anything else you need?"
The woman looked up from her book,
"I think I'm okay for now, thank you, David, you're a saint."
"Anything for my little sister, how's everything going?"
"Fine, I was thinking of getting out in the garden a bit more now the weather's nicer."
She moved to stand by the window, her faded blue dressing gown draped open to reveal worn and tired-looking joggers and a stained sweatshirt. She gestured towards the small area of long grass and rampant shrubs outside the window.
"Well, don't go overdoing it, you don't want to make yourself ill again. I can get someone to come around and tidy it up a bit if you want. Anyway, I'll be off if there's nothing else."
The woman turned toward him,
"There's no need, I'll have a go at it myself."
They both knew that she wouldn't. David smiled,
"Okay, is that all?"
"Actually, there is something," she crossed the room to pick up a bulging carrier bag. "I've been making some space on my bookshelf. Could you donate these to the library or something, please?"
A brief flash of irritation crossed David's face, unnoticed by Angela.

"Of course, I'll do it on my way to work."

He took the bag from her and turned towards the door.

"Thank you, David, I would do it myself, but…you know?"

David knew the chance of Angela leaving the flat was slim to none – the same as it had been for years, since the accident. Even though the physical injuries were long gone, reduced to faded scars and an imperceptible limp. Angela told him that she sometimes went out in the garden in the evening when it was quiet, but he didn't believe her.

"It's not a problem. Do you need any new ones to replace them?"

Now Angela smiled,

"It's like you read my mind, yes, please."

"I'll see what I can do then. Have a good day."

He left the flat, throwing the bag of books onto the back seat of his BMW. He thought he'd have Courtney from reception drop them off at a charity shop and take a trip to the bookshop later. She'd have a better idea than him what books to get for his sister.

CHAPTER THREE

Joe was waiting on the balcony again, at least today it had stopped raining. He mumbled a greeting to the neighbour and smiled at her little boy as they passed. In return, she smiled back.
"Locked out again, eh?"
"Yeah, waiting for Mike."
"Well, I hope he's not too long," she replied as she steered the pushchair inside her front door.
At that moment, two texts came through on Joe's phone,
'Running late again back at 7'
'Sorry'
Joe sighed. he couldn't really complain, Mike was doing him a favour after all. But he also couldn't hang around here in the cold for nearly two hours. He returned to ground level and then walked the short distance to the row of shops, where he could at least gaze in some windows and sit in the little café with a mug of tea while he killed the time.

As he walked, he thought of the neighbour and her little boy. The woman, young with shoulder-length blonde hair, had looked slightly frazzled each time Joe had seen her. He idly wondered if there was a dad somewhere in the picture – or if she was managing life's trials alone.

When Joe was in primary school, his dad had abandoned the family home one snowy Wednesday. Or, to be more precise, he just hadn't come home. That day, he went to work and never returned. At first, Mum panicked, thinking he was caught in the snowbound traffic outside of town, and then the worrying thought that he may have come to harm set in. It didn't occur to either of them that he had decided to go and live somewhere else – with someone else. Later that night, as Joe lay listening to the non-sound of the blanket of snow outside, the phone rang. He heard it being answered, his mum's voice – angry – then the sound of crying as he tucked his head under the pillow and went to sleep. His mum never told him what had been said, and Joe didn't ask; he just accepted it as a thing that was. He didn't miss his dad's outbursts of anger anyway, nor being reprimanded for everything and anything. He certainly didn't object to the cessation of the frequent sound of the evening arguments that had often drifted up the stairs when he was in bed.

He was so deep in thought that it took him a moment to realise that the shop he was standing outside was still open. A small charity shop brimming with other people's cast-off belongings: shelves of ornaments, racks of clothes, stacks of CDs and DVDs, and a wall full of books. He stepped inside, where the slightly musty smell was easily forgiven as the waft of warm air enveloped him.

The woman with long red hair behind the counter greeted him,

"Hello, love, I was just about to lock up. I can hold on if you want."

Joe didn't want her to do that; there was nothing he needed, and he was nearly broke. But she had seemed so keen that he should have his opportunity to browse through the remnants of other people's lives that he didn't like to refuse her.

"Thanks, I won't be long."

"No problem, I'm just finishing up here, so you've got about five minutes."

Now, there was a time limit imposed Joe was not sure where to start. He glanced around, then walked to the stuffed shelves with their rows of books, each brightly coloured spine competing with the others for the privilege of being picked up. He was standing in front of them and realised that this could be a godsend; instead of draining his phone battery at the café, he could read something. Sensing the clock ticking on his allotted time, he started to scan the titles on display to see if there was anything that appealed to him. Some of the authors were familiar to him, but most weren't. He trailed his finger along the titles, stopping once or twice to take a closer look at something that looked like it could be okay, but nothing captured his interest.

Aware that his time was running out, he started to rush, hoping that he would find something if only he looked at as many books as possible. There seemed to be so many romance and spy novels, the descriptions on the backs all melding together after the first few, and who knew so many people had written entire books about how depressing their childhoods were? He didn't think they would be the right reading matter for him today, or any day, really.

There were so many it was a sensory overload. He was on the verge of giving up, thanking the lady and leaving the shop. Just then, he spotted a slim volume that he recognised, John Steinbeck's Of Mice and Men. He'd read that at school. He remembered being engrossed in it, despite it being less than cheery; it had taken him to a different place. Next to it was another book by the same author, The Grapes of Wrath. It was a good, thick book, with enough story to keep him busy for ages if he liked it. Without reading the blurb, he took it to the counter.

"Oh, good choice," said the shop lady, "I loved this. Have you read any other Steinbeck?"

"Er, no, only Of Mice and Men."

"Well, I hope you like this as much, that's fifty pence, please."

He fumbled in his pocket and produced the required coin. They both thanked each other, then she followed him to the door, ready to lock it behind him.

"Have a nice evening,"

"Thanks, you too."

It wasn't much, but it was the most interaction he'd had with anybody all day. He half wished he could have stayed and talked to the red-headed lady about books for a while, maybe she could have given him some guidance. Instead, he walked to the small café further along the arcade of shops. A faded sign above the door proclaimed it to be Stan's Place, it was near the taxi rank and bus stop; it stayed open later to catch the trade of people who were left waiting for rides home or cab drivers waiting for fares to turn up.

Inside the faded white painted walls of the café, he collected a mug of tea from the diminutive, taciturn man behind the counter who he assumed was Stan. He settled himself at a table with his book placed next to his steaming drink, ready for him to test the shop lady's recommendation. All the time, he was trying to ignore the rumbling in his stomach that the smell of cooking bacon had triggered.

When Mike rang to tell him he was back, Joe's mug was long since empty, and he was fully immersed in the commencement of Tom Joad's journey across America. He tucked a paper towel from the dispenser on the table into the book to mark his place and left for the flat.

Mike decided to turn in early that evening; he'd had a long day and needed to be in for another early start the next day.

"I'll try and get a spare key cut tomorrow, sorry I didn't get a chance today."

"No problem, I'll manage."

"Okay, help yourself to stuff, you can pay me back when you're on your feet again."

"Cheers, Mike, I really do owe you."

"No worries, goodnight."

Mike shuffled off to get ready for bed. Joe hated relying on him right now, even though he was grateful. That afternoon, he had visited as many places as he could in the hope that someone would require his skills. He would have been hard-pressed to say what they were precisely, but it didn't matter as the places that didn't give him an outright no suggested he drop his CV into them. The problem with that was that he didn't have one as such. He had started to write one, but there was precious little to go in it; padding it out with larger fonts had only got it to three-quarters of a page, and that included the headings. Anyway, even if his CV was worth anything, he didn't have enough money to print any copies off.

He was glad Mike was going to bed early; he was itching to get back to his newly acquired book and the American Midwest. He settled himself into the cushions and wrapped himself in the sheets and blankets that made up his bedding, then began to read.

A few pages from where he picked up the story, he turned the page to reveal a surprise. On the facing sheet, the text finished halfway down the page, and in the blank space was a beautiful illustration. It did not seem to represent anything. It was, nevertheless, a stunning series of swirls and eddies that coalesced into a vortex of pencil strokes. In places, he felt he could almost see the long dusty road, a horse's head, and the silhouette of a man, but when he looked closely, none of these things were properly there. They were just whispers and suggestions in the hypnotic patterns that filled the space.

He checked the front and rear covers but found no note of this being an illustrated edition, and then he turned back to the picture. He ran his fingers gently over the lines and felt faint ridges and bumps, leading him to believe that maybe somebody had drawn this in here. He thumbed through the pages of the book and found several more gaps that had been filled in a similar style to the one he had just found. All were just as detailed, emotive and beautiful as the first one he had found. For a while, he found it hard to continue reading, being compelled to turn, flick through and stare at the pictures regularly. Eventually, he left Tom, now reunited with his family and travelling West, and lay in the darkness of Mike's flat.

After his dad had left, they soon got used to his absence. They had formed a tight little unit, sticking together and weathering the storms that life sent their way. The lack of money was hard, but it just meant they had to manage without the little luxuries that his friends took for granted: new clothes, bikes, meals out, holidays – anything that would not fit their tight budget. Even though Joe complained about it sometimes, he understood, and Mum tried to make up for it in different ways. She would take him on the bus to visit the free museums in town. There were picnics in the park on sunny days and an occasional weekend trip to the seaside, where they would stay on the sand all day, dipping in and out of the sea until it was time to eat some fish and chips on the sea wall before taking the train back home. Joe enjoyed those outings and liked having Mum to himself.

In the darkness, he sniffed back his tears. It was what it was; crying wouldn't get back what he had lost.

CHAPTER FOUR

It had been a good night for Angela last night. She had waited until it was fully dark, there was no moon, and there weren't likely to be any late-night dog walkers out on the street – she'd been caught out by them before. After opening the front door and listening for a few minutes, she had been as certain as she could be that there were no people or cars around.

Leaving the front door wide open, she had taken two tentative steps along the front path, gaining her confidence before making a rush for the green wooden gate that marked the edge of her small front garden. After leaning over and looking up and down to make sure she was alone, she opened the gate with a clank that sounded enormous in the still of the night. She edged out onto the pavement and then stopped, looking around at the houses in her street. Although she could see them from her windows, they looked different from here, bigger, more life-like, without the glass screen of her window in front of them, all of them filled with unknown people. They were a source of intrigue: who was behind the dark windows? What did those people do with their days? What were their names?

As she paused and considered this, a tabby and white cat had sauntered out from behind a hedge, appearing from the shadows by her feet. For the shortest moment, they had stood and looked at one another, and then Angela had turned and bolted back into her house. She assumed that the cat had made a similar hasty retreat. Standing with her back to the closed door, she could feel her heart beating as she tried to balance the fear and the exhilaration. Sleep had been a long time coming.

Now, long after the street had been brought to life again by the rising sun, she sat in her kitchen with a mug of tea. She had recognised the cat; it was the one that lived in the house opposite, the one with the blue door. She often saw it from her upstairs window, sitting on the front wall, accepting strokes from passing strangers. When its owners' car parked in front of the house, it would spring down and follow them indoors with its tail held high as it twined around their legs, threatening to trip them with every step they took.

She wondered what the cat's name was and if maybe she should get a cat. She thought she might talk to David about it and ask for his opinion. Of course, he would probably tell her it wasn't a good idea, and he would probably be right. Still, it was a nice thought.

CHAPTER FIVE

Joe heard Mike leaving the flat. He could hardly not, given that the flat was so small. Not that Mike had been unduly noisy or clumsy; he was just in the same space as him. After Mike left, he could hear the sounds of the woman next door trying to persuade her little boy to get ready for the day. It was muted by the walls, but he could tell she was getting exasperated by the tone of her distant voice.
Being witness to everybody else's busy starts to the day made him feel guilty for still being under the covers in his boxers and tee shirt. He got up and made himself some tea in the kitchen while he decided what he should do with his day. He hoped it would end up being more productive than yesterday, as he didn't want to have to ask Mike for a loan. He decided that today he would focus on cafes, pubs, and restaurants; he was willing to do anything: washing up, peeling potatoes, scrubbing floors and toilets, if it meant he could start getting back on his feet.

When he had moved into his last place, it had been okay at first. A single room in a house shared with three other people was fine, mostly quiet apart from the muted sounds of music, TVs, and computer games that came from behind the closed doors of the other bedrooms. The only time Joe and his housemates came into contact with each other was in the kitchen, where brief, stilted conversations took place in transit. As Joe didn't cook anything complicated, most of these interactions only lasted as long as it took for the microwave to finish microwaving. Evenings were mostly spent watching TV and scrolling through his phone in his room, occasionally messaging his friends or sending unanswered texts to his mum.

It was at work that things started to go pear-shaped. One Wednesday morning, the shop had been short-staffed and the manager, 'Call Me Geoff,' had asked Joe to work on the tills. This wasn't his favourite job, and this morning, he was in a bad mood after his mum had not responded to a single one of his messages the previous evening. He had tried to get away with the minimum of interaction with the customers as he scanned their shopping and slid it down towards the end of the till. Only there was this one woman who persisted in trying to engage him in conversation, asking him to check how much things cost, getting him to double-check the labels to make sure she had the right things. All the time, she was smiling and offering snippets of information about her day, then poking her nose into his business, asking what he had been up to. It was fairly fucking obvious what he'd been up to, he'd been at bloody work. He barely managed to resist the urge to tell her that in those exact words, but the woman persisted,

"Do you think you could help me pack the bags, love? It's a bit hard with my arthritis."

He looked at the queue that was starting to form behind the old woman, then down at the small pile of shopping and let out a long sigh,

"I suppose," he grunted, throwing the items indiscriminately into two bags.

"Thank you so much, dear, you've been so helpful. Here, this is for you."

She handed him a pound coin. He took it with another grunt, glanced at it, and then put it in his pocket before turning to the next customer.

The next day, he was summoned to Geoff's office as he arrived for his shift. Geoff didn't spend much time on niceties, asking him outright,

"Did you take money from a customer?"

He'd completely forgotten about the irritating old lady by then,

"No."

"Well, Joe, I think the CCTV would suggest otherwise." He pressed a button on his computer and turned the monitor so that Joe could be reminded of his encounter with the old lady. Now he saw it, he recalled how irritated he'd been by her, how he'd just wanted her to go away. It was why he didn't like being on the till, the customers tended to annoy him. Except, on the screen in front of him, the woman looked smaller, more frail and vulnerable than he remembered. As the video clip ended, with her shuffling out of view, he felt ashamed of how short he had been with her. Watching the scene back, he now wished he hadn't been quite as grumpy with her as he had been; it wouldn't have hurt him to be nice, would it? The thought made him angry again, this time with himself.

"There it is," said Geoff, "you put whatever it was she gave you into your pocket. Now...."

"It was a bloody pound," Joe told him.

"Yes, but the store policy is..."

"I know, put it in the charity box. I'm not bloody stupid."

"I wasn't suggesting you were, it's just..."

"Well, bloody sack me then," he stood up and tried to pull off his name badge. The pin got stuck and wouldn't come undone, adding to Joe's feeling of anger at being ridiculed by Geoff.

"Nobody's going to sack anyone, I just wanted...."

Joe had crossed the room, he stood by the door and looked back,

"You can't sack me, I quit." He walked out, leaving the door swinging open behind him, and Call me Geoff left sitting in his chair, looking dumbfounded.

With no money, he quickly realised that living in a shared house was reliant on paying the rent on time. He tried to get another job but didn't find it as easy this time as he had before. By the time his most recent rent payment was due, he had a small amount of cash and an empty bank account. Rather than face the shame of being thrown out, he packed up his meagre belongings into two bags and called Mike.

As he finished his drink, he picked up the book. The temptation to start reading again was huge, but instead, he was overwhelmed by the desire to flick through and look at the beautiful illustrations once more. He was tempted to pull them out so he could look at them all side by side, but the thought of tearing up a book did not sit well with him. Instead, he used his phone to take photos of them so he could scroll through them quickly and easily.

He reluctantly put the book down for later, got dressed and started tidying Mike's flat. He was neat by nature, and he felt it was about time that Mike got his stuff unpacked and sorted. He set to work cleaning and tidying the kitchen, quickly settling into a rhythm and working his way around the rooms – not Mike's bedroom, of course, that would be wrong. After a couple of hours, he had cleaned around the dusty surfaces, unpacked the remaining boxes and found places and spaces for all the bits and pieces that made the flat look more homely. Years of practice, helping keep the flat he shared with his mum clean and tidy, had instilled good housekeeping habits in him. The only thing that still irked him was that there were no pictures on the bare walls; if it were his flat, he would have to do something about that.

Now, he sat reading and drinking tea, following some more of the Joad family's travels as they made their weary way towards their next destination. He wondered if he should try going back to Call Me Geoff and asking for his old job back; he was pretty sure some humble apologising and a bit of grovelling would do the trick. But he knew he wasn't ready for that yet. He also didn't know how he'd cope with the rejection if it didn't go to plan, he knew that keeping his temper wasn't one of his stronger character traits. Sighing, he put the book in his backpack, rinsed out his mug and set off into the world to see if he could find his fortune, or at least enough money so he could move into another house share. Even buying something for Mike to thank him would be a good start.

By mid-afternoon, he was, once again, considering going cap in hand to Call me Geoff. His efforts in gaining employment had been as dismally unsuccessful as the previous day. The weather had improved today, it was warmer and, more importantly, drier. He sat in the precinct and weighed up his options for the final part of the afternoon before Mike got back from work. Deciding that there was little else to do, he got his book out of his bag and started reading. At least, that's what he meant to do, but he kept getting pulled back to the drawings that filled the spaces between the words. Then it hit him; he could print those off to go on the wall in Mike's flat.

Putting the book away, he walked back to a print shop he had passed earlier. Inside, amongst the displays of picture frames, oversized family portraits, mugs and cushions with pictures of smiling children and family pets, he approached the counter.

"How much is it to print out pictures?" he asked the smiling, dark-haired woman behind the counter.

She gave him a price, and he blanched; his dwindling funds would take a serious hit if he paid that much. He thanked her and was turning to leave when the woman said,

"It'd be cheaper if you just did photocopies; it depends on what sort of quality you want."

"How much cheaper?"

She told him what the revised price would be, and he smiled. That was more affordable, taking his phone out of his pocket, he replied.

"That'd be perfect, can we do that?"

She walked him through the process, and a few minutes later, after some button pressing and clicks and whirs, he was ready to leave the shop with an envelope containing A4 copies of the pictures from the book. At least now, he wouldn't have to keep thumbing backwards and forwards through the pages to find them.

"Thanks," he told the woman.

"You're welcome; they're beautiful pictures, I can see why you wanted prints of them."

"They are, aren't they?" he stood by the counter and told the story of how he had come by them inside his charity shop book.

"Wow, so you don't even know who they're by?"

"Not a clue, just one of those weird things, I guess."

"You should try and find out; they're really good."

Joe paused, running this idea through his mind,

"Yeah," he answered, "I might do that. Thanks for your help."

He left the shop, wondering how he would go about tracking down the previous owner of the book.

CHAPTER SIX

After the excitement of the previous evening, Angela decided to have a quiet morning. She had things to do, but there was no rush, nothing that couldn't wait until the afternoon. Maybe she would have a little reading time or listen to the radio. She could even go back to bed for a while to do those things, although that idea felt a bit decadent now that she was already up.

She had thought over the idea of getting a cat and had almost decided against it now, predicting that it would be too much responsibility. She needed David's help just to get through her days; the idea of keeping another living creature here seemed too daunting. That didn't stop her from thinking about the cat from last night, though, the way they had managed to scare each other in the darkness seemed funny now as the sunlight came in through the kitchen window, and she sipped her tea. The fleeting contact with a living being that wasn't David, even if it wasn't human, had been oddly uplifting.

This would have been unthinkable before, even as recently as last year. Then again, so would leaving the house. Her recent forays, first into the darkened garden, then towards the street, had been becoming more frequent as she began to look outwards to the world she had shut herself away from for so long. Recently, she had been spending more and more time sitting in the upstairs room on a small wooden chair, watching the comings and goings in the street. She knew the routines of the family opposite, the one with the little girl and the cat. She knew what time people left for work and roughly when they would return. The dog walkers all had regular routines, greeting one another and trailing behind a variety of different-sized and shaped animals with a clutch of plastic bags in all weathers.

When they were children, she and David had a dog, a small brown bundle of fur called Bobbin, that would jump on their laps and lick their faces at any given opportunity. They had taken on the responsibility of walking and feeding Bobbin, sharing the tasks equally between them. Together, they had taken him to the local park, morning and evening, rain or shine, playing on the swings and slides while Bobbin ran around excitedly sniffing, peeing and barking in equal measures. Then, one day, the gate to the garden was left open, and Bobbin ran off to explore by himself.

They were bereft, of course, walking around the local street calling his name (which must have sounded ridiculous to passers-by, but what did they care?) and putting up handwritten posters on lampposts. When he was finally located by someone who had seen one of their posters, it was by the side of a busy road. Dad had to go and sort Bobbin's body out; she and David both cried for the best part of a week. After making a little shrine in the hallway with his lead and some photos, Angela had weeks of bad dreams, envisioning poor Bobbin getting crushed beneath the wheels of various vehicles. Their parents didn't agree to any more pets after Bobbin.

Angela wasn't sure if this was a happy memory or a sad one, maybe both. She knew for sure that she didn't want another dog, who would take it for walks for a start? There were probably one hundred and one other considerations that she hadn't thought of. Cats seemed altogether easier – although she had mostly decided it was not a good idea, she would keep it under consideration.

CHAPTER SEVEN

It was still too early for Joe to go back to the flat. He had checked his messages, but Mike hadn't given him any clues about what time he would be back today. He didn't fancy sitting on the cold floor of the walkway to wait again. He walked back to the row of shops, deciding he would browse the charity shop where he got the book from yesterday. Maybe he would find another mini art gallery hidden in the pages of another book if he was lucky. As he entered, the same woman from yesterday greeted him,

"Hello again, finished that book already?"

"Not quite," he smiled back, "you were right, though, it's good."

"I'm glad you're enjoying it. Let me know if I can help with anything."

"Sure, thanks," answered Joe as he reached the bookshelf and started lifting down various books and flicking through the pages.

He didn't have a system; he just lifted down random books, looking for empty spaces that had been filled with beautiful drawings. As he worked his way along the top shelf, he started to think that this had been a stupid idea. Why would there be more than one book like the one he had stumbled upon before? He was ready to call an end to his folly as he took Great Expectations down from the shelf. He flicked through with no expectations of his own – and there it was, a gorgeous series of swirls and lines that created an almost landscape. A quick look revealed at least two more pages whose blank areas had been filled with elaborate designs. He tucked the book under his arm and continued to look through the shelves.

He found one more decorated book, a copy of To Kill a Mockingbird. He took both books to the counter, where he was greeted with a smile from the red-haired woman.

"You're really going for the classics, aren't you? Good choices, though."

Joe was a little embarrassed, both because he hadn't chosen the books on their literary merits and because he hadn't read them before. He liked reading, but there just always seemed to be so many other, easier things to do. He decided he was going to read both books once he had finished Steinbeck.

"Yeah, thanks. Actually, I had a different reason for choosing them."

He paused, trying to think how he would explain about wanting the drawings. In the end, the simplest explanation seemed best.

"The book I got yesterday had drawings in it."

"Oh no, I'm so sorry. Do you want a refund?"

"No, no, nothing like that. The pictures are gorgeous; I just came in to see if there were any more."

He patted the two books he had placed on the counter and smiled,

"I found some."

Picking up the top book, he flicked through to the first piece of artwork and showed it to the woman. She took it off him and examined it closely, running her fingertips over it as Joe had yesterday to ensure it was not part of the design, even though she knew it wasn't.

"It is stunning," she smiled, "good find."

"Thanks."

"I want one for myself now. I'm going to have to look through all the books until I find one unless you've taken them all."

Joe blushed,

"Here, you can have one of these."

"No, you take them. I'll be glad to have a little mission to distract when it's slow in here."

"If you're sure, I don't want to be greedy."

"Really, it's fine. You have them – they are wonderful, though."

"They are," a thought occurred to Joe, "do you have any picture frames?"

The woman laughed,

"I've got a whole box of them out the back; we can't sell them at any price. What size are you looking for?"

Joe took the photocopies out of their envelope and put them on the counter next to his books,

"Big enough for these."

"Oh, are these the ones from the book you got yesterday?"

"Yes, I got them printed to go on the wall at my mate's flat. He's just moved in."

"What a lovely idea, hang on, I'll go and look. By the way, my name's Janet."

"Joe," said Joe, "it's nice to meet you, and thanks."

Janet went back into the back room, returning moments later with a box full of picture frames as promised. At that moment, the door opened, and a young woman started to fight her way in with a pushchair in hand and a toddler in tow. Joe stepped over to hold the door for her, and Janet greeted her with an offer of help. She then joined the new customer in the quest for suitable children's toys and shoes. One a bribe to gain cooperation for the other, Joe guessed. He flicked through the frames, looking at old prints of pastoral scenes and faded cartoon figures smiling and waving.

He finally settled on a selection of empty frames that were almost perfect A4 size; he moved them to one side as the new customer came to the counter to pay for her purchases. After she had finished, Joe returned to hold the door for her once more. As it closed, he turned back to see that Janet had started unclipping the back of the frames, ready to put the pictures in.

"There's no need to do that, thanks."

"It's no problem, just as well to get it done here, then they'll be ready for your friend."

"Thanks, here I'll help."

Together, they got the pictures assembled in the frames; Joe thought they looked stunning. He hoped Mike would like them. It wasn't much, but it was something.

"Do you live nearby?" Janet asked.

"Yeah, well, at the moment. I'm staying with a friend while I get back on my feet. I lost my job."

He didn't hint at his part in his downfall; some things are hard to share.

"Oh no, that's awful. He sounds like a good friend."

"He is."

He reflected on the truth of this, Mike had agreed to Joe staying without a moment's hesitation. There may have been some sympathy involved; he'd been friends with Mike since they were at primary school together, and Mike knew what had happened with Trevor when they were near the end of their schooling.

"I've known him for a long time."

"What sort of job are you looking for?"

"Anything, anything at all. I don't want to have to start signing on."

Janet took a pen out of the pot on the counter and started writing something on a piece of paper.

"You seem like a pleasant young man; anyone who reads Steinbeck can't be all bad. I've got a friend who's looking for someone to help out for a bit. Give this number a call and ask for Tom. Tell him Janet said to ring."

Joe took the offered piece of paper. He was taken by surprise and didn't know what to say,

"Thank you, thanks very much."

"You're welcome; I'll let him know you're going to call, shall I?"

"No, that's okay, I'll ring him first thing tomorrow."

Just then, Joe's phone chimed, it was a message from Mike saying he was home. Another customer came into the shop, Joe collected his pictures, thanked Janet and left.

Back at the flat, Mike proudly presented Joe with a key,

"I had it cut in my lunch break. Now you won't have to sit out on the balcony in the rain."

Joe smiled,

"Here, I got something for you, too."

He presented the framed photocopies to Mike,

"I thought the walls were a bit bare."

"Thanks, mate. Wow, these are great, where did you get them?"

As they made some tea and found some food, Joe told him the story of the book he'd bought and everything that happened afterwards.

"That is so random. So you've got no idea who drew them?"

"Not a clue, but the other good thing that came out of it is I might have got a job."

"That's great news, what doing?"

"I don't know yet, I've just got a number to call."

"Well, I hope that comes off. But you're still welcome to stay as long as you like."

"I know, thanks. I just don't want to have to ask Trevor for anything; you know how it is?"

Trevor was Joe's mum's new husband. They'd got on fine when he was just her boyfriend, but when things started to get more serious with Trevor and Mum, it had changed. Trevor had two children, twins, from his first marriage. Joe had assumed that they would find a bigger place if they wanted to move in together, wrongly, as it turned out. Trev and Mum had sat him down one evening and told him that Trevor would be moving in before they got married.

"The thing is," Trevor said, "there won't be room for all of us and the twins."

Joe couldn't see where the conversation was going or what was expected of him here. Trevor smiled and continued,

"We thought it would be good for you to have some independence and get a place of your own."

"But I'm in the middle of my exams. Mum, are you kicking me out?"

"No," she assured him, "you'll always be welcome here, there's just not enough space for us all to live together."

"I've already found you a place," Trevor supplied helpfully, "it's all paid up, and we'll pay the rent for you while you're still at school. We'll give you a food allowance as well."

And that was it; it had all been decided. Joe was moved into a bedsit and left to his own devices, which pretty much ruined the small chance he had of doing well in his exams as he started to navigate adult life at the age of sixteen. He hadn't spoken to Trevor since then and only occasionally to Mum when she replied to his messages, or on the rare occasions she rang up to check how he was doing – as if she cared.

Mike did know how it was; he had tried to help Joe as much as he could, inviting him to tea at his house, spending time with him, and getting him things he needed. But there was only so much he could do. In the end, Joe had been on his own in the world, the safety net of family effectively cut away from underneath him. Joe knew that worse things happened to other people, but it still sucked. And it still made him angry. His previously good school work had diminished in direct proportion to his feelings of anger and betrayal.

"Come on," Mike said, "I'll buy you a beer."

CHAPTER EIGHT

The following morning, Mike scrambled to leave the flat. One beer had, inevitably, turned into several, and he had struggled to wake up. Joe waited until Mike was gone before he started his day, folding the blankets and putting them in a pile at the end of the sofa before sorting himself out.

Once he had some tea in a mug and his clothes on, he picked up his phone and rang the number that the lady in the shop had given him. It was answered promptly, a man's voice sounding bright for the time of the morning.

"Hi, Tom speaking. How can I help?"

"Umh, I was told that you had some work going."

"Were you? Who by?"

"The lady in the charity shop gave me your number."

"Oh, Janet. Okay, in that case, how long will it take you to get here?"

"Where?"

"Did she tell you what the job was?"

"No."

Tom laughed on the other end of the phone, a rich, friendly sound,

"That's so Janet. Okay, it's probably easiest if you come over and I show you what it is we want, then you can decide if it's right for you. The guy who came last week only lasted an hour."

"I need the work. Can you send me the address, and I'll get there as soon as I can."

"Sure thing, I'll see you when you get here."

He hung up and then waited for Tom to text the location through. It was on the right side of town for him and would only take him twenty minutes to get there. It was within walking distance, which would save on a bus fare, much to Joe's relief. He made sure he had his new key with him and then left the flat.

Following the directions on his phone, he eventually arrived at a small block of offices at the edge of an industrial unit. He pressed the buzzer marked 'Griffin Graphics,' which was next to a picture of a lion with wings, which he assumed was a griffin, that he had been instructed to. Immediately, a metallic voice spoke to him through the grill underneath.

"Come on up; it's the second floor. I'll meet you there."

The door made a buzzing sound. He pushed it open and started to scale the stairs. At the top, he was greeted by a mountain of a man whose face was mostly beard.

"Joe?"

"Yes, I'm here about the job."

"Fantastic, I'm Tom. Any friend of Janet's is okay by me. Come on in," he held the door open and ushered Joe inside, "take a seat."

Joe sat on the sofa he had been directed to. He looked around at the plush office, rows of desks with drawing boards, computers and cupboards full of sheets of paper. A large printer was busy in the corner, and people moved purposefully and quietly around the space, some on phones, others in conversation and a few working alone at their stations. At the reception desk sat a girl not much older than Joe with cropped hair and a pierced nose. She was on the phone but looked up and waved a greeting as she was speaking. Tom pulled over a chair and sat himself in front of Joe.

"So, first up, did Janet tell you what the job was?"

Joe shook his head.

"Okay, we'll get to that in a moment. How's your reading?"

"Um, fine, I guess."

"Good, the last lad didn't seem to know his alphabet, if you can believe that."

Joe couldn't. He thought everybody learnt that at infant school. He shook his head slightly,

"I'm pretty good with my ABCs."

"Good. Here's the thing, we only just moved into these offices," he swept his arm around behind him to show Joe the office. "It took two removal trucks to shift everything from our old places to here. All the expensive equipment in this room arrived unscathed, so we could get up and running. The other truck had all our archives, files, folders and paper records in it, and it wasn't as lucky. On the way here, it got into an argument with a lorry, a big lorry. Nobody was hurt, thankfully, but all the packing boxes burst open. Everything had to be scooped out and put into another van for the rest of the journey. In a moment, I'm going to show you a room that would be the stuff of nightmares to someone with OCD; it's literally a mountain of paper. The job is sorting it out and filing it. I've already had two people who told me it's impossible and walked out, as well as the lad who couldn't figure out the system. You, Joe, are my final hope. Well, for today, anyway. I reckon it'll take at least a month, and I'll pay you a fair rate. Do you think you might be up for that?"

"Just sorting stuff out?"

"Yes, don't underestimate it. The task is Sisyphean."

Joe had no idea what that word meant, but he needed the work.

"Yeah, I'm up for it."

"Great, come on, let me show you where you'll be working."

Tom led the way to a windowless storage room at the back of the office space. He flicked the lights on, revealing a mass of paper spilt all over the floor in bundles and piles, spewing from the sides of burst boxes and cascading to all corners of the room, which was lined with alphabetised filing drawers. Joe now thought he had a better idea of what Sisyphean might mean. He looked at Tom,

"All that?"

"All that," Tom agreed. "Each sheet has a code on it in the top right corner. For now, it just needs to go into the right drawer; we'll work through and sort them out once that's done. Still up for it?"

"I guess, shall I get started?"

"You hero, I'll get you a coffee. If you need more, there's a machine by reception; just help yourself."

Joe took his jacket off, laid it on top of the nearest drawer and started sorting.

As the day wore on, Joe soon found himself immersed in his task. What had, at first, seemed daunting quickly became a personal mission. He found that many of the sheaves of paper were already in order; they went directly into their allotted spaces. Other similarly grouped sheets were clumped close together, enabling him to locate pieces fairly quickly. Some were orphans; he started arranging them in piles ready to file when they found their accompanying sheets.

When the crop-haired girl came in with a fresh drink, he asked her if she had any tape to repair the damaged sheets.

"I don't think that you need to do that; we can sort that out later."

"I might as well do it as I go, otherwise, they'll get more damaged. It makes sense."

She left the room, returning moments later with a large spool of tape in a bright red dispenser,

"Here, you can borrow mine. My name's Steph, by the way."

"Hi, Steph, I'm Joe. Thanks for the tape."

"You're welcome; let me know if you need anything else."

Joe resumed work, becoming deeply engrossed with his task once again. He looked up in surprise when the door opened, and Tom beckoned to him.

"Come on, lunchtime."

"Er, I'm alright, thanks." He hadn't thought to bring anything to eat with him and knew he didn't have enough cash left to buy anything.

Recently, he had not always been able to eat and was getting used to being hungry.

"No, I insist. It's Pizza Day; everyone joins in."

"Well, the thing is…" Joe started, patting his pockets.

"No, Pizza Day is on me. Keeps everyone working hard." He winked and held the door open, revealing a group of staff surrounding a small table which had been cleared to make way for a selection of pizza boxes. The office staff were all standing nearby, helping themselves to the feast.

"Quick, before they eat the lot."

Joe felt self-conscious standing amongst this group of strangers. Steph came over and took his arm in hers. She led him around the assembled designers, introducing him as 'the man who has come to save your archives'. This seemed to meet with widespread approval. The loss of the work in the storeroom had been problematic for them. One tall, curly-haired man asked if he had seen anything with a GTL prefix on yet, half smiling as he looked at Joe.

He had.

"Yes, do you want me to get it for you?"

"Seriously?"

"I don't know if they're the right ones, I'll get them."

He was about to put his plate down, and Tom appeared at his side.

"Let him finish his lunch first, Gary, he's on a break." He turned to face Joe,

"Well, Janet was right to send you to us. You might just save our lives."

It turned out the sheets he had found were the work that Gary needed; he was cheered back to the store room while being bombarded with requests as he went. Steph came to his rescue again,

"I'll put a sheet on my desk, write on anything that you need urgently, then Joe will be able to keep an eye open for it," she announced to the room. She turned back to Joe, "Is that okay?"

"That's fine. I'll do what I can. Thanks."

"No problem, let me know if you need anything else."

The afternoon disappeared as quickly as the morning had. Tom came and looked around the room.

"Excellent start, well done. See you tomorrow?"

Joe looked at the room. It barely looked any different to him despite the fact he had been working on it all day. He knew now why Tom had said it would take a month. He took some satisfaction from knowing that he had managed to provide two other people in the office with folders that they had been looking for.

"I'll be here at 8."

"Don't be, we don't start until 9. Here, this is for you."

He passed two twenty-pound notes to Joe,

"It's not your pay; it's just to tide you over because you're broke. We'll talk about your wages tomorrow."

Joe thanked him, he put the money in his pocket, planning to buy some food and beer on the way home and give one of the notes to Mike as a thank you.

The next few days followed a similar pattern: stacking, sorting and filing the files and folders in the tiny stock room. Steph came in regularly to update his list and stop for a chat. She even found time to give him a hand when it was quiet at the reception desk. He found himself liking her; she was funny and smart, and it was good to have occasional company in the room. Tom also popped in from time to time to check he was okay and make sure he was taking breaks.

"We don't want you to crash and burn before you finish," he joked.

On Friday afternoon, Tom came to the store room again,

"I hope this is okay," he said, handing Joe an envelope.

Joe took it and looked inside. It was filled with cash.

"It's only for now. Next week, I'll get Steph to take your details, and we'll put you on the payroll."

"On the payroll?"

"Yes, we don't want to piss off the taxman, do we?"

"But I thought I was only going to be here until this was done."

"Well, maybe we need to have a chat about that. This is going to take at least another three weeks, maybe more; then, we'll need someone to make sure it doesn't get messed up again. You've seen what that lot out there are like, haven't you? Also, Steph could use an occasional hand on reception; business is going well, and we could use a useful person around the place – like yourself."

"You're offering me a job? You don't even want to know what my exam results were, or anything?"

After what had happened with Trevor, his schoolwork had taken a nosedive. His exam results were less than impressive. Also, there was the thing he didn't want to tell Tom: he'd been in a bit of a scrape with the police. Nothing serious, stupidity mostly, combined with his fiery temper. He'd been lucky to get away with a caution, but he knew he'd have to tell Tom sooner or later. Call Me Geoff at the supermarket had said that he was 'all about second chances', and he hoped Tom would be as understanding when he told him. He decided that was a conversation for another day.

"That's the gist of it, yes. You can tell me about your exams another time, you're smart and hard-working, and that's good enough for me for now. Unless you don't want to work with us, which is also fine. You've been doing a really good job here anyway, thanks."

"Yes, yes, please. I would like to work here, thank you so much."

Joe put the envelope in his pocket. He and Mike were definitely having a takeaway tonight or maybe even going out for tea. He turned back to the pile of paper he was currently working his way through.

"I know you're keen, but it's Friday. We finish at three on Friday; it's the weekend."

"Seriously?"

"Seriously, go home. I'll see you on Monday, and we'll talk about your salary."

Joe couldn't believe it: a job offer. In one week, he'd gone from homeless–okay, technically, he still was at the moment, but that was a detail–to being a man with a salaried job. He had to tell someone and share his good fortune. It was way too early for Mike to be back, so he decided to go home via the charity shop to see if Janet was there.

As he walked through the shop door, he was pleased to see that she was. She looked up from the pile of clothes she was pricing up and smiled when she saw him come in.

"Well, hello to you. I've got something to show you."

She stopped what she was doing and reached down under the counter, pulling out a stack of three thick books. She opened the top one to reveal another of the beautiful drawings that were now familiar to both of them.

"Wow, you found more."

"Yes, I've been hunting them down. I don't know whether to charge more for them or keep them for myself."

"I wonder who drew them?" Joe said, "They could be someone famous, that'd make them worth a bit."

"I know. I do remember; now I've seen all the books with the drawings in, the woman who bought them in. She was smartly dressed and had a whole carrier bag full of just books. If she comes in again, I'll ask her if they were hers."

"Fair enough, anyway, I only came in to say thank you."

Janet tilted her head to one side,

"For?"

He told her about her friend Tom offering him a job at Griffin Graphics.

"That's great," she told him. "Tom's lovely, I've known him since we shared a house at university. He's not easily impressed, either. You must have done a good job."

Joe described the task he had been given, the disastrous unfiled files that had not made it to the new office in one piece, and Janet laughed.

"Well, that sounds like a job and a half."

"Oh, I kind of like it. Getting everything in the right place, making sense of the mess."

Janet gestured around the shop,

"Maybe you should come and volunteer here. I could do with someone with organisational skills."

"I could come in on Fridays, like now. We finish at three, so I've been told."

"That's so Tom, you don't have to, I was only joking."

Joe looked around the shop,

"No, I think I will. I can see how this could be better, look."

He started to rearrange some of the items on one of the shelves. At first, it just looked to Janet as if he was moving things randomly, and then she started to see what he was doing.

"Oh, you've made it easier for people to see everything. How did you know to do that?"

Joe shrugged, then he took off his coat and put it on the stool behind the counter.

"Come on, I'll help with the clothes racks."

CHAPTER NINE

Angela leaned with her back against the front door, now firmly closed behind her. She was exhilarated and exhausted. Part of her had been terrified, a large part. But another smaller voice kept telling her she should be proud of herself, proud of what she had achieved.

It was dark outside; she had just returned from a trip to the lamppost up the road. She knew it wasn't much, really, but it was the furthest distance and the longest time she had been away from the house since she could remember. The entire round trip hadn't taken more than five minutes, constantly checking up and down the road for passing strangers as she went and breaking into an almost run as she got back to the garden gate.

Next time, she decided, she would see if she could get all the way to the corner. Even as she decided this, she gave an involuntary shudder, unsure if she would be able to follow through with her plan. She wondered if she should tell David about her exploits, then decided against it; she didn't want to cause him any more worry or bother than she already did. Also, she wanted it to be a surprise for him. One day, she would turn up at his gallery, swan in through the front doors and watch his face light up with pride when he saw what she had done.

Fat chance of that, though, not while the corner of the road still felt like it was such a distance. She resolved to try again to get beyond the lamppost tomorrow night. She also decided that she should try a trip during the day, not yet, but soon. She would be able to check that the street was empty from the upstairs window before she did.

All of these plans, together with the adrenaline rush from her earlier excursion, almost guaranteed that she would not sleep for some time yet. She walked through to the kitchen and put the kettle on while deciding which of her projects she should work on while she recomposed herself.

CHAPTER TEN

It had been a busy couple of weeks. Joe was in the backroom of the charity shop, sorting out the bags of donations that had been left that day. Other people's junk fascinated him; he could see very well why people didn't want some of the items in their homes anymore. Occasionally, people dropped off really good quality, unused things that he didn't understand why they didn't sell them themselves. There was also a fair amount of what could only be classified as junk. Still, most of it went out onto the shelves, and most of it got taken home by a new owner. One man's treasure and all that he supposed.
He had been talking to Janet through the open door, telling her how far he had battled his way through Tom's document pile. He wasn't there yet, but it was starting to look as if he had made a difference. You could see more of the floor of the storeroom, and the drawers and trays were neatly organised and accessible, although he was having to act as a gatekeeper to them to make sure they didn't get rifled through by any impatient designers who would not care if they upset his system.

Tom had sorted a contract out for him at the end of his second week; his new official title was 'clerical assistant', and the job description was vague enough to ensure that he could be asked to do just about anything. They had agreed on a salary that seemed enormous to Joe after his meagre supermarket pay. Tom assured him it wasn't, it was just standard pay for someone at entry level, like Joe. But there would be, he told him, bonuses when things were going well, and pay was reviewed every March.

Joe still hadn't mentioned his criminal past, justifying this by telling himself that Tom had never asked. It bothered him; he didn't want Tom to find out accidentally, but it never seemed to be the right moment to talk about it. He let it lie, deciding that he would know when it was time. But not yet.

All in all, his life had taken a turn for the better. Mike had seemed a little disappointed when he realised that Joe would probably be moving out, then had cheered up again when Joe had assured him that he wasn't in a rush and, anyway, he would need to save up for a deposit first. He had blown some of the money Tom had given him on a second-hand fold-out bed. It was more comfortable to sleep on than the sofa and less intrusive in the main living space. He'd set it up in the corner of the sitting room, so it looked and felt like he had committed to staying with Mike for a little while longer.

In the shop, Janet was telling him about a disastrous date she had been on earlier in the week (her prospective partner had arrived late, forgotten their wallet and stopped halfway through the meal to take a phone call), when Joe heard the shop door open. Janet's voice, normally quiet, suddenly raised in volume as she greeted the customer. It was clear to Joe that she wanted him to hear what was being said, so he stopped what he was doing and moved closer to the doorway that led to the front of the shop.

"Hello," Janet greeted the newcomer. "How lovely to see you again, you're the lady who bought in the books the other week, aren't you?"

There was a slight emphasis on the words 'the books'. Joe got it straight away, she was talking about The Grapes of Wrath and all the other ones with the drawings in. He picked up some ceramic animals that were ready to go on display and went onto the shop floor. There was a woman in a business suit who was handing a carrier bag to Janet; it didn't look like books this time, too bulky with soft bulges. Janet was making small talk about the weather, about how good it was to be approaching the weekend and about whether the woman lived nearby.

"Oh no, I live further out of town. I work in a gallery on Stinnel Street; the boss asked me to pop these in on my way home."

"Well, thank you, and thank him." Janet looked in the top of the bag, "We always need more men's shirts, especially good ones like this."

"Yes, he's a bit funny about his shirts, insists on having new ones every month – says it's the first thing people notice."

"Oh, I thought that was shoes."

"Me too, but it's his money, so what can you say?" She shrugged, and her and Janet both laughed.

"Okay, have a good weekend then."

"You too, and thank you for the donation."

Almost as soon as the door had closed, Joe had made his way to the shop counter where Janet was typing Stinnel Street into the map app on her phone. She turned the screen slightly so they could both see it clearly and went onto street view. About halfway along, there was a gallery between a jeweller's and a Tapas place. Joe must have walked past it a hundred times but never noticed it, probably because he'd never been looking for an art gallery before now.

"Desidero Gallery, that must be it. Look and see if it has a website."

"Okay, give me a chance," answered Janet. She clicked on the link that opened the page for the gallery and started scrolling.

The webpage had rows of thumbnail images. Some were quite mediocre landscapes and scenic views, not that Joe was any kind of expert. But the others were the familiar swirls and suggestions of images that Joe had found in the margins of the books, only better. These pictures were in vivid, glorious technicolour, taking up large areas of canvas that they were able to explore and expand into.

"Well, we've found our artist," said Janet. "How fantastic are those pictures?"

"They're wonderful. I may go to the gallery tomorrow and have a look at them in the flesh. How much do they cost?"

Janet clicked on the link on one of the pictures; the information came up next to it: Rapid Descent by D. Hacer - £2,398.

"Wow, I don't think I'll be buying one anytime soon. I might still go and have a look, though."

"No, it's a bit out of my budget, too. I wonder what the ones in the book are worth?"

"Well, if it's that much for the big ones... If they are worth something, I'll bring them back; I'd feel bad otherwise, they were given to charity, after all."

"Don't worry, we've still got the others, and we'd never have known if it wasn't for you."

"Well, even so…"

He left the sentence hanging while they both looked at the picture on the phone screen. Janet put it down on the counter.

"Come on then, let's get packed up and switched off for the night, then we can all go home for tea."

She smiled, and Joe went back and put everything in its proper place while Janet cashed up the till. They walked out together, switching off lights and locking the door.

"Night then, I'm going to tell Mike about the gallery so he knows what prestigious artwork he has on his wall."

"I hope he appreciates it; I'm going to have a bath, a glass of wine and an early night. See you next week."

"Yep, see you."

They went in different directions, both happy at last to have solved at least part of the mystery of the illustrated books. Joe still wondered how they came to be in the books in the shop. Was it deliberate? Did they forget they were there? Or was it some kind of publicity thing?

*

The following day, Saturday, was not a work day. Joe didn't like to admit to himself that he was a bit disappointed; he liked having something to do, and he was keen to get to the end of Paper Mountain. He lay on his new fold-out bed for a while and scrolled through a selection of memes and videos on different social media sites, then sent messages to some of his mates. Everybody he talked to was up to something, but nothing that appealed to Joe enough to persuade him to ask if he could tag along. Mike had left the house early to get the coach to some town or other in the north. His passion for following the local football team had always been the source of teasing from their mates. Mike didn't care; now he was earning money, his enthusiasm for supporting them had intensified and often included long coach trips or railway journeys to different parts of the country.

Left to his own devices, Joe got up slowly, had something to eat and went out. He still had plenty of cash for now, so he thought he might go and get something more respectable to wear for work. Not that anyone had commented on his tracksuit and hoodie; it just felt like the sort of thing he should do. He walked to the bus stop and waited for the next Blue Line bus that would take him into the town centre.

Two smartish jumpers, a couple of shirts a new pair of jeans and a burger later, he was ready to get the bus back. Before he got to the bus stop, he realised that he was now quite close to Stinnel Street. He walked on past the stop for his return journey and made his way to the more bohemian shops that populated the Stinnel Street area.

He knew he'd arrived when he got to a shop whose window display was filled with copper pots and embroidered scarves, with a smell of incense wafting out through the open front door. Directly next to this was a window filled with what was labelled as vintage clothes. Pausing to look, Joe saw little difference between their stock and some of the clothing they sold at the charity shop, apart from the prices. It gave him the idea of setting up a vintage corner in the shop; he'd talk to Janet about that next week.

Eventually, he came to the gallery. The smell from the tapas bar next door made his mouth water, despite the burger he'd eaten earlier. He looked at the huge canvas hanging in the window, once again mesmerised by the beauty of the lines, the grace and precision of the patterns and the impact of the work. Tearing himself away, he went inside to let his eyes feast on the other pieces that were hanging there. He bypassed the watercolour landscapes and seascapes with barely a glance.

The woman who had come into the shop yesterday was sitting behind a desk. She briefly looked up from her phone call but didn't show any signs of recognising him from their brief encounter. Her voice faded into the background as he stood in front of the wall of technicolour paintings. As he looked, the pictures seemed to morph, turning into something different but still not anything he could quite put his finger on.

The smaller drawings in the books had hinted at things they might be suggesting, giving clues as to what they were about. Snippets of information that didn't quite make sense. The larger works were trying even harder, urging Joe to concentrate, to see more. He stood motionless in front of the largest work, one hand in his pocket, the other holding his shopping bag.

"Is there anything I can help you with?"

The voice broke him out of his trance; the receptionist had finished her call and was standing beside him.

"These are fantastic, aren't they?" he responded.

"Yes, they're really pretty," she replied in an almost nonchalant manner. Joe wasn't sure pretty was the right word; it seemed to reduce them to the level of decoration. He looked at the receptionist and realised that she meant it, that was all she could see in them, colours and patterns that might go well with certain décor.

"Is the artist local?"

"Yes, he's the owner of Desidero. Everything here is his work."

"What all of ...?" Joe swept his hand around, taking in both the large canvases in front of him and the smaller, more traditional pieces."

"Yes, David Hacer, they're all his work. It used to be all in the style of these pieces," she waved her hand in the direction of a large picture of a fishing harbour. "I really liked them; then, he started to introduce these abstract works. They're incredibly popular."

"I'm not surprised; I love them. They're a bit out of my price range, though. Well, a lot, actually." He laughed, and the receptionist laughed with him, but in a way that said she had heard this a thousand times before.

"Does he do any smaller pieces?"

"No, not at all. He only works on this scale, sorry. I guess you'll just have to save a little longer. We can arrange payment plans if you want, though."

Joe was almost tempted by this; he loved the work so much. But he hadn't even got his first paycheque yet, and he knew that getting somewhere to live had to be his priority.

"I'm seriously tempted, but I can't afford it now. Maybe in a few months, thanks."

"You're welcome." The receptionist was losing interest in him now and looked almost relieved when the phone she'd left on her desk rang, and she went to answer it.

Joe paused to take one last lingering look at the largest of the pictures before he left. Then, as he turned, he saw it in the corner of his eye. It was fleeting, and he almost ignored it, but he turned back and looked again with fresh eyes.

He wasn't mistaken; it was there. It had been there all along; he just hadn't been looking properly. Now, he looked at it again. He could see what the painting was and what it wasn't. He realised now that he must look odd, standing open-mouthed in front of the picture. He forced himself to move, pausing again by the picture closest to the door, then standing in front of the gallery window, examining the painting that hung there. He waited until he was sure the receptionist wasn't looking and took a picture of it on his phone before walking back to the bus stop.

On the way home, Joe continued to look at the picture on his phone, scrutinising every detail. Being able to zoom in on sections made it easier to examine, but it still didn't compare to the near-overwhelming experience of standing in front of the real thing, seeing the bumps and contours of the rough paint that brought the canvases to life. He wanted to tell someone about his discovery and share what he had found, but it would be hours before Mike got back, and he would probably be worse for wear when he did. He had

Janet's number; she had given it to him so he could let her know if he wasn't able to get in on a Friday. He didn't think this would count as enough of an emergency to disturb her on a Saturday. Aside from them, he couldn't find any contacts on his phone that he could talk to about the paintings. Once upon a time, it would have been Mum he turned to first; of course, Trevor had successfully shut off that avenue. Thinking about this made him clench his jaw and feel unwelcome emotions rush to the front of his mind, where they had to compete with the overwhelming feeling that sat there. It was a feeling that he had found it hard to put a name to at first. But now he had come to recognise it for what it was – loneliness.

CHAPTER ELEVEN

Another few feet, and she would be there. She hesitated, considered turning back, and then took two rapid steps, stopping herself with her hands on the top of the gate. She clenched the strip of wood with both hands, gripping it tightly as she tried to decide if she was terrified or elated. Both, she decided as she looked out into the deserted street. She had timed this for after everyone had left for work or school and before those left behind started to make their way on their errands and odd jobs for the day. Her observations from the upstairs window had helped her decide that this was the optimum moment, a dead time in the busy lives of those around her.

She knew most of them by sight: the cat family with the little girl opposite her, the house full of teenage boys and harried parents next to them. Her neighbours, Tracey and Jim, on one side and the young couple with the baby on the other. She couldn't remember their names, although she could hear them in the dead of night, tending to the infant's nocturnal needs. Not that she had ever met or spoken to any of them, David would occasionally stop and chat with them when he visited, then pass on what he had discovered to her when they were sitting at the kitchen table together.

As her panic subsided, Angela started to realise that there was something else – it was that feeling of pride again. For most other people, this would not be a big deal; she knew that. But coming this far out of the house in broad daylight was a challenge that she had not thought she would be up to. The street looked different from here, more real and alive, despite the absence of people. The colours of the flowers and plants in the front gardens looked vivid, the remaining cars still parked outside the houses were garishly bright, and the slight waft of a breeze carried rich scents to her.

She looked back over her shoulder to make sure the door was still open and ready if she needed to retreat, then looked back out to the road. She started to feel herself relax very slightly as she held onto the gate and leaned slightly forward for a better view. She was so absorbed in drinking in the atmosphere that she didn't notice the small movement in the hedge to her right until she felt something brush against her leg. She lifted a hand to her mouth to stifle a scream and started to turn back towards the open door. As she did so, she looked down and saw the tabby and white cat, the one from over the road. It was standing, looking at her, poised in the same ready-to-run position as her.

Heart pounding, she stopped herself.

"Only a cat," she said to herself, "it's only a cat."

She bent and offered her outstretched hand to the animal, who tentatively stepped forward and sniffed it before striding confidently forward and brushing itself lightly around her ankles, with its upraised tail nudging the frayed hem of her dressing gown.

"Hello again, we must stop meeting like this. What's your name then?"

She lightly scratched the cat's head between the ears, causing it to intensify its gentle assault on her legs.

"Well, you're a cutey, aren't you? I can see why your girl is so fond of you."

Just as she finished speaking, she heard a bump from up the street, a front door closing and the sound of footsteps on the path. She glanced up quickly, but did not see anybody yet, it sounded like it had come from several houses further down the road. She felt her heart start to race and she began to perspire slightly. She looked down at her new friend,

"Sorry, cat, I've got to go."

She hurried back up the path and returned to the safety and sanctuary of her house, closing the door firmly behind her. Breathless, she made her way to the kitchen and made herself a drink before going upstairs to the back bedroom. Pausing in the doorway, she looked in, smiled and muttered to herself,

"Time to do some work then."

CHAPTER TWELVE

Mike had got home late and drunk, as predicted. He didn't emerge from his room until the middle of Sunday afternoon, a sheepish smile on his face,

"That was a good day yesterday. It just seems to take so long to get over it. Is there anything to eat?"

It was a rhetorical question. Before Joe could answer or even put down The Grapes of Wrath, Mike was spreading some margarine on some slices of bread and cutting a chunk of cheese to go between them.

"Good match then?"

"Epic, three–nil. We played them off the pitch. Bloody long coach trip, though; I'm getting the train next time. Anything would be quicker than the M1. How was your day?"

"Alright, I got some new clothes. I thought I'd better have something decent if I'm going to be a clerical assistant."

"You should have held on for a job at our place; you get a free polo shirt and fleece."

He smiled around his mouthful of sandwich as he sat down beside Joe,

"Call of Duty?"

"Uh, yeah, okay."

Joe put down his book and collected the game controllers. As he switched the TV on, he decided it might not be the right time to talk

55

about his visit to the art gallery; he would mention it later. Only later never came; after they finished annihilating one another in the blasted war zones on the TV, Mike wanted to go out and get some energy drinks to help clear his head. Then he had to go out again for the bread and milk he should have got when he went out earlier, before getting his clothes ready for work the next morning. Sunday just drifted away with no real chance for Joe to tell him about what he'd discovered. He knew it had to be the right time because he still wasn't entirely sure that he could explain it. It would need both his and Mike's full and undivided attention, which he certainly wasn't going to get today.

*

The following day, Joe was back at his task. He had looked up what Sisyphean meant by now, of course, and could see why Tom had called it that. Regardless, he was making progress. As he was getting closer to the bottom of the heap, the amount of damaged paperwork was increasing, taking up more of his time. It was also using more of his tape, as he got to the tail end of another roll, he went out to ask Steph for some more.

"Another one? Are you eating it?" she asked, looking at the empty roll in his hand and smiling.

"I wish I was. I'm ravenous," he answered.

"Well, take a lunch break then. Come on, I'll treat you." She started to put on her denim jacket, which had been hanging on the back of her chair.

"Shouldn't we tell Tom or someone?"

"No, the answer phone can pick up the slack for us. Burger okay for you?"

Joe didn't need to be asked twice; he collected his coat from the storeroom and followed her out.

As they sat at their table, waiting for their food to be served, Steph asked him,

"So, Joe from the store room, what do you do when you're not at work?"

"Umm, not a lot. I help out in a charity shop once a week," he added as he struggled to define his non-existent social life. "I read, and I'm interested in art." All technically true, but hardly the habits of a lifetime.

"Wow, you are a man of culture and compassion. What are you reading at the moment?"

"The Grapes of Wrath."

"Oh, I love Steinbeck. Have you read Cannery Row?"

"No," he confessed, "only Of Mice and Men."

"Well, that's a good place to start. I'll bring in my copy of Cannery Row if you want to borrow it."

Joe thought he did. He was enjoying the book he was reading (if enjoy is the right word for something so bleak), he just hoped the book he had been offered wasn't quite such a hefty tome. He was also curious as to what Steph thought was a good book; she was interesting. Her close-cut hair and black clothes gave her an almost punky look but with none of the hard edges. She was pretty without trying to be.

It turned out, over lunch, that she was also interesting and pleasant to talk to. As the minutes ticked away, long after they had finished eating, he found himself deep in conversation with her. She had studied art at college but realised early on that she had neither the skills nor the temperament to be an artist. She was, however, happy doing what she was doing while she figured out what she might try next. She knew it would be something creative; she just didn't know what yet.

When she asked Joe about his own story, he dried up. There was much he was embarrassed about: his dysfunctional family, his inability to keep a job, his lack of academic success, his still undisclosed involvement with the law and the fact that he was sleeping on someone's floor. He tried to avoid answering some questions, changing the subject or giving vague non-answers. This, of course, had the opposite effect, intriguing Steph and prompting more follow-up questions. In an attempt to change the momentum of the conversation, he told her about the drawings in the book. He tried to describe them to her, but couldn't find adequate words. Instead, he got out his phone and showed her the photos he had taken. She took the phone off him and stared at them, not talking at all as she took them in.

Before she could speak again, there was a cough beside the table, designed to draw their attention. Joe's heart sank; it was Tom. This was where he got fired before he even started his new job for taking too long for lunch – how long had it been anyway?

"It's quite busy in here. If you two have finished, do you mind if I grab your table?"

"No, we were just on our way back now. Are you okay to pay for us? Trade for the table," answered Steph.

"No problem, see you back at the office," Tom replied with a smile and a small shake of his head.

"It's okay," said Joe, "I'll pay for mine."

"Don't be daft, go on, off you go so I can sit down."

He didn't know what he was more surprised about, that Steph had asked him to pay or that Tom had agreed.

Steph seemed to have moved on from the incident completely,

"I like those drawings. Can you bring the books in for me to have a look at?"

"Sure, I'll bring them in tomorrow. There's more to the story, though; you won't believe it."

"Ooh, some intrigue. I'm looking forward to it now. We should go for a drink after work sometime – so Tom doesn't come and interrupt us while you tell me the rest."

Joe agreed. He wasn't sure if he was being chatted up or not, but that was okay; he liked Steph. He went back into the stock room with two more rolls of tape and a smile on his face.

The afternoon was over before he realised it; he fixed and filed while he thought about how he would retell the series of events to Steph so that it made sense. He eventually decided that just a blow-by-blow account would be best, trying not to leave out anything. He knew from previous experience how hard it could be to articulate something that seemed straightforward in your head if the person you were telling had none of the extraneous information that gave it context. It had been like that after he got arrested.

Steph stuck her head around the door as he was getting ready to leave for the day,

"So, what time are we meeting then? And which pub?"

When she had said they should go out for a drink, he hadn't realised that it would be straight away.

"What, tonight?"

"Yes, unless you're busy. I want to hear the rest of the story."

"Oh, okay. Do you know The Travellers Rest in town?"

"Yes, seven o'clock?"

"Sounds great."

"Okay, see you there then."

Joe was left feeling like he had been ambushed, not that he minded. He hadn't been out on many dates since he had been homeless, none in fact. He guessed that this was a kind of date, although he still wasn't completely sure how it had happened. He hurried to get home so he could shower and put on one of the new shirts he'd bought at the weekend, maybe the blue-striped one, which was a good mix of smart casual.

*

Because it was a weeknight, the Travellers wasn't too busy, he spotted Steph straightaway, standing at the bar in a pair of jeans and a Nirvana tee shirt with a hoody over the top. He was glad he had changed out of his work clothes, but worried now that he might have overdressed. Steph didn't have a drink yet, so she had only just arrived. He walked up to her,

"Hi, get you a drink?"

"Yes, please, a cider would be lovely. Are you sure you don't mind, you haven't had your first pay yet?"

"I'm fine." He was; he still had plenty of cash left from the money Tom had given him, despite having forced Mike to take some and paying for the week's shopping. "Anyway, you got lunch."

"Well, Tom did, actually."

"Okay, yes. But you offered."

He ordered the drinks, and they found a table slightly away from the hustle and bustle of the bar area.

"How are you finding it working at Griffin?" Steph asked.

"Yeah, I like it so far. I can't believe Tom gave me a job, though."

"Why not?"

"Because I don't know anything about graphic design or record keeping. I don't really know what I'm supposed to be doing once I've cleared up the moving mess."

"Nobody does when they first start a new job. We'll all make sure you're on the right track. Tom wouldn't have offered you a job if he hadn't seen a glimmer of what he thought you were capable of, trust me."

"I guess I'll have to. Cheers." He raised his glass, and Steph tapped her own against it before they both took a drink.

"Anyway, don't tell me you don't know anything about art when you found those beautiful drawings. Come on, tell me the whole story; don't leave anything out."

He told her the whole story, trying his best not to leave anything out. Despite his best efforts, she still had to ask him to explain things once or twice and show her the pictures on his phone again. He got to the bit about the art gallery, and by the end, he realised he was starting to drift into a jumbled explanation of his feelings when he found the large paintings. He stopped and showed her the picture from the window on his phone.

"It's beautiful."

"That's nothing; you should see it in the flesh; it's breathtaking."

"Do you want another drink? My round."

He looked down, almost in surprise, at his near-empty glass.

"Yes, please."

Steph went to the bar and came back with two fresh pints.

"I haven't even got to the weird bit yet," he said.

"What, there's more?"

"Yes, when you look at them the right way, the pictures tell a story."

"A story?"

"Yes, I know it sounds weird. You have to look at them just the right way, like those magic eye pictures."

"I know the ones you mean."

"So yeah, a bit like that."

"So tell me about the one on your phone."

He unlocked the phone again and went around the swirls and semi-impressions with his finger, explaining what he thought they meant. The ones in the books were easier as they all related to the content of the stories. He did not make eye contact with Steph while he did this; he was still unsure that he had seen what he thought he had, and he didn't want her to think he was losing the plot. When he did look up, he saw that she was staring at the picture on his phone intently.

"I see it," she told him, "at least I think I do. It doesn't make sense, though, not completely."

"No, you have to see the pictures next to each other, I think. Except in the gallery, they weren't in the right order; that's why it took me a while to figure out."

"So what's the whole story?"

"I don't know yet, it's all just fragments and suggestions. I need to see more of the pictures. But look at the ones on the website," he opened the Desidero page to show her the other pictures, "can you see them now?"

"Oh my god, yes. This one's something to do with a locked door, isn't it?"

"I think so, yes. And this one's about a birthday party."

"Wow, did you figure this all out by yourself?"

"Well, kind of."

"See, I told you Tom was right to give you a job. Can you bounce the pictures through to me, please?"

Joe did that; then they started to talk about other subjects. Joe was thankful that Steph didn't ask about his family or how he came to be cast adrift at such a young age. By the time he'd finished his second drink, he knew that would have to be his last of the evening if he intended to get up for work the next day, which was a shame because he was finding Steph to be good company. She must have felt the same,

"Well, thank you for such an educational evening. I kind of need to head off now. I know it's still early, but we've both got work tomorrow. Next time, I want to find out about the real Joe."

Joe thought the part about next time sounded brilliant. He was not so keen on the other bit. Still, he guessed she'd know about him sooner or later; they were working together now, after all. He waited at the bus stop with her for the short time that it took for the number 7 to arrive, then walked briskly back to the flat. He had loads to tell Mike about now.

CHAPTER THIRTEEN

After her second encounter with the cat, Angela's mood was buoyant; she even caught herself singing in the bathroom – and she couldn't remember the last time she'd done that. The tune that had inserted itself into her subconscious was the old music hall song I Do Like to be Beside the Seaside. As it had been more years than she could remember since she had been to the seaside, it seemed a bit weird. Nevertheless, she embraced it, giving the tiddly om pom poms some extra gusto for good measure.
Her good mood carried on into the kitchen while she made some breakfast and drank her morning tea. She left the table, having finished her cereal and went to look out of her front window. Across the road, she could see the cat, which was sitting on the front wall of the house, seemingly asleep. The façade ended when the front door opened and the cat jumped down, arching its back and waving its tail as it demanded to be made a fuss of by the girl as she passed.

She thought that maybe the road didn't look as foreboding as it had a few weeks ago, although nothing had changed. Well, that wasn't strictly true. Nothing had changed on the road, but something had changed in her. Her nightly escapades had emboldened her to the extent that she was now contemplating going outside in the broad daylight again, or at least the penumbra of evening, before it was fully dark. But this time, she would leave the garden.

Summoning the spirit of Neil Armstrong landing on the moon, she muttered to herself 'Small steps for a man, but giant leaps for Angela.' Inside the house was where she felt safe, the place where she and David had grown up, and she had lived for almost her entire life. The years she had spent at university had been transient, but she had always thought of this as home. After that, there were several years when she lived in a fourth-floor flat closer to the middle of town as she stretched her wings of independence once she finished her studies. But this house was the place where she had spent the last three and a half years.

When she moved back in, it was supposed to be a short-term emergency measure. Their parents had died within twelve months of one another, twelve awful months when she and David had been fully occupied. First, there was the nursing and caregiving, which was hard on both of them. The rapid decline of their mother's health, followed by their dad's fall and subsequent short illness, left little time for introspection. This was followed by arranging two funerals in rapid succession, sorting through paperwork to locate wills that had never been discussed and informing everybody in officialdom who needed to be informed about the deaths.

They had jointly decided to take a breath and some time for themselves, some time to mourn and grieve properly, before starting the daunting process of clearing and selling the house. A lifetime of possessions and belongings that would need to be rehomed, recycled or otherwise disposed of filled the house. Neither of them had the heart to begin the process straight away, leading to the decision to procrastinate. It was during this hiatus that it became untenable for Angela to continue living in her high-rise flat; moving back in had been the only realistic option. They couldn't have known at the time that it would be where she remained ever since.

She looked at the clock in the kitchen and decided she would make her next trip after tea. Maybe at seven, when the light was starting to fade and people were inside watching TV and winding down for the evening.

CHAPTER FOURTEEN

Predictably, Mike had found plenty to say about Joe's date.

"I'm not sure it was an actual date; we just went out for a drink."

"That's what a date is, stupid."

"No, it wasn't like that. She just suggested it after we'd had lunch."

"Lunch? So you've been on two dates?"

"No, well, not really. She's just being kind, I think."

"Sounds like a date to me. Anyway, I'm glad you're enjoying your new job. Even if you have to put up with older women chasing you around."

"Shut up."

"Ooh, touchy."

"Anyway, I was going to tell you about the pictures."

"You went to the pictures as well?"

"No, the drawings," Joe pointed at the framed pieces on the wall, and Mike grinned back, showing that he had known full well what Joe was talking about.

"What about the pictures?"

Joe explained, as best he could, about the larger artwork in the gallery and about the way you could see things in them. He showed him the paintings on his phone, pointing out the details he had made out. The flashing blue lights, the hospital equipment and the mysterious hooded figure.

"Do you see them?"

Mike tilted his head, squinted at the phone in his hand, then zoomed in on a section. He looked up at Joe with a small shake of his head and was about to speak when he glanced back at the phone. His half-open mouth closed again, and he stared at the screen,

"Fuck me, I see it, Joe. How could I not have seen it?"

"I know, it's weird, isn't it? But it's not right, it's only fragments and scraps."

"Yeah, I get that. Do you think there's more in the other paintings?"

"I'm sure of it. Steph's going to help me try and find out more."

"Sounds like the sort of thing a girlfriend would do if you ask me."

"I told you it's...." he looked up at Mike's big, stupid grin and then smiled with him. "Just for that, you're getting thrashed at Forza tonight. He put down his phone and picked up a controller.

"In your dreams, mate, in your dreams," answered Mike as he picked up the other controller and dropped onto the settee.

Joe didn't get to speak to Steph when he arrived at work the next day, she was already on the phone with a client. He was beginning to realise what his new job might entail now. As he got closer to the bottom of Paper Mountain, he was being interrupted at regular intervals by designers looking for specific documents. By and large, he was able to help them find what they were looking for with a minimum of time or effort; he knew where everything was because he was the one who had put it there. He had also found a need to create a drop-off system for new files that needed to be added to the collection to ensure that current projects found the right place to live. All in all, it was keeping him very busy, more so than usual, as it was Friday and everyone was trying to wind up for the week.

"You haven't stopped once this morning, have you?"

Joe looked up to see Steph standing in the doorway, a mug in each hand.

"I don't think so, no. Is one of those for me?"

"Of course," she passed him one of the mugs, which he took and sipped from.

"Thanks, I needed that."

Joe briefly thought about Mike ribbing him last night and felt his face get warm, he hoped he wasn't blushing. Steph continued,

"You're welcome. I was looking at those pictures again, I think I may have an idea about how we can find out more."

"Yeah," he took another slurp of his tea. "What's that then?"

Joe was now leaning against the drawers. Steph had come over and joined him, leaning no more than a few centimetres from him. He was starting to wonder if Mike might have been right.

"No clues. You'll have to invite me out for another drink before I tell you."

He was certain that he blushed when she said this; he hastily took another drink so his mug would at least partially cover his face. He looked at Steph and saw that she was grinning.

"That's so cute. Do you always go that colour?"

"No, I did it especially for you."

Now, Steph laughed before taking a sip of her drink and carrying on,

"We could ask Tom, he knows all the local artists."

"Tom, the boss?"

"Of course, Tom the boss, who else?"

"He'd be too busy for that. And he's the boss, so…I don't know, it would feel funny."

"Why?"

"Because he's the boss."

At that moment, one of the design team came in with an untidy bundle of papers. Joe put down his drink and took them from him. Steph started to leave,

"We'll revisit this; let me know when we're going out for that drink."

The rest of the day stayed busy, Joe absorbed himself in his work while his brain reran the conversation he had just had with Steph. He thought that maybe Mike had been right, that Steph did like him. He wondered where a good place to invite someone for a date would be, he was seriously lacking in experience in the matter. And he thought about what she'd suggested, about asking Tom to help. He liked Tom, and he was still keen to make a good impression. Presenting him with a weird theory he had about some doodles he'd found in a book didn't feel like the right way to cement their new employer/employee relationship.

By the end of the afternoon, he'd formulated a plan. As everybody was getting ready to leave the office, he paused at the reception desk and spoke to Steph,

"Are you busy tomorrow afternoon?"

"Not particularly, no."

He felt his cheeks start to get warm again and began speaking quickly to try to stem it.

"Would you like to come and see the exhibition at the museum tomorrow?"

He had remembered seeing a poster for it in town at the weekend, something about Russian art. He didn't know anything about it other than what he'd seen on the poster, but he was sure Steph would.

"Yes, I was going to try and get to that. Shall I see you outside at eleven?"

"Sure, we can get a bite to eat afterwards if you want."

"That'll be great. I'll see you there."

*

"Can I ask you something?"

Joe had stopped by the counter and was looking at Janet.

"You can ask me anything," she replied, "whether I answer or not is a different matter."

Joe paused as he thought about what he was going to say. It felt a bit odd asking for dating tips from someone he didn't know that well. But it was the kind of thing that he thought he would probably be asking his mum if they'd been talking. On the evidence of last night, Mike was hardly likely to be much use either, so Janet had become the lucky recipient of his quest for advice. He explained the situation with Steph as clearly as he could, ending with the planned gallery visit the next day.

"So, do you think she likes me?"

He thought Janet might laugh when he finished talking, but he didn't know what he would do when this happened. He looked up at her and saw a look of deadly earnestness on her face.

"I think she might do Joe, yes. Why wouldn't she? You're a good-looking young man, as well as being sharp as a tack. The gallery sounds like a good idea, just one suggestion though…"

Joe braced himself.

"Maybe get your hair trimmed up a little bit beforehand if you've got time."

He ran his hand over his head, pushing his fingers through his hair. Janet was right; of course, he had been meaning to do it. A combination of a lack of money in the first instance, followed by a lack of time, meant it had turned into a bit of a bird's nest.

"Good advice, thanks," he smiled.

CHAPTER FIFTEEN

Making sure the door was propped open- it would be a disaster if it slammed shut behind her- Angela walked down to her garden gate. She managed to do this with big, confident steps, she had been building herself up for it all day, after all. It was nearly dusk, and the noise of the sparrows squabbling over roosting places in the hedge at the side of the garden was surprisingly loud. She leaned on the gate and looked up and down the road to check that it was deserted. Once she was sure that nobody was about, she took her next steps.
Her hand rested on the latch and trembled slightly as she pushed it down and pulled the gate towards herself. Before she knew it, she was standing at the end of her path, on the brink and ready to step onto the pavement, in daylight, for the first time since she could remember. She had thought that this would be the point when she would start to panic, that her flight response would kick in, and she would scurry back into her sanctuary. Surprising herself, she did not turn and run but stepped out over the boundary. First one foot, then the other, then pausing to check again that she was still alone.

Her original plan had been to walk to the lamppost like she had the other night, maybe as far as the corner if it went well. But her plan had never been written in stone; in her heart of hearts, she hadn't even thought she would make it this far. Now that she was here, she made a spontaneous decision to go in the other direction, towards the park – although she would not go that far, obviously, just close enough to see the trees and then she would come back again. Just thirty or so steps away from the house, she knew she could do it. She turned right and started to walk in that direction, her steps slightly less confident now, her limp more pronounced.

She counted out thirty paces, which got her as far as number 42, stopping to look at the beautiful ceramic plate displaying the numbers on the gatepost. She turned and looked over her shoulder in the direction she had come from. She could still see the birds, small shadows flitting in and out of the hedge, and her wide-open front door spilling light into the street. The neighbouring houses looked different now. From this direction, in this light, they seemed friendlier somehow. She had forgotten how welcoming her road looked, even though she had known it all of her life. The houses were not overbearingly imposing or crammed together, it was just an ordinary road with no illusions of grandeur, a place that people could call home.

Looking in the other direction, she could now see the tops of the mature trees that stood sentry at the edge of the park. Dark in shadows but made visible by the ebbing light that glowed behind them, she suddenly felt a desire to see them properly. She imagined herself standing beneath them, smelling the scent of the leaves and feeling the rough bark under her fingers, crinkled and ancient with bits flaking off at her touch. She had thought the wide open space would be terrifying, she had avoided it for so long that it had become more imposing and insurmountable with every passing month. But now she was here, she could smell the flowers in people's gardens, see the flickering lights of TV screens through the windows of the houses and hear the one hundred and one tiny noises that work together in harmony on a late spring evening.

All those delicate sounds were suddenly drowned out, washed away by the impossibly piercing roar of an engine. Behind her, a car had turned onto the road. It growled and grew louder as it approached her, obliterating the sound of her involuntary scream. The headlights cut through the darkening night, wiping away what little colour was left in the day and dazzling her as she turned to watch its approach. She felt its mass as it passed her, felt the speed and solidity of the metal dragon displacing the air around it and then moving away as quickly as it had arrived.

In its wake, the red glow of its tail lights lit up the figure of Angela, crouched at the base of the gatepost and gripping the corner of the brickwork with both hands. She stayed there until the car had completely disappeared around the next corner, then she got up and ran back to her house, her dressing gown flapping around her legs and her shoes slapping against the pavement. In her panic, she nearly ran straight past her open gate. She stopped in time and got back inside the door, which she closed firmly behind herself.

"Stupid woman, it was just a car. Stupid, stupid woman. You see them all the time, they drive up and down the road every day, you stupid, stupid woman."

As she admonished herself, she moved into the kitchen and put the kettle on. Her rational mind knew that it was just an ordinary car, driving at an ordinary speed. No bigger, faster or louder than any of the other cars she saw every day. But when she had been outside her rational mind had not been in charge, a deeper more primitive part of her had taken over.

"You are useless," she told herself, "you can't even go for a walk to the park, how are you ever going to get to David's gallery?"

The truth was, she didn't know. But now she had set herself this target, she was determined to reach it, somehow. She promised herself that she would break free from this self-imposed prison sentence, and she would get to the gallery – one day.

CHAPTER SIXTEEN

The art exhibition turned out to be wonderful, exceeding whatever expectations Joe may have had for it. Steph had been waiting outside when he arrived fresh from the barber shop; they had gone in together and toured the three rooms of paintings and posters for over an hour. If he had been by himself, he might have walked briskly around deciding which things he liked and which he didn't before buying a postcard from the gift shop. He may have even paused to read one or two of the small plaques under any pictures that he particularly liked.

Steph read all the plaques and talked knowledgeably about some of the work. She wasn't an expert, but she knew a little about Russian art and a lot about the context of what was happening in the world of art in the timeframe they were curated from. Joe would readily admit that he didn't understand everything that she told him, but he could still have listened to her for the rest of the day. He was almost disappointed when they got to the end of the last room. Almost but not quite, they still had lunch to get, so he would spend more time with Steph and have something to eat too. It was a win-win situation.

Enough time had passed now that they had missed the lunchtime rush, Steph ignored the museum café next to the gift shop and led him around the corner to a little tucked-away café in a side street. It didn't look like the kind of place that Joe would normally stop in, meaning it was not a burger and chips type of place.

"I love this café," Steph told him, "they do the best coffee."

Joe didn't argue the point, he had no better suggestions after all. They went into the tiny space and found a table. The interior was filled with mismatched tables and chairs, and notices about community events competed for space with a selection of paintings by local artists. The menu was chalked on a board above the counter, with information about where the various drinks and food items had originated from. There were things that Joe had never heard of, although he could figure out roughly what they were from the descriptions. Whether he would like them or not was another matter entirely. Steph saved the day,

"I'm having a coffee and sourdough with brie," she told him, "It's the best sandwich in town."

"That sounds great," he replied, "I'll have the same."

They placed their order with the waitress and talked about the exhibition they had just seen while they waited for their food to arrive.

Joe had to admit that the sandwich was probably one of the nicest he had ever eaten, apart from the ones he used to eat on the beach with Mum, of course. He leaned back in his chair, smiling, and asked,

"Did you think any more about how we could see more of the pictures?"

"I did, I still think Tom is our best bet, he knows everybody."

"Yeah, I still feel a bit funny about that. You know, he is the boss after all."

"I think you'd be surprised, he's really quite helpful. I'm certain he won't mind."

Joe wasn't sure why she would be so confident of this; she seemed to have absolutely no doubt at all. He still thought it would be a bit weird to approach someone as busy as Tom with such a mundane request for help.

"I'll think about it," he replied.

"Good, I'm just going to pay for this, where shall we go next?"

Joe was unprepared for this, he hadn't thought beyond the initial part of the date. He couldn't invite her back to Mike's flat, even though he had made it more habitable than it had been a couple of weeks ago, it was still a bit of a mess. It was a nice day outside, he tentatively suggested a walk in the botanical garden. He knew it was nearby, even though he had never actually visited – apart from a school trip once when he was a kid, which didn't count because all he did that day was mess around with his mates without taking in any of his surroundings. If he remembered rightly, the coach trip was his favourite part of the day.

Steph agreed with the idea enthusiastically. They spent the next couple of hours in the grounds and greenhouses of the gardens, where Joe found that simply strolling around looking at plants and flowers was a soothing and relaxing way to spend a sunny afternoon. At some point on one of the many meandering paths, Steph slipped her hand into his as they walked. The contact was unexpected, and the warmth of their interlaced fingers made him simultaneously nervous and excited. He liked Steph more and more as he got to know her, but he hadn't believed that she would like him with his numerous faults and insecurities. He was still dreading the inevitable time when she would find out more of the truth about who he was.

As they finished the circuit of the gardens and reached the large ornate gates, Steph turned to him,

"This is the nicest date I've ever been on, thank you."

She leaned forward and kissed him on the lips, catching him unprepared. She stepped back slightly.

"Sorry, was that too much? I just thought…"

Now it was Steph who was starting to blush. Joe closed the space between them again and kissed her back. It took all his nerve as he entered this largely uncharted territory, but it was worth the effort.

"I had a great day too," he said when they parted again, "can I see you again sometime?"

"I thought you'd never ask," she smiled, "how about tomorrow?"

"That's fine, I'm not doing anything else."

"Oh, so I'll do then, will I?"

"I didn't mean it like…" he realised that she was teasing and stopped, then kissed her again.

"Where do you want to go?"

"You can come round to my house for lunch if you want."

The thought of some home-cooked food was tempting,

"Okay, that would be good."

"I'll text you the address, see you around midday?"

"I'll be there."

They parted at the bus stop, and Joe walked back to the flat with a smile on his face and a spring in his step. Mike was still not back when he arrived, but he would be there soon as the team were playing at home this week. Joe didn't want all the good-natured ribbing that was sure to come, but he was bursting to tell someone about his afternoon. He even thought, briefly, about calling his mum, but decided that even if she answered, which wasn't a certainty, she would probably not be that interested. So he made a cup of tea and waited for Mike to get home.

Despite his good spirits, he still felt like an impostor, as if the good things that were happening in his life right now were undeserved. Steph didn't know about his past, and when she did, she probably wouldn't be as keen on him as she appeared to be right now.

She didn't know that he had been expelled from school, only being allowed back on-site to take his exams. His frequent angry outbursts in classrooms had been a contributory factor, that and the fact that he was not turning up to his lessons on anything more than a part-time basis, treating the school sixth form like a drop-in centre when he managed to get up in time to make it there. Then there was the fight. Gareth Grantly, posh prick that he was, had started making comments about how Joe's mum should wash his clothes more often so he wouldn't look like a homeless person. Now, Joe realised that was probably a badly executed attempt at a joke at his expense. At the time, it had seemed very much like an invitation to punch Gareth in the face. So even though he wasn't much of a fighter, that's what

Joe did. The ensuing fight had been what finally led to him being asked not to come back.

Like most incidents, there had been one chain of events leading up to it and another leading away. When they found out what had happened, Mum and Trev came to talk to him at his bedsit. Mum was full of concern and worry; she had looked upset and kept asking what she could do to help Joe sort out the situation he had got himself into. It was the last time he saw this bit of his old mum, the mum that had been his sole flatmate and confidant for all those years after Dad left.

Trev had been angry; he had interrupted his Mum over and over to let Joe know what a huge disappointment he was, what a waste of space that would never amount to anything. He berated and belittled Joe, and, unlike Gareth Grantly, he was way too big for Joe to even consider fighting – although he also seemed to be inviting a punch in the face. Joe had sat with his jaw clenched and teeth gritted while Trev told him he had until the end of the month to get a job because after that, he would not be paying the rent anymore.

His resentment continued to simmer long after they had left him alone in his room. It was still simmering a week or so later when Joe spotted Trev's car parked up on a quiet side street. The car, a stupid Ford Escort, was Trev's pride and joy – washed, polished, pampered and a garish yellow colour that made it easy for Joe to notice.

His blood was racing as he picked up some bits of rubble from a small area of scrubby wasteland nearby. By the time he had broken all the glassware and used a sharp rock to gouge the word 'cunt' in big upper case letters across the bonnet he could barely see through the tears that were welling in his eyes, tears of anger, rage and frustration. When the police arrived, he had already climbed up onto the roof of the car and was jumping up and down, stamping it into a new shape. He stopped as the blue and yellow car pulled up alongside, climbing down and then meekly getting into the back seat under the guidance of an officer.

Mum had come to see him by herself at the police station, Trev had been too upset and angry to even consider it. She was pretty cross too; she told him she didn't understand why he would do such an awful thing, and when Joe tried to explain, she seemed to glaze over, not hearing or listening to what he was saying. That was the last time they had spoken other than her occasional brief responses to his messages, he thought that Trevor was probably the main reason that her responses had dwindled in the last year.

He did not get taken to court on criminal damage charges, although that was what Trev had pushed for. The police had told him that it would not be in the public interest, which had probably infuriated him even more. But Wendy, the police lady who had helped him down from the top of Trev's car and then arrested him, had somehow managed to persuade everyone that an official caution would be the best resolution in this case. She had taken him aside afterwards and given him some firm advice about working on his anger management, not unsympathetically, but meant to guide him.

Mostly, he had been managing to keep his inner rage inside since then, even when it was hard. Until the day he had stormed out of Call Me Geoff's office, he had been doing okay. Now things were going well again, he was scared that his past might catch up with him at some point, or that history would repeat itself in a flurry of unexpected fury that he was unable to contain. He knew that at some point Steph would need to know some, or all, of this, and the shame of having to admit it, along with the fear of how she would respond, was paralysing.

As he finished his tea, his phone chimed and he opened the screen to see Steph had sent through her address as promised. He took a deep breath, it would be what it would be, he supposed. Sooner or later, he would have to tell her, so he should make the most of it while it lasted.

CHAPTER SEVENTEEN

"Hi, how is everything?" David called out as he let himself in through the front door.
Angela stopped what she was doing and came through to the kitchen where David was already switching on the kettle,

"It's all fine, I'm keeping busy."

"Pleased to hear it, what've you been up to?"

"I've been trying some new things."

"Sounds interesting, like what?"

She had been about to tell him about her trips out, but decided at the last moment that now wasn't the time. She would wait for a bit and then surprise him with an invitation to go for a walk together, maybe even all the way to the park. She didn't know if having David beside her would make that easier or harder; besides, her gut feeling was that this was something she needed to do by herself.

"Just this and that, nothing major. Did you bring me some new books?"

David pointed to the bags he had set on the kitchen table, two bulged with the food shop that he collected for her each week. The third sat slightly apart from the others. She started to pull out its contents, examining the covers of each book as she took it out. She always suspected he didn't choose these himself; he never seemed to know what any of them were about if she asked. She didn't mind, though; it was good that he reliably and regularly bought her a new selection.

She looked forward to his visits; he turned up twice a week, usually on Mondays and Fridays and usually at around mid-morning. There had been a few times in the last year when he hadn't been able to, then he would call her instead, causing her to hunt for the seldom-used phone, locating it by a kind of echolocation system as it repeated an irritating and strident electronic sound. On those days, he would usually send his assistant Courtney, who Angela suspected was the one who chose the books, with some essential supplies. She would watch through the window as the smartly dressed woman rang the bell, put the bags on the doorstep and left without waiting to see if they were collected or not.

She wasn't sure if David's visits were the product of fraternal love, duty or guilt. Whichever it was, he had been consistently turning up week in and week out for years now. Of course, he had needed to be there all the time initially, as her bones healed and she recovered from her injuries. It had been a dark time, one that she would happily forget – if only she could. She didn't want to get her hopes up too much, but she did think that maybe she had been sleeping better since she started her trips into the outside world. But that might have just been her imagination.

Whatever, she thought she wouldn't say anything to David right now. She would wait and see if she could make it any further than number forty-two, see if this was just a passing thing or if she really could manage to do more.

CHAPTER EIGHTEEN

Joe had come to a decision, he was going to tell Steph about himself. Not everything, just some edited highlights, he didn't know if this was going to turn into a proper relationship, but he knew he had to be honest with her from the start, or it would be doomed to failure from the outset. He didn't know yet how he was going to broach the subject, telling someone you're homeless and that you sometimes have anger issues didn't seem like it would be a comfortable thing to do. He'd told Janet at the shop that he didn't have a permanent address, and she'd been lovely, sympathetic and understanding, but he wasn't planning on being romantically involved with her, so it was different.
He ran through what he was going to say in his head as he rode the bus across town, trying to think of ways that he could make things sound less bad than they were. He was so engrossed that he almost missed his stop, then he thought he might be in the wrong place as he looked along the row of large detached houses and double-checked the directions on his phone. He guessed that either Steph lived in a house that had been divided up into smaller flats, or that she still lived with her parents. Arriving at the end of her drive, he decided that it was the latter–unless she was somehow extremely wealthy.

The door opened before he had even rung the bell, and he was greeted by a smiling Steph who didn't even invite him in before she kissed him. Once inside, she led him to the kitchen where she put the kettle on,

"Drink?"

"Yes, please, this is a nice place."

"Yeah, I'm stuck here with Mum and Dad for the moment. I should be looking for a place of my own, but this is rent free and I don't have to pay the bills."

"Fair play, I don't blame you." Joe looked around the grey and red kitchen, everything clean and a full range of working appliances and felt a pang of irrational jealousy.

"It's better than where I'm staying at the moment."

Now he added guilt to his jealousy, he hadn't intended to speak badly of Mike's flat, it had just slipped out. Steph was now pouring boiling water into the mugs,

"Why, what's wrong with it?" she asked.

"Well, nothing, it's just…it's kind of complicated. Can we talk?"

"Sure," Steph put the drinks on the island and sat on one of the stools, "what's up?"

"Well, like I said, it's kind of complicated," Joe started, then told his story.

Although he had thought it was going to be hard, he found that once he had got started, it was not. He began with Trevor moving in and him moving out, and although he hadn't intended to tell Steph the entire story, he ended up giving her a full synopsis. Expressions of surprise and disbelief crossed her face at regular intervals, accompanied by short articulations of 'No?' and 'Really?' and 'That's awful.' He took a large swallow of his tea.

"So that's how I came to be living on the sitting room floor of Mike's flat, and I thought you should know that I'm probably not as nice a person as you might think I am, before we get involved."

There was a quiet pause. He looked away from Steph, certain that she would have been appalled by what he had just told her.

"Oh, Joe, that's awful," was her first response, followed quickly by her climbing down from her stool and coming to hug him. The feel of the warmth of her body and her touch, combined with the raw emotions that had bubbled under the surface when he had been telling his story. He burst into tears as she wrapped her arms around him and tried to hide his face as the tears streamed down his cheeks.

"You poor thing, that's…well, it's shit."

Joe disentangled himself and started apologising, wiping his face with his sleeve and trying not to make eye contact with Steph.

"So anyway, that's who I am. I got chucked out of home, I blew my exams, I got in trouble with the police, I blew my job, and I'm homeless. And I'll probably mess it up at Griffin too, so maybe it's best if…I don't know, I'm not really the sort of person…"

Steph took a step back, drew a breath then answered him. Her tone was firm, and she held her closed fist in front of her as she spoke, unfolding one finger at a time with each point she made,

"Okay, let's just recap. From what you've told me, what happened to you was shit, that shouldn't happen to anybody. I'm not surprised you were angry, I'd have been bloody furious. You shouldn't have been having to do that by yourself; nobody should. It's not your fault you have nowhere to live; it can happen to anyone. I'm glad you've got a good friend like Mike. I happen to know, because Tom told me and I've seen it myself, that you are doing fantastically at Griffin. Tom talked to me yesterday and asked me to check that you were happy, because he really doesn't want you to leave. Lastly, I think I can judge for myself whether you're the kind of person I want to get involved with."

Joe didn't know what to say. Steph put her now open palm on his shoulder and touched his cheek gently with the back of her other hand.

"If that's the worst of it, I've had the misfortune to date men with nastier skeletons in their closets, and I had to find out the hard way," she told him. "I'm sorry those things happened to you, but thank you for telling me, maybe you can start to put some of that behind you now."

"But what will happen when Tom finds out?"

"Nothing, except maybe he'll help you get back on your feet. He's a nice guy."

"How can you be so sure?"

"Because I am, come on, let's get these mugs refilled."

She went back to the kettle and refilled it while Joe finished wiping his face with a tissue he took from the box on the counter. Steph spoke to him over her shoulder.

"So was the car really trashed?"

"Eh? Oh, yes, it had to be written off. The stupid bastard hadn't insured it, he got done for it, which made him even more pissed off with me."

Steph laughed out loud when he told her this, a good hearty guffaw that felt at odds with the recent conversation. It brought a smile to Joe's face.

"Do you want to know the worst bit of all?" he asked.

"Go on."

"I'm not even sorry, it was worth it, even with the police and everything."

"Good for you," Steph answered, "sounds like it served the bastard right."

They both grinned when Steph said this, then she suggested they go through to the front room and see if there was a film to watch. Lunch was going to be a bit later when her parents got back from the supermarket. Joe followed her through, and together they settled on an old black and white film that Steph assured him was good, although he'd never heard of it. He was sitting on the sofa with Steph curled up next to him when a voice came from the doorway,

"Casablanca? You should have waited, we'd have watched that with you."

Joe hadn't heard anybody come in; he guessed they must have used the side door. He looked around and saw an older version of Steph standing there.

"Hello, you must be Joe, I've heard so much about you recently, it's nice to finally meet you. The food will be ready in about twenty minutes or so, Dad's just putting it on."

"Thanks, Mum," Steph answered.

"Hi Mrs.... um." Joe looked at Steph, realising that he didn't know her surname. Steph grinned,

"Just call her Sally, I'm sorry, I should have said that before. I'm not much of a hostess, am I?"

"Hi Sally," Joe finished.

As soon as they were alone again, Steph asked him,

"You okay now?"

"Yeah, just not used to being around families, he answered.

"Come on," she paused the film and leaned over to kiss his cheek, "let's go and give a hand in the kitchen."

She led the way, with Joe following close behind, as she entered the kitchen. She wrapped her arms around the person standing at the counter,

"Hi, Dad."

He turned to greet her, and Joe froze in the doorway, looking from Steph to Tom and back again.

"Tom!" he stuttered.

"Hi Joe, how's things?" Tom asked.

Joe looked at Steph,

"Tom's your dad?"

"Well, yeah."

"Your dad's the boss?"

"Only at work," Steph grinned, "I assumed you knew."

"No, I didn't, how would I have known?"

"Because everybody at the office knows."

"I didn't."

Tom stepped in,

"I'm sorry, Joe, that's probably my fault. Let's start over. Joe, this is my daughter, Steph."

"Shut up, Dad," Steph smiled as she said it, then looked at Joe, "I'm sorry, I genuinely thought you knew, I didn't mean to make this awkward."

"No, it's fine, just a surprise, that's all." Joe was inwardly embarrassed, his first reaction had been a familiar and unwelcome flash of anger, thinking that he had been tricked or manipulated in some way. It passed in an instant but left a nagging feeling that he was not altogether in control of himself or events.

"Anyway," Tom said, "It's about time I got to know the newest member of the team a bit better. I hardly see you at the office, you're always working so hard. I'm making omelettes, so I hope you like them."

"Dad thinks he makes the best omelettes in the world," Steph told him, "it's his speciality."

"I love omelettes, so I'll let you know where they stand in the world rankings later," Joe answered.

The slight tension broke, and the three of them gathered around the counter to help chop ingredients and select fillings. Soon, the smell of cooking filled the kitchen as the omelettes began to appear, drinks were poured, and the table was set. Joe quickly found he was enjoying being in the middle of this scene of domesticity; he hadn't realised until right now how much he had missed home and family life. Steph and Tom argued good-naturedly about the best way to make the omelettes while Sally did her best to make Joe feel welcome as they prepared some salad together.

By the time they sat down to eat, Joe was feeling comfortable; his flash of anger and earlier rush of emotion were forgotten as everyone talked about their weekends and plans for the week ahead. The omelette did live up to its hyperbolic introduction, and his plate was soon wiped clean.

"I can wash up if you want," he offered.

"You could," answered Steph, "but the dishwasher would feel left out. Shall we go and watch the rest of the film?"

"What film?" asked Tom.

"Casablanca."

"Well, wait for us, that's one of my favourites, how far in are you?"

"About fifteen minutes."

"That's fine, we're joining you."

"You can't talk through it. Joe hasn't seen it before."

"Hasn't seen it? Oh my god, Joe, you are in for a treat. Come on, Sally, before they get the best seats."

Joe smiled to himself as he watched the family scramble towards the sitting room. He joined Steph on an armchair that was comfortably big enough for the two of them as Tom and Sally took the sofa. The film was good, he wasn't sure why he'd never seen it before and was glad he had now. As the titles rolled, Tom announced;

"The Maltese Falcon next week, you up for it, Joe?"

"Eh?"

"It's another Bogey film, you'll love it."

"Leave him alone," Steph said, "what makes you think he'll want to come back here after that horrible omelette?"

"Ooh, I know who's cleaning the staff drinks area next week now."

"Gary, he's the one who messes it up."

"Fair enough. Joe, it was nice to see you outside the office. I hope you're settling in okay and that Steph isn't making you do all her work for her while she slopes off."

"No, it's fine, I'm enjoying it."

"Good."

"Actually, Dad, Joe had something he wanted to ask you," Steph said.

Joe had a panicked moment when he thought Steph was going to tell Tom he had nowhere to live,

"Do I?" he asked.

"Yes, tell him about the pictures."

He had been reluctant to go to Tom about this yesterday, but now that he knew Steph was his daughter, it put a slightly different slant on things. He retold the story as briefly as he could for such a convoluted tale, showing Tom the pictures on his phone. He finished with the large picture from the gallery window.

"So you can see other pictures in this painting?"

"Yes."

"Like anamorphosis?"

Joe looked at him blankly.

"Sorry, I mean, do you have to look at it through a lens or a mirror or something?"

"No, you just have to look at it the right way. I don't really know how to explain it; it just kind of happens if you look for long enough."

"Send me the image, and I'll put it on the big screen."

Steph sent him her copy, and he opened his laptop and got it up on the screen.

"Show me what you can see."

Joe pointed to some of the elements he had seen within the swirls of lines and colour. Tom studied them carefully, leaning in to look carefully at the screen. Eventually, with a small shake of his head, he sat back.

"Nope, I'm not seeing…"

He stopped talking abruptly and leaned back in,

"Bloody hell, there it is. David Hacer, you sly old dog."

"You know him?" Steph asked.

"I was at college with him, nice bloke but all he ever seemed to paint were washy watercolours, rural idylls and that sort of thing. He's definitely upped his game since then."

"He still does the landscapes," Joe said, "but they're nothing like this."

"No," Tom agreed, "these are stunning as they are. The hidden pictures make it even more intriguing. I really like this."

"I think the hidden pictures are telling some kind of story, but everything's muddled up. The ones in the gallery are in the wrong order, and there are gaps."

"Really?"

"Yes, but I can't know for sure unless I can see the others."

"I've got boxes full of old trade magazines in my office at work. I'll get them out on Monday and see what I can find. I like a challenge; it can be my new project. David Hacer, eh?" he shook his head again. "I haven't seen him for years. He had a little sister who used to hang around with us sometimes. She was studying maths, I think. There was something that happened with her, but I can't remember what it was; it was after we'd all finished college."

He closed his laptop, and there was a moment of quiet. Steph broke it,

"Fancy going for a walk, Joe? I could do with some fresh air."

It was a nice afternoon, still sunny and dry, and Joe readily agreed.

"I'm so sorry about that. I thought you knew Tom was my dad."

They were walking along the footpath next to the canal that cut along the edge of town, overshadowed by old warehouses that had been converted into luxury flats.

"It's okay, I was just surprised. I'd have worn a better shirt if I'd known it was a work thing."

"It wasn't…" She looked over at his half smile, "You're winding me up now, aren't you?"

"Maybe, what about David Hacer, though? I think we should do a bit more research."

"I think so too, it's weird, isn't it?"

"Yeah, I wish I still had my laptop; it would be easier than looking stuff up on my phone."

"What happened to your laptop?"

"I sold it when I started to get behind on my rent, along with a lot of my other things. I should have kept hold of them; it was never going to be enough."

They stepped to one side to let a cyclist pass, and Steph put her arms around him,

"You'll get back there, Joe, it won't take long."

"I feel like I'm already on the way, mostly thanks to you – and Tom, of course."

He kissed her; he would have liked to stay just like that for the rest of the day, but the light was ebbing away, and he supposed he ought to get back to Mike's. He would have plenty more to tell him tonight.

"I'll walk you home."

"Don't be daft, I'll walk to the bus stop with you, it's only around the corner."

He didn't argue about it, they walked the rest of the short distance, then Steph waited with him until his bus came. They kissed,

"See you tomorrow then."

"Tomorrow, have a good evening."

"Steph waited on the pavement and waved to him as he passed before going home with a smile on her face and a spring in her step.

CHAPTER NINETEEN

The cat was sitting in the middle of the path as she came out, almost as if it were waiting for her. She wedged the door open and stepped out into the sunshine as the cat came to greet her, winding around her ankles and waiting for her to bend and scratch its ears. As Angela fussed over it, she heard the distinct sound of purring in the stillness of the afternoon. She stopped, and the cat turned to follow her as she walked the remaining distance to the gate.
"Which way, cat?" she asked.

The cat's answer was to twine itself around her legs again, disappearing under the frayed edges of her dressing gown.

"Well, you're no help, are you?" She looked up and down the road, then opened the gate and started to walk towards the park, determined to go further than she had last time. She took a couple of steps forward, the cat started to follow her and then sat down in the middle of the pavement with its tail wrapped around its feet. Angela glanced back at it,

"I suppose I'll have to do this on my own then," she set her sights on her previous best, the gateposts with the ceramic numbers, and started to walk along the road towards them. She knew she was right; this was something she would have to do by herself. She clenched her jaw and kept putting her feet one in front of the other, surprising herself with how quickly she covered the short distance. She passed number forty-two and kept going without pausing. As the trees on the edge of the park started to get bigger, she became more confident, increasing her stride as she swept along.

A car entered the road, she could hear it approaching from behind her. She knew if she looked around, she would panic. Instead of letting that happen, she held the top of a garden wall and stood with her eyes closed, listening as the car approached, passed, then became quieter as it left the far end of the road. She opened her eyes again as it was turning left, and abruptly burst into tears.

Wiping her eyes on her sleeve, she admonished herself.

"It's just a car, they drive up and down here all the time. It's just a car."

Frozen in place, she realised that she had not considered the fact that she would need to get home again, and she didn't think she could now. She started crying again as she realised that she was now stranded, the only way she would get back would be if she managed to get her stupid emotions under control again and rediscover the courage that had brought her here in the first place.

"Are you okay?"

She turned, surprised. The noise of the car had masked the sound of approaching footsteps from behind her. The woman looked concerned, she stood holding the hand of a young girl and was about to speak again when Angela recognised her, it was the lady from across the road.

"Do you need a hand?"

She admitted to herself that she did need a hand; she badly wanted to be back at home again, safe indoors, and she wiped her face with her dressing gown sleeve again.

"I do, I need to get home again, would you mind walking with me?"

The lady smiled,

"Not at all, it's only a short way, come on."

She gently placed her hand on Angela's shoulder and started to guide her slowly back in the direction of home. With every step, she found herself feeling calmer as the panic subsided, inwardly chiding herself for being so foolish.

"Why was the lady crying, mummy?" the little girl asked in a whisper that was loud enough for Angela to hear clearly. She answered,

"I just got scared. It's been a long time since I've been for a walk. Thank you for helping."

The girl smiled at her,

"It's okay, we were going to the park, but we can go later. My name's Elsie."

It had been a long time since Angela had had this much interaction with someone other than David, the girl's innocent introduction was something she would have found the thought of terrifying a few months ago. But now that it was happening, she found herself relaxing a bit more. The house was now no more than a few steps away.

"Well, hello, my name's Angela. You're the little girl with the cat, aren't you?"

"Yes, she's called Misty."

They were at the gate now, Misty was still on the pavement outside. She walked over to Elsie, who picked her up and started making a fuss of her. The cat looked as though it might try to wriggle free before changing its mind and settling into the crook of Elsie's arm.

"See, she's got misty eyes."

"So she has," Angela answered. She thanked Elsie's mum, who introduced herself as Deb.

"We don't see you very often. Are you okay now?"

"I'm fine now, thank you so much. I just don't go out very much usually."

Angela thought this must be the understatement of the decade,

"But I'm trying to get out more, it's just…well, it's difficult."

"Well, if you need any help, just ask. You can always walk with us sometimes if it helps."

Angela thought she was going to start crying again, but this time through gratitude. In her isolation, she had forgotten how kind people could be.

"Me and mummy are making cookies this afternoon, do you want me to bring you some?"

Elsie looked up at her, and Angela felt her eyes start to well up,

"That would be lovely, thank you. I do need to go back inside now. You have a lovely time at the park."

"Are you sure you're okay?" asked Deb.

"I'm fine now, thank you again."

"It was nothing, let me know if you need anything, won't you?" she smiled, then looked down at Elsie,

"Come on, you, put Misty down and we'll go to the park."

"Can't she come with us?"

"She wouldn't like it, there are dogs there, it would be scary for her."

"Oh," Elsie answered. She placed Misty on the pavement and took Deb's hand as they started to walk back the way they had originally been headed. Elsie looked over her shoulder as they went and gave Angela a small wave and a smile. Angela looked down at her old towelling dressing gown and the well-worn clothes it was draped over. She wondered what they had seen when they found her beside the road, a slightly mad old woman perhaps? Or an eccentric recluse maybe? Whatever it was, she was glad they had come to her aid.

CHAPTER TWENTY

The cardboard box next to the laptop on Tom's desk was stuffed full of catalogues and magazines, some creased at the edges, others bulging upwards as if they were trying to escape.

"I'm pretty sure you'll find some of David's work in some of these; I remember seeing them. I couldn't tell you which ones, though; I'm afraid there's going to be a bit of detective work involved for you."

"That's okay, I don't mind a project. Thanks for looking them out for me."

"No problem, I think I got the easy part of the job though."

Joe picked up the box, and as he did so, Tom picked up the laptop and placed it on top of the uneven edges of the pages.

"This is for you as well, Steph said You needed one, it's a spare old one that was gathering dust."

He wondered if Steph had told Tom what had happened to his last one; he hoped she hadn't but suspected that Tom now knew a lot more about his new employee than he had before the weekend. If he did, he didn't show any outward signs of being bothered about any of it.

"Thanks, I'll let you have it back once I've got another one."

"There's no need, consider it a gift."

"Well, thanks, I really do appreciate it."

He took the box and laptop back to the stockroom, where he placed them out of the way before getting back to sorting out the car crash paperwork. He had only just started when Steph came in,

"Power cable for the laptop," she announced, placing it on top of the pile.

"Why did he give me a laptop?" Joe asked.

"Because I told him you needed one, and he had that old one doing nothing."

"Did you tell him about… You know, everything?"

"No, I said yours was broken."

"Thanks, it's not that I'm trying to hide it, it's just, you know?"

"I know, you don't want to announce it."

Joe was glad she understood; he was also grateful for the loan of the laptop.

"How's it going anyway?" Steph gesticulated towards the remaining boxes of paper.

"I think I'm nearly there, a few more days maybe. It'll be done by the end of the week."

"That's good."

"It is, I'm still not quite sure what I'm supposed to do afterwards, though."

"Don't worry about that, there's always plenty to do."

Joe nodded as he looked at the returned folders that needed refiling. He wasn't quite sure how they had appeared between Friday afternoon and now, but there they were.

"Some of this stuff is really good," he told Steph, holding up a mangled piece of paper with a ship logo on it. "Are they all things that people have ordered?"

"To be honest," Steph replied, "a lot of it is stuff that was rejected by customers; it just sits here until it can find a way to be adapted and reused somewhere else."

"So nobody has ever used them?" he asked incredulously. He opened a drawer and pulled out an elaborately detailed drawing of a dragon. "Even stuff like this?"

"Yep, all filed away in case it can be given a second life."

"But there's loads of it."

He shook his head slightly and put the dragon back in its drawer.

"Do you want to help me look through these catalogues sometime? There are loads of them."

"By sometime, do you mean tonight? I can come round to yours if you want."

"Well, Mike's, but I'm sure he won't mind."

"Okay, how are you going to get them there?"

Joe hadn't thought of that, he didn't fancy lugging them on the bus.

"I'll put them in Dad's car and get him to drop me around, about seven?"

"Sounds perfect, I'll make sure the kettle's on."

With that decided, they both went back to their respective jobs and worked their way through a busy Monday.

*

Joe was waiting outside when Tom dropped Steph off. He took the box and carried it up the three flights of stairs.

"I could have carried them up myself, you know."

"I know, I could've let you, but it wouldn't have been very nice, would it?"

"I suppose not, thank you."

Joe pushed open the door with his shoulder and stepped aside to let Steph in. Mike had been fine about her coming over, he had even helped make the place look presentable, cleaning the kitchen and putting his games and CD boxes into regimented piles. The room was too small to ever look properly tidy, particularly when Joe's fold-out bed and possessions took up such a large part of the area.

But they had done the best that they could. He had looked at the bed and raised an eyebrow,

"Are you sure that's going to be up to it?"

"Shut up," Joe replied, "We've only just started going out."

"Yeah, but you know what those older women are like."

"For goodness' sake, I hope you're not going to be like this when Steph's here."

"Best behaviour – I promise."

He was good to his word, welcoming her in as she came through the door, offering to make a drink and inviting her to take a seat as Joe brought up the rear. She sat on the settee. Joe put the box down on the floor and joined her.

"Where do we start?" she asked.

"With a cup of tea and proper introductions. Steph, this is Mike, my hero and saviour. Mike, this is Steph, my work colleague and…friend."

Steph smiled and put her hand on top of his,

"It's okay, you can say girlfriend."

Until that moment, Joe hadn't been 100 per cent certain, as he'd never actually asked Steph out, he hadn't wanted to take it for granted. Mike moved past the moment, asking Steph if she'd seen all the pictures. This led to a Steph and Mike conversation about how great they were, and how cool it was once you could start to see the hidden pictures. Joe listened in as he put the kettle on and got a mismatched selection of mugs out of the cupboard. Soon they were all sitting around the box, Joe and Steph on the settee, Mike on an old wooden chair which he had procured from his bedroom.

"So we just flick through them all looking for any pictures that look like the ones from the book?" Mike asked.

"Yeah, but when we find any, we need to try and make sure we get them in date order, I think," Joe added, "I had a look in the box earlier, they're all jumbled up."

"Let's get started then," said Steph, "dive in, last person to find one makes the next cup of tea."

It was Steph who had to pay the forfeit, mostly because she had picked out a stack of older magazines, she made the tea and produced a packet of chocolate biscuits from her handbag. Most of the old trade catalogues were now in a pile on the floor at the side of the settee, spread out on the carpet between them all were about half a dozen, opened to pages that showed pictures like the ones Joe had seen in the gallery. They were arranged in a line, in the chronological order of the publications.

"What do you think, picture whisperer?" Mike asked Joe, "You're the expert."

Joe was studying them intently. He grunted back but did not break his concentration. Mike looked at Steph over the top of Joe's hunched shoulders and shrugged, She raised her eyebrows in return before turning her own attention back to the pictures.

The quiet of the room was broken when Joe leaned forward and swapped the position of two of the magazines. He sat back, looked for a moment, then asked,

"Are there any of those biscuits left?"

Mike passed over the nearly empty packet,

"Well?" he asked.

"It's still not complete, but there's more of it now. The ambulance needed to go before the hospital, I think."

He pointed at the pictures he had swapped. Mike and Steph both looked then, almost simultaneously, let out audible sighs of recognition.

"I see it," said Steph, "you're good at this. But what is the story?"

"I don't know yet, there's still not enough of them to tell properly."

"You could ask the guy that painted them, David Whatshisface," suggested Mike.

"I could, but look," he went through the pictures, including the ones they had copies of, and explained what he had worked out so far.

They disregarded the ones from the books as they had already figured out that they were just reflections on the contents of the stories they accompanied. With Joe guiding them, and showing them what to look for, Mike and Steph started to understand the fragments of the story he had pulled together so far.

"The pictures in the gallery were all in the wrong order, and their titles had nothing whatsoever to do with what they're actually about."

"How about we all do some background on David Hacer?" Steph said, "See what we can find out."

"What, now?" asked Joe.

"Good lord no, that was plenty of work for one evening. I think it's pub o'clock now, don't you?"

Both Joe and Mike agreed readily, putting on their jackets and flanking Steph as they left the flat. There was no more talk about paintings that evening, just three young people drinking a tiny amount more than they should have on a work night, laughing a lot and finding out a bit more about each other before moving on to the chip shop and then the bus stop, where Joe and Steph parted ways for the evening.

As Joe and Mike walked back to the flat, Mike nudged him,

"Nice one mate, you've done alright there."

"Thanks, I like her."

"If you ever need me to be out for the evening, just let me know and I'll make myself scarce."

"Okay, thanks mate," Joe answered, although he couldn't imagine having the audacity to ask Steph to stay at his friend's flat. In the back of his mind, however, he did not rule the possibility out.

CHAPTER TWENTY - ONE

The cookies had been delicious. Elsie and Deb had delivered them later in the afternoon on the day they had met, the misshapen rounds of chocolate bearing the evidence of Elsie's involvement in their creation. The little girl had passed them over with a smile, they had been carefully wrapped in some sheets of kitchen paper. When she had unfolded the paper, Angela had found the words 'I hope you're ok now' written on them with a red pencil in the stunted, carefully formed but imperfect letters that only young children can master.

Today, she was on a mission. Her bedroom floor was knee-deep in clothes. She pulled things from the wardrobe to try and find an outfit she would be less embarrassed to be seen in than the scruffy ensemble she had been sporting the day she met Elsie and Deb. She had finally settled on a blue jumper, some jeans and a pair of trainers that she had forgotten she owned. She looked in the mirror and decided it would do, it was just a shame about her hair, which she had been taking care of herself. By taking care, she meant hacking bits off with the kitchen scissors when she got fed up with it. Her dogged resistance to David's suggestion that someone should come in and do it for her meant she bore a striking resemblance to Worzel Gummidge. She brushed it as best she could, but had to admit to herself that there was no real way to salvage it at this point.

Downstairs, she picked up a package from beside the front door and left the house, walking as far as the gate before she paused uncertainly. Now she was about to do it, she was having second thoughts. She was ready to turn around and go back inside, but feeling the weight of the package and remembering how good the cookies were – not just the taste of them, but the thoughtfulness behind them – spurred her on.

Two steps and she was across the pavement and standing by the kerb. She looked up and down the empty road but didn't move, checking again and again, straining her ears for the sound of approaching traffic. She was certain nothing was coming, but still couldn't quite force herself to take the next step. For a moment, she stood with her eyes closed, taking deep breaths. She opened them again and repeated her careful scrutiny of the empty road, then, with tiny, hurried steps, scurried quickly across the short distance.

Once she was there, she stood by Elsie's gatepost, using it to help support her weight as she took deep breaths and her legs trembled. She was looking back at the road, a harmless width of black tarmac that had seemed like an insurmountable object in her head, an impossible mission. Except now she had done it, she was across it and had completed the first part of today's challenge. She smiled as she wondered what David would think of it if he knew, uncertain if he would be delighted or horrified.

Steadier now, she turned and looked at the house, not opposite now but right here in front of her. She opened the gate and walked up the path while Misty watched her from her perch on the inside window ledge. She reached out tentatively, holding her finger over the doorbell for a moment before pressing it. The sound from inside the house seemed enormous to her, almost causing her to panic and race back. She held fast and saw Misty jump down as the curtain was pulled to one side and a small face peered out at her, disappearing as quickly as it had arrived and being replaced by a loud shout from indoors.

"Mum, Mum, it's Angela, the lady from over the road, can I open the door?"

There were more muffled voices from behind the door, which swung open to reveal Deb holding Elsie under her arms as she lifted her to reach the door latch. She placed her back down, and they all stood on the doorstep for a moment before Elsie broke the standoff,

"Hello, do you want to come in?"

The thought sent a chill down Angela's spine; that would be too much, she had already done enough for one day.

"No, no thank you. I came to say thank you for helping me the other day, and for the delicious cookies."

"You're welcome," said Deb "Elsie insisted. I hope they were okay."

"I think they were the most delicious cookies I've ever eaten in my entire life."

Angela wasn't sure how it was happening, but the lady and her little girl were having the same soothing effect on her as they had previously. She smiled and lowered herself to Elsie's level.

"I thought such a kind and thoughtful gift deserved something in return," she told Elsie, "this is for you."

She passed the package to Elsie, who took it with both hands and big eyes,

"Can I open it now, Mummy? Can I?"

Deb looked at Angela, who nodded back at her,

"Of course you can, sweety, let's have a look, shall we?"

She prised her small fingers underneath the edges of the brown wrapping paper and clumsily pulled it open to reveal a stream of bright colours that swept from one edge of a small canvas to the other. She dropped the paper and held it up in front of her face,

"It's Misty," she said, her voice rising in pitch, "It's my cat, thank you."

She handed the painting to her mother and stepped forward to wrap her arms around Angela's legs. Deb took her turn to look at the gift,

"My goodness, so it is, thank you, it's beautiful. Where shall we hang it, Elsie?"

The girl had now released Angela and taken back possession of the picture.

"In my room," she answered.

"I'm sorry it's not more, it's just a hobby of mine, I hope it's okay."

"It's more than okay, it's wonderful, do you want to come in for a cup of tea?"

"No, thank you, I need to get back now."

Deb gave her a look that told Angela that she understood, or was starting to. She waited until the door was closed and she could hear the sound of feet on the stairs inside, then returned to the road. There she stopped and waited. She could see her front door now, directly in front of her. It wasn't going to take more than a few seconds to cross over and go back inside. She looked around and then waited again.

"Come on, you stupid woman," she muttered to herself, "You did it once today already, you can do this."

There was another long pause, and then she half ran across the road, up her path and into the house, where she stopped and leaned with her back against the door, breathing hard and smiling to herself. Behind her, the net curtain in the upstairs window dropped back into place.

CHAPTER TWENTY - TWO

On a tiring afternoon towards the end of the week, Joe reached the last few remaining tattered files from the bottom of the broken boxes. As he finished fixing and filing the very last one, he smiled and then stood back with his hands on his hips, surveying the now tidy room. Steph chose that very moment to come in with a drink for him. She realised immediately that Joe had finally come to the end of his task, putting the mugs down, she wrapped her arms around him and kissed him.

"Well done, you, you've done it."

"Yeah, that's it. So what happens next?"

"You go home early, that's what," a voice behind them said.

They looked around and saw Tom's beaming smile. He looked at Steph,

"Okay, you too, even though Joe did all the hard work."

"I helped, he couldn't have done it without my Sellotape and cups of tea."

"I know, you two seem to make a good team."

He took out his wallet and pulled out a twenty,

"Treat yourselves to something nice to eat, we'll talk about what you'll be doing next tomorrow, Joe – if that's okay?"

Joe didn't have a chance to answer; Steph spoke first.

"Actually, Joe has an idea he wants to run by you."

"Does he?" answered Tom.

'Do I?' thought Joe.

"Yes, it's about the archives."

"Well, if what you've done so far is a measure, I'll be happy to listen tomorrow. Go on, off you go the pair of you, I'll man the phones."

Steph grabbed Joe's hand and started to pull him towards the door,

"Come on, before he changes his mind."

*

"What idea?" asked Joe once they were outside on the pavement.

"The one you talked about yesterday, about using the rejected pieces."

"It wasn't an idea, just an observation."

"I know, but there's an idea in there. Let's go and get something to eat, and we can talk about it."

They went to the same café they had been to previously, it was quieter now that the lunchtime rush had ended, with plenty of free tables. They were sitting in a quiet corner, waiting for their food to arrive.

"So come on, what was my idea?"

"It was about all the old artwork we aren't using."

"That wasn't an idea, I was just saying it's a shame."

"True, but you're right. We could select some of the best of the unused pieces and try to reuse them, we could offer them to new clients at a reduced rate. They're all done and ready, so it could make for some quick turnarounds, and you've got a good eye for it."

Joe thought for a moment,

"That's actually a good idea, do you think Tom will go for it?"

"I'm pretty sure he'd let us give it a try; it'll be another part of the business. It'll get the artists more money – and recognition if it goes well."

Their food arrived and they started to eat.

"Do you want to do some David Hacer research when we're done here?" Joe asked through a mouthful of burger.

"Yeah, I haven't had the chance since we last met up. Have you?"

"Not really, just a couple of quick searches. I need to spend some proper time on it."

"Well, let's make the most of our time off then, eat up, and we'll go to your flat."

"Mike's flat."

"Yeah, whatever, it's a plan."

*

The Wi-Fi had been one of the first things Mike had sorted out when he moved into the flat, his main priority in fact. Joe had connected his newly acquired laptop to it, but had hardly had time to sit with it since then. They sat together on the sofa as Joe searched and Steph offered suggestions about how to extend or broaden the search. Before long, they had a row of tabs open along the top of the browser, but nothing that told them any more than they already knew. It was mostly about the gallery in town with occasional references to his time spent studying at the local college and some images of him, along with some thumbnails of the artwork. They were all pictures they'd seen before.

They carried on digging through the internet, gradually finding some new pictures they didn't have in their collection. They saved copies of these to a folder on the desktop to look at later. The many David Hacer landscapes they found did not interest them, they were not part of the story.

Joe stopped to make drinks, and Steph followed him into the kitchen area where they shared a long, passionate kiss as they waited for the kettle to boil. She pushed the weight of her body against him, making him wish that he had some way of knowing when Mike might come through the front door; he was fairly sure it would be any moment now. Nevertheless, he pushed back against her, pressing his own body against hers and holding her closely, enjoying the sensuousness of the situation and the thrill of anticipation for the potential for more intimate contact in the near future. Without warning, Steph stopped and stepped away from him.

"Did I do something wrong?" he asked, worried that he had overstepped some boundary.

"No, nothing. I didn't want you to think I was rushing things. I liked you from the first time you came into the office; you looked like a startled rabbit. Tom couldn't believe you'd take on such an awful job; nobody thought you would stay and see it through. I'm not always good at small talk, but it was easy talking to you."

"I liked you too, but I didn't think you'd be interested in me. Also, I didn't know you were the boss's daughter until it was too late."

"Would it have made a difference?"

"I don't know, I guess so – maybe."

"Well, that's definitive," she laughed. "Are you sure you don't want to be more ambivalent about it?" she kissed him.

"No, I'm glad you made the first move, though, I wouldn't have been brave enough."

"Well, I'm pleased too."

"Although I don't know why you'd be interested in someone with no job and no home, someone who's messed up so bad."

"You've got a job now, Mike's doing a sterling job of keeping a roof over your head until you get your own place, and I don't think you can take all the blame for everything that's happened to you. You got a pretty raw deal."

"Well, I might have to own some of it; nobody made me do some of the stupid things I did."

"Fair enough, but don't let it define you. Anyway, finish making my tea, we're not getting far with our research yet, are we?"

"No, I don't know where to look next. I guess we just keep digging."

They dug a bit more but didn't find anything that added to what they already knew. Finally, when Mike got in, they called it a day.

"I'll see you at work tomorrow. I've got to go with Mum to my aunt's house this weekend, it's her birthday. Not that I mind going, I like Aunty J, but I'd like to see you too."

"Me too, but I've got the charity shop after work tomorrow, then I have to do my laundry and go shopping this weekend, or I'll have nothing to eat and no clean clothes to wear next week, that takes most of Saturday. I guess we'll have to work on this again next week."

"I suppose we'll survive without each other."

"I'll try. Can you do me a favour?"

"What is it?"

"Don't remind Tom about the prints, I want to think about it a bit more first."

"My lips are sealed, see you tomorrow."

CHAPTER TWENTY - THREE

The letterbox shut with a metallic thud that Angela heard from the kitchen. It seemed way too early for the postman to be delivering mail; he didn't usually arrive until nearly lunchtime. She would see him wheeling his trolley down the road, wearing his shorts regardless of the weather and stopping to chat with people as he passed over their letters and parcels. It was probably a circular asking if she wanted new windows or a conservatory, or maybe someone asking her to vote for them in an upcoming election. Whatever it was, it surely wasn't urgent; she left it until she had finished what she was doing.

When she finally remembered and collected it, she was surprised to find not a letter, but a piece of lined paper folded in half. Opening it, she found a note of two halves; the top of the page was inscribed with what was probably Elsie's best handwriting, carefully formed letters arranged into, mostly, correctly spelt words. Beneath this, Deb had transcribed the note and added extra detail.

'This is to say thank you for the picture of Misty. We think it is gorgeous. We are going to the park after lunch, and Elsie wanted me to ask you if you wanted to come with us?'

She looked at the letter in her hand, re-reading it several times while she considered its contents. It had been so long since she had had an invitation to anything that she was unsure what she should do. The thought of going all the way to the park, along with the memory of her previous outings, made it a daunting prospect. But she also recalled how comfortable she had felt walking alongside the mother and daughter when they had come to her rescue, and she didn't want to let the little girl down. The clock in the kitchen showed that it was eleven thirty. Angela decided that she should go upstairs and start getting ready if she was going to join her new friends.

By twelve-fifteen, she was standing by her garden gate. She was wearing a blue and white striped shirt with a pale blue cardigan over the top, some black trousers and an old pair of plimsolls that she remembered as being comfortable. None of these clothes had seen the light of day for some time. She had looked in the mirror and decided they were fine before brushing and pulling her hair into some semblance of respectability. It had been a while since she had tried to dress like this – like an ordinary person - and she hoped that she would pass.

Elsie saw her waiting as soon as she came out of her house. She waved and ran down to her gate, smiling and waiting for Deb to catch up. When she did, there was some discussion about looking both ways, holding hands and being careful when she crossed. Elsie complied with all the instructions until a few feet from the edge of the road, when she broke formation and ran to meet Angela.

"I knew you'd come. I told Mummy you would because you said you wanted to come to the park with us."

Deb had now caught up,

"Well, we don't know that yet, do we? And anyway, Angela may not want to go all the way to the park today. Do you remember we talked about this?"

"Yes, because she might get scared again, like she did before."

Deb looked up apologetically, but Angela had started to smile, enjoying the interaction of mother and daughter, and the honesty of Elsie.

"I might yes," she answered, "sometimes I find the outside really scary. But I think it might be easier with you to help."

"Why do you get frightened of the outdoors? Is it because of the dogs?"

Deb gave the same look again, the one that said, 'Kids – what can you do?'

Angela did not try to hide her smile,

"It's a long story," she told Elsie. "It's not the dogs, no."

"I like stories."

"You may not like this one. Come on, are we going to walk or not?" She opened her gate and joined them on the pavement. Together, they started to walk in the direction of the park. Angela felt a small hand slip into her own and smiled down at Elsie in her bright red sweatshirt. She was more than a little surprised when she felt another hand slip into her free hand. Deb gave a gentle squeeze with her fingers,

"We'll just go as far as you like, say if you want to turn around."

It was at that moment that Angela knew she could make it, that she would get to the park. Although it was only a short distance from the house, it was a big first step towards showing her brother, and the world, that she was getting better.

Inside the park gates, Elsie let go of Angela's hand and ran onto the grass, picking up a twig to wave like a magic wand. Angela stopped and looked at the vast expanse of open space in front of her, a huge ocean of grass, punctuated by trees and stretching out in every direction. She didn't realise how long she had been standing, staring at it, until Deb spoke,

"How long has it been?"

There was no need for her to elaborate; it was clear to both of them what the question meant. They had moved in across the road when Elsie was small, but had never seen Angela out of the house until recently.

"Three years," she answered. "Nearly four."

"Are you okay right now?"

"I…I think so, but I don't think I can go much further."

It was true, she was excited and happy, but she could feel her heart beating at what felt like a hundred miles an hour, she was perspiring slightly, and all her senses were on high alert. She knew, from reading about it, what hypervigilance was, and this was it: fight, flight or freeze. She was working hard to override her instincts, to tell herself that it was safe, that it was okay. Deb seemed to sense at least some of this,

"It's alright, I'm here and the house is only a short way away."

She was still holding Angela's hand, and she increased her grip by the smallest amount, and Angela felt a little calmer. A gentle breeze blew across the tips of the grass, making ripples of light and dark green around the trees and the scattering of people who were enjoying the afternoon. Ahead of them, Elsie had crouched down and was examining something on the ground. She stood up, turned and ran back to where the two women were standing. With a smile, she held out her hand,

"These are for you," she offered a tiny posy of daisies that she had collected from one of the many patches that were spread across the grass. Angela took the handful of tiny blooms carefully, using both hands to make sure she didn't drop any.

"Thank you, Elsie, they're beautiful."

They were, possibly the most gorgeous thing Angela had seen in years. Not that she didn't see flowers regularly, David often bought a bunch to brighten up the house, but none that had been given in such a spirit of kindness and friendship as the daisies. She felt a small tear start to form in the corner of her right eye and her vision became fuzzy, she wiped it away and told herself not to be so ridiculous.

"Do you want to pick some?" Elsie asked.

Angela looked out at the expanse of space, a place where anything could happen, where she would be exposed and vulnerable. She wanted to stay here by the fence, but she also wanted to join Elsie. She had already done so much today, though, so why not take just one more step? She pointed at a patch a few feet away,

"Why don't we sit down over here? Just for a little while."

They walked to the spot that Angela had indicated, Deb with her hand gently on Angela's shoulder and Elsie leading the way with her magic wand stick, and sat in the warm sunshine. She felt the coolness of the earth beneath her hands as she lowered herself to the ground, the texture of the grass on her fingertips, and the smells and colours of the outdoors invaded her senses. She realised now how much she had been missing this while she hid inside; she liked it, and she wanted more.

Elsie had wandered towards a small slope and was climbing to its summit, reaching the top she lay down and rolled back down the incline through the grass.

"She'll get messy," Angela said to Deb.

Deb shrugged and smiled,

"Sometimes life is messy, she's having fun, and we've got a washing machine."

Angela remembered this after she had been escorted safely home again. She had declined Elsie's offer of a drink of juice but agreed that they should go to the park again another day.

"Tomorrow?" Elsie had asked Deb hopefully.

"We'll see," had been the answer.

Angela put her small handful of daisies in a shot glass on the window ledge then lay down on the sofa and closed her eyes. 'just five minutes' she told herself and was soon snoring gently, with a twitching smile flickering across her sleeping face.

CHAPTER TWENTY - FOUR

When Mike got home, the pictures were still spread across the floor. Joe apologised and went over to start picking them up. "No, leave them for a minute, they're not hurting. I like looking at them, especially since you showed me how to find the different elements in them."

Joe was pretty sure that Mike would have figured this out by himself eventually, he was one of the smartest people he knew. At school, he had cruised through all his subjects, or at least he would have done if he'd ever managed to stay out of trouble for long enough. Not big trouble, nothing malicious or egregious, just a near-continuous succession of minor indiscretions. Mike was one of those restless souls who never seemed to settle into one thing before he was onto the next. He wasn't suited to sitting in quiet rooms for long periods listening to teachers explain things methodically and slowly. His boredom threshold was easily breached, and that was when his decision-making skills appeared to desert him.

His current job suited him, a combination of physical labour and a constantly changing environment, along with a group of co-workers who would tolerate, if not enjoy, his occasional detours off into Mike-land. Joe would not be surprised if Mike ended up running the company or starting one of his own one day. For now, he seemed content to work all the shifts he was offered and let the money accrue in his bank account. Aside from the flat and following his beloved football team, he had few outgoings and seemed the most content that Joe had ever known him.

"How did you get on with the research then?" he asked.

"It was okay, we found a few bits. There was nothing from more than four years ago, though, it's like they only started being painted then. I don't know, maybe they did."

"It does seem a bit weird to suddenly change from paintings of the countryside and beaches to the other ones overnight. There must be something else to it, something that came before."

"That's what I thought, but I can't find anything. Still, we did get a few more different pictures to add to what we had already. If I'm honest, the new bits just make it more confusing."

Mike was now studying the pictures with him.

"Yeah, I see what you mean. It just doesn't quite make sense, does it?"

"Not yet."

"How's it going with Steph?"

"It's okay, I really like her."

Joe braced himself for some ribbing that never came.

"That's good, I like her too, she's nice – and good-looking. The offer still stands if you need the flat to yourself."

"Thanks, I'll keep it in mind."

"Pub?"

Joe didn't answer, just started to put his trainers on as Mike, who hadn't waited for an answer, put his jacket back on and they left the flat together.

The next day passed quickly. Joe was busy at work, ostensibly going through the drawers to check that everything was now in order, although he had an ulterior motive. He kept a notebook close to hand, stopping occasionally to scribble a reference number in it before continuing. The pages soon started to fill with his list of numbers and dates. The rest of the office didn't notice what he was doing. Friday was a day to finish projects and meet deadlines before the weekend, which kept everybody busy.

He had a snatched lunch with Steph, between the two meetings that she had been asked to sit in on. It was a muted affair as they both contemplated having to spend the weekend apart,

"I think I've got a plan for Tom. I'm working on it anyway, I'll tell you about it next week," said Joe.

"No, don't leave me hanging, tell me now."

"I can't yet, I'll have something more definite by Monday if you want to come over to Mike's."

He didn't want to talk about it at work or at her house with Tom around, not until he was ready.

"Monday it is then, I've got to go to my meeting now, I'll see you next week."

Joe finished his afternoon and left for the charity shop, where Janet greeted him with her usual cheery smile. She had left a section of the shop for him to organise in his inimitable way, he set to it while he thought about how he was going to approach his plan. In the end it was Janet that started the conversation.

"You seem quiet today, are you okay?"

"Sorry, just thinking, that's all."

"Okay, anything I can help with?"

"Well, it's funny you should ask that,"

Joe explained his idea to her as she made tea in the background. It didn't take long, Joe finished and then looked at her to see what her response would be. He had steeled himself for a range of options, from dismissal to laughter and everything in between. What he had not anticipated was the delighted enthusiasm that he received.

"I love the idea," Janet told him, "I think Tom will too. Explain it like you just did to me. I'm sure he'll think it's a great idea."

"Really?"

"Yes, it's brilliant."

"Well, it's just an idea at the moment; there's still a lot to do."

"Honestly, I've known Tom for years; he'll love it."

"Do you think so?"

"I'd bet my eye teeth on it."

Joe spent a lot of the subsequent weekend typing up his proposal. It was arduous work, requiring a lot of thought and a little research. What he didn't want to do was approach Tom with half an idea; he knew that would just mean being sent away to add more detail or just being dismissed out of hand. He finally understood why they had tried so hard to teach him some of those things at school – skills that he'd never imagined that he would need at the time. He finally arrived at what he thought was a reasonable representation of what he had wanted to say. He would show it to Steph next week; that would be the acid test. He hoped he had got it right; he didn't want to make a fool of himself.

CHAPTER TWENTY - FIVE

After lunch strolls became something of a routine for Angela, Elsie and Deb. It hadn't been every day, but several times Elsie had been supervised while she crossed the road to deliver a handwritten invitation for Angela to join them; she had watched her from the upstairs window, her spirit lifting when she saw her coming. The days and times weren't predictable, so Angela found that she was starting to dress properly in the morning just in case. Clothes that hadn't seen the light of day for years had come out of their long hibernation, and the tatty old dressing gown now spent more time hanging on the back of the bedroom door than anywhere else. Being up and dressed for the day made a difference to how Angela felt about herself and how she approached her days. Now she felt like she was getting up with the prospect of doing something, and the days didn't all just merge into one unending mass.

David had called, as he usually did, and expressed surprise at what she was wearing – a spotty dress that she had remembered wearing on a trip to the beach once, probably there were photos somewhere to prove it. She had, of course, told David she could wear whatever she chose.

"I know," he replied, "it's just that you usually choose that grotty old dressing gown."

She couldn't decide whether to be insulted by his description of her robe or refreshed by his honesty. She chose not to waste energy being offended, not when things were going so well. She was still planning on walking right into his gallery one day and seeing the look of disbelief on his face. Not yet, but it did feel like she was on the way at last. Her walks to the park were getting bolder, venturing further inside the perimeter. Elsie had asked if they could feed the ducks next time they went; the pond was visible from the gate, just. Angela had been uncertain but had tentatively agreed that they would one day. She was hoping Elsie would appear with a note today; she had decided that it would be a good day to feed the ducks, and she had even set some crusts aside for the visit.

She wasn't rude, but she didn't want David to still be here if Elsie turned up. She kept hinting that she might have things to do and that maybe David should be making sure the gallery was okay or making more art. Eventually, he left, and not a moment too soon. As his car pulled away, the door opposite opened, and Deb and Elsie stepped out. Elsie had her note already written and looked disappointed when she saw that Angela was already outside her house. Deb sent her carefully over anyway, to pass the note to Angela. She didn't need to read it. Elsie announced that they were 'going to the park in a half of an hour' if Angela wanted to come with them.

"I'd love to," she told her. "I've got some bread for the ducks inside. See you in thirty minutes."

"Half of an hour," corrected Elsie.

"Okay, half of an hour, see you outside."

The ducks squabbled, pushed and quacked their way forward, surrounding Elsie's feet and making her squeal with laughter. The laughter was infectious. Deb took photos on her phone, and Angela watched the spectacle, ready to step in if Elsie needed rescuing. There was no need; when the bread ran out, they lost interest and plopped back into the water where they preened themselves with their beaks and waited for their next meal. The procession of splashing ducks started Elsie off giggling again, and the two women joined in. Once it was quiet again, Angela pointed to the kiosk on the far side of the pond,

"Who wants an ice cream then?" she asked.

"Me," shouted Elsie, looking up at her mum as she answered.

"That's fine, Els, are you sure, Angela?"

It was much further than they had walked before, a long trip around the pond. But Angela had planned this; she knew she needed to start making bigger steps and was getting impatient now. At home, she had hunted through her belongings, eventually tracking down her purse. There was still money inside this little-used artefact from a previous life; she had tucked it into her pocket before she left the house.

The further they got from the house, the more comfortable she became. Elsie walked between her and Deb, holding both of their hands, and they made their way to the kiosk. She chatted all the way, about what she had been doing at preschool, what her friends' names were, which flavour of ice cream was her favourite and so on. On a previous trip, Deb had confided to Angela that she was dreading Elsie starting full-time school and that she was determined to enjoy every day that she could still spend with her. Angela had felt honoured to be included in this quality time, she had tried to repay this kindness by bringing along some drawing materials and showing Elsie how to create her own pieces of art. Elsie had been more keen on collecting the examples that Angela made for her. Deb said that she had been carefully sticking them into a scrapbook. She, however, had been fascinated, watching Angela carefully, asking questions and trying her hand at it herself.

They arrived at the wooden hut, and Deb ordered two drinks and a banana-flavoured ice cream. Angela handed over the money to the young girl behind the counter, feeling proud of herself for doing something that she had done herself a million times before, that anybody, even a child, could do. Ridiculous, she knew, but nevertheless, there it was. They sat at one of the small metal tables, sipped their drinks and licked a banana ice cream as they recalled how funny the flock of hungry ducks had been.

There were only two tables by the kiosk; most people took their drinks and snacks and went to sit on one of the many benches surrounding the pond. Angela had sat on the chair that faced away from the second table, so she didn't see the two young men approach the hatch, order drinks and sit at the empty table behind her. She only realised they were there when one of them laughed out loud at something the other man had said. There was nothing untoward or unpleasant about the sound, but Angela tensed. She glanced behind her and then quickly turned back. She gripped her mug of tea with both hands, her body rigid and her head a frenzy of conflicting instructions. She started to look around, hunting for an escape route.

On their previous trips, they had not come into close contact with any other people, only passing dog walkers and other parents with their children, all from what Angela considered to be a safe distance. This was different, she knew now that she had been rash. She had overstepped a boundary and was paying the price.

Elsie carried on licking her ice cream and delivering a monologue about why ice cream was the best thing ever, oblivious to the fact that nobody was listening to her anymore – if they ever had been. Deb had been talking about a planned holiday to Greece, one last fling before they got tied into the rigid structure of school holidays and overpriced flights. She noticed Angela look behind her and saw how her demeanour suddenly changed. No longer the confident and outgoing woman from a few minutes ago, but the same scared person that she and Elsie had rescued from the street a few weeks ago. She leaned across the table and put her hands on top of Angela's.

"It's okay," she said, "it's safe, you're safe."

Elsie noticed now, she looked back and forth between the two of them before speaking to Deb,

"Is Angela scared again, mummy?"

"Yes, dear, but she's going to be okay." She looked at Angela, "We're going to take her home now, I think she's had enough today."

Moments before, Angela hadn't known whether to scream, run, hide under the table or cry. Maybe a combination of all of the things she had thought, as her mind raced to decide what to do. Deb's calm voice and gentle touch grounded her again, slightly. She took a brief look back over her shoulder, the two men sat drinking their coffees and chatting, oblivious to what was occurring on the table next to them. They were just two ordinary men enjoying a walk in the park and a catch-up; they probably hadn't even noticed the three of them sitting at the table next to them.

She started to cry, not loud sobs, but silent weeping; tears ran unchecked down her face, and she started to shake. Elsie looked alarmed as if she, too, might start to cry at any moment. Deb took control. She moved around the table and positioned herself between the two of them, putting an arm around each of their shoulders. She spoke to both of them,

"It's all okay now, whatever it was, it's over now, nothing's going to hurt you here and now. You're safe."

Elsie buried her sticky yellow face in her mother's armpit, and Angela started to relax fractionally,

"I'm sorry," she said, "I'm so sorry, it's so stupid."

She took a handful of napkins from the dispenser on the table and started to dab at her face.

"It's not stupid, whatever it is. We've got you, haven't we, Els?"

Elsie's face reappeared, filled with concern and still not certain that she wouldn't cry,

"I'm sorry, I dropped my ice cream."

Now, small tears did start to appear in the corners of her eyes. Both women turned their attention to her, reassuring her that it was okay and that they weren't cross.

"It's okay, Els, it was nearly finished anyway. We can make some banana bread when we get home. Angela can have some too, if she likes it."

Elsie looked at Angela, her big, wet eyes asking the question for her.

"I love banana bread," she answered. "It's my favourite thing."

"I thought you liked cookies," she said accusingly.

"They're my favourite thing too," Angela told her, now starting to regain her composure.

"You can't have two favourites," she was told accusingly.

The seriousness of Elsie's face as she told her this elicited smiles from Angela and Deb.

"Who told you that? I have lots of favourite things."

"Yes, but…" Elsie was, unusually, lost for words. Angela felt herself regaining the composure and confidence she had felt earlier. She looked back at the other table where the men were showing each other pictures on their phones. She turned to Deb,

"Thank you," she mouthed, almost silently.

"Okay now?"

"Yes, thank you, yes."

"Shall we start walking back? I've got banana bread to make."

They both smiled at this, then got up and started the walk back. Angela's legs felt unsteady as they set off; the adrenaline wasn't leaving her body as quickly as it had arrived, and she felt a bit wobbly. Walking past the men at the other table did not set off any other triggers or warnings from her subconscious; it had just been the surprise of seeing them there. It was fine, everything was fine now.

At her house, she was pestered by Elsie to come over later and have some banana bread.

"You would be welcome to," Deb said. "You could meet Gareth. Elsie's told him all about you."

"I'd love to," Angela replied, "But first, I think I need a little rest."

"See ya later then," Elsie smiled and turned to Deb, leaving Angela standing, watching her new friends as they returned safely to their banana bread appointment.

CHAPTER TWENTY - SIX

Mike answered the door and let Steph in. He glanced around to check that the flat was still relatively tidy and decided that it passed – just. It was one of the things he liked about having Joe to stay, he was one of those people who seemed to enjoy tidying and organising – neither of which things were Mike's strengths. There was some washing up by the sink, nothing too shameful, and the pictures were still spread out on the floor. They had been carefully walking around them since they spread them out the other day, occasionally pausing to look at them and see what else they could pick out from them.

"Hi, Mike," Steph came in and made a beeline for the prints.

"Joe just popped out to get some milk, he'll be back in a minute."

"Okay, is it alright if I wait?"

"No problem, I'll put the kettle on."

"Thanks. How are you doing anyway?"

"Fine, thanks, and you?"

"All good, a bit tired. I may have had too much to drink at my Aunt's birthday."

"I can relate to that. Tea or coffee?"

"Coffee, please." She looked over at Joe's neatly folded clothes next to his bed. "You're a good friend to Joe, he's lucky you could put him up."

"Joe's great. I wish he could just move in. If I could afford a two-bedroom place, I would. I might ask him if he wants to start looking once he starts getting paid regularly. He really needed a break. I'm glad your dad gave him a chance."

"I'm pretty sure Dad's pleased with how it's working out, too. I just don't get why someone's parents would turn them out like that. It's not right, is it?"

"It was more, Trev, his mum used to be okay when we were kids. She'd always give us something to eat if we came round, and made sure Joe had everything he needed. I like her."

"Do you think Trev's stopping her from speaking to him?"

"I'm sure of it, he's a real bigmouth, thinks he's something he isn't. He works out at the airport; he tells people he's security, but he just checks people's tickets when they're boarding. He's a real prick."

Steph paused thoughtfully, then they heard the key in the lock as Joe returned with supplies.

"Hi, Steph, I was just out getting milk," he held up the carton as if to prove it. "How are you?"

"Fine, getting over the weekend. You?"

"All good. Tea or coffee?"

"I've already got that under control," Mike told him. "Sit down, and I'll bring them over." He took the milk from Joe and turned back to the kitchen area.

Joe sat with Steph on the sofa, and Mike carried across two steaming mugs.

"So how did you two get on with the detective work the other day?" he asked.

"It all turned into a bit of a dead end. We didn't find out much else," Steph answered.

"No, there's not a lot about it online," Joe added.

Mike looked thoughtful for a moment, then asked, "Did you just carry on looking at the art and auction sites?"

"Yes, that's where we're most likely to find stuff. But we ran out of anything new."

Mike collected his mug from the counter,

"Just the art sites?" he asked.

"Yes," Steph replied.

"Didn't you try going through the news archives? Local paper and all that?"

Steph and Joe looked at each other, mirroring a look that said, 'We should have thought of that.'

"No," they answered together. Joe got up and collected his laptop from beside his bed. Mike pulled over the folding chair, and they huddled around the screen as Joe typed into the search bar.

"I can't believe I didn't think of this," muttered Steph.

"Me too," Joe replied, "look at all this stuff."

A page of articles, all linked in some way or another to David Hacer, had appeared on the screen. Joe scrolled through, opening several to see what they were about. Mostly, they were to do with the opening of the gallery, special exhibitions and articles about local businesses. There were very few copies of the pictures that had ignited their curiosity, and none that they hadn't seen before.

"Well, it was worth a try," Mike said as Joe clicked onto the second page of results.

"Yeah, I wonder if there's anything else we could try," Steph said.

Joe stopped scrolling and clicked on a link,

"What's this?" he asked as the page opened. The article included a mention of David, but it wasn't about him or his gallery; it was about his sister. The three friends read the brief article together. Under the headline 'Artist's Sister in Critical Condition' was a brief write-up about Angela Hacer, who had been admitted to the hospital after being hit by a car. Joe immediately linked this to one of the paintings on the floor, the headlights, the ambulance in the background, and the view looking up through the branches of a tree. He showed the others.

"Tom said she had a sister," Joe said to Steph. "Remember?"

"So it's about her, not him," Steph said, try searching for her name instead of his."

What came up were several stories from the local paper, all about Angela Hacer, sister of a local artist, who was involved in an awful incident nearly four years ago, just before the first paintings started to appear. The three of them read them, mostly the same information retold in slightly different words, but with the same details. The serious head injury, the induced coma and the damage to her lower limbs and pelvis featured heavily in most of the write-ups. They started to find the links between the pictures they had and various elements of the story. Some parts appeared several times; the hospital appeared in several pictures, in a slightly different form each time. Various figures identifiable as doctors, nurses, and police officers appeared in numerous places through these early artworks. The newspaper stories begin to fizzle out after her recovery was reported, leaving the newer works as mysterious as they had been to begin with.

"So he was painting what happened to his sister?" Mike asked.

"Looks like it," answered Joe. Steph nodded.

"Well, why would he do that?" Mike asked the others, looking to them for an answer that they didn't have.

"I guess we've still got some detective work to do," said Steph.

"Have you tried talking to him?" Mike asked.

"No, not yet," Joe answered. "It's just weird how the titles he gives them have nothing to do with what they're about."

"Shall we go to the gallery next week?" Steph suggested, "It can't hurt, can it?"

"How will we know when he's going to be there?" Joe asked.

"I'll ring them up and ask if we can talk to him as part of our university course," said Steph.

"But we're not at university," Joe replied.

"You know, you're pretty stupid for someone so clever," Mike told him.

Steph laughed, and Joe made an 'I guess so' gesture with his hands and shoulders as he went to put the kettle back on.

CHAPTER TWENTY - SEVEN

The men in the park, as unthreatening and benign as they were, had freaked her out. As always, she felt stupid now that the incident had passed. But at the time, her fear had been a real and raw response over which she had no control. It was why she had spent so much time shut away inside her parents' old house, hiding from the world and hiding from the things that scared her. At first, her injuries had stopped her from going anywhere, but as time went on, everything changed. Outside had become a terrifying place, all after that night four years ago. David had been great, of course, looking after her, nursing her back to health, making sure she had everything she needed and providing some company when she felt the need for interaction.

She was never quite sure if he provided this support out of familial duty, brotherly love or guilt. In her darker moments, she blamed him for what happened, so why wouldn't he blame himself? She knew it wasn't his fault, and heaven knew he'd apologised enough times, but there was always an unspoken acknowledgement that his caregiving was a part of his penance.

Petulant thoughts that she could not silence, asking questions that could never be spoken aloud – and would not be satisfactorily answered even if they were. The fact remained that David was supposed to have been driving her home that night, had offered to, in fact.

She had always been a little afraid of walking alone after dark. Who knew what dangers hid in the shadows and lurked in the empty spaces? Not monsters, but men capable of monstrous things, men who would hurt and humiliate her, or worse. She knew, of course, that not all men were like this. Most were kind, thoughtful and gentle. But the ones who weren't were exactly the sort of men who would skulk in dimly-lit back streets and alleyways like cowards, waiting for weak and vulnerable prey.

She had called David fifteen minutes after he had failed to show up. The leaving do for one of her work colleagues was winding down, and people were drunkenly climbing into taxis or leaving in small groups. She had assured them all she had a lift, and so they had departed, confident that she would be able to get home safely.

On her third attempt to ring him, he had eventually answered, slurring and apologetic, explaining that he had forgotten and was now too drunk to drive. Too drunk to do anything much at all. He suggested that she get a taxi, or 'gerra taskie' as he put it. It was the time of night when taxis begin to be in short supply, and being alone with an unknown man made her nervous anyway, which David knew. So, bracing herself, she set out to walk the two miles to her flat.

The distance would not have been an issue, more of an inconvenience than anything else. But walking among the drunks and revellers through the city centre was not an appealing thought. There was a slight chill in the autumn evening air, but at least it wasn't raining. She set off into the night, muttering under her breath about what a useless idiot her brother was. She fully intended to give him hell tomorrow, probably with an early morning call that would upset his hangover, followed by a demand that he take her out somewhere for lunch. He could pay for it, of course.

As she walked, her breath came out of her nose and mouth in thin ribbons of vapour. When they were kids, she and David used to roll up their bus tickets on the way to school and pretend they were smoking on chilly mornings, taking elaborate puffs of their bits of paper and blowing thin streams out through their pursed lips. Her shoes clapped on the pavement, she would have worn trainers if she had known she was going to have to walk home. The sound broadcast her position in the now rapidly emptying streets.

Once she was past the well-lit and, thankfully, not too busy centre, she got to the part of her journey she had been dreading. Her flat was close to the canal; 'a desirable dwelling in an up-and-coming area' was how it had been described to her when she had first moved in. She quickly realised that up and coming was letting agent code for 'stuck in the middle of a less desirable area'. The excitement of seeing the sparkling new flat in the refurbished mill building had meant she had been blind to the boarded-up houses and crumbling edifices that she had passed on the way to view it. She noticed them now, though, on this dark and frigid night. Only one in three streetlights seemed to be working, slivers of light crept through the occasional gap in a curtain, and there was rubbish piled on street corners. The only sound she could hear was the clacking of her shoes, echoing between the rows of terraced houses.

She paused at the end of a long road, then cursed David silently under her breath again. This was the quickest way home, but the thought of running the gauntlet on this dark and foreboding road was too much. She decided that, despite her feet hurting in her clicky-clacky shoes, she would walk the longer route. It was better lit, and even at this time of night, there would still be traffic on the main road and possibly even other people returning home after a night out. She turned right and started walking.

The lights cast a yellow glow through the curling wisps of mist that had started to form around their tops. She pulled her jacket closer around herself as the chill of the evening started to set in, and with more urgency, increased her pace despite her shoes being more for show than go. A bus passed, going in the opposite direction, back to the depot. She looked enviously at the few passengers who were sitting in warmth and comfort, deciding that she might have a late night bath when she got home – what the hell, it was Saturday tomorrow.

The houses here were set further back, behind high fences and long gardens that provided a buffer from the noise of the traffic. The road curved gently along its length, so Angela didn't see the figure in dark clothes leaning against a garden wall until she was some distance along her route. It was the movement of the glowing tip of a cigarette that she first noticed, then the smoke being blown out in a plume that hung slightly in the cool air. It was too far to turn back, and crossing over was not an option as there was no pavement on the far side of the road. Steeling herself, she moved to the outside of the pavement as she approached and quickened her step slightly, just wanting to get by as fast as she could.

He watched her approach, his face benign as he took another puff of his cigarette and let the smoke out in a cloud that surrounded his head like a halo. As she drew closer, he spoke to her, his voice almost lost in the night air,

"Been anywhere nice, love?"

She glanced over at him, then looked quickly ahead again. There was nothing about the man that suggested he might be a danger to her, medium length hair, glasses, half a smile and his head cocked to one side as he spoke. She didn't answer him but just kept on walking past him with her eyes fixed on the buildings at the end of the road, which were now in sight. The middle building was home, she would be able to swap her shoes for slippers, make a cup of tea and maybe watch TV in bed as she wound down for the day; she could save the bath for tomorrow morning. She didn't know then that she would never see the inside of her flat again.

Behind her, she heard footsteps. She didn't need to look back to know that it was the smoking man; she could see him in her mind's eye pushing himself away from the wall and starting to walk along behind her. She tried to shrug it off, telling herself he just happened to be going that way, that he had been taking a rest and was now on his way home. Still, she wished he weren't quite so close behind her. She increased her pace slightly, hoping to widen the gap between them, still looking towards home. But if anything, he sounded even closer, she could now hear him breathing and the sound of his jacket rustling as the fabric of the sleeves brushed against his body. She wasn't sure what to do next. Her instinct was saying 'run!', but she knew that wasn't an option in these stupid shoes. She was passing an old warehouse that was being renovated, a building site really, with nowhere to go and no one to call for help. Hoping that the man was intending to walk past her, she moved to one side of the pavement. He was closer now, much closer. He spoke again, louder this time,

"Didn't you hear me, love? I asked if you'd been anywhere nice?"

This time, his tone was different, not as soft. She carried on walking, on the verge of breaking into a trot. He called to her again, and this time, his voice was almost beside her,

"Are you ignoring me? I spoke to you nicely; why are you just blanking me?"

Angela felt him put his hand on her arm, and she pulled away,

"Leave me alone, I just want to go home."

"Well, you could stop for a chat with me, couldn't you? It wouldn't hurt you."

Now, he had moved in front of her, forcing her to stop. She could see that she had been mistaken about his benign appearance; the hair was greasy and fell over his eyebrows, half covering his dark eyes. What she had mistaken for an attempt at a smile now looked more like a sneer, and his breath smelled of a mixture of tobacco and beer. She reached into her pocket for her phone, although she had no idea who she might ring. The police? 'Hello, a man talked to me. Can you send a car?' She tried to step around him and continue on her way, as the screen of her phone lit up.

"You stupid stuck up bitch, what do you think I'm going to do? Rape you?"

The moment those words left his mouth, Angela's fear turned into full-blown panic. She turned and ran, despite the shoes that weren't designed for it. As she turned, she saw car headlights approaching on the previously deserted road, and she ran into the road so it would come to a stop, and whoever was inside could help her. She waved her arms above her head and started to shout, even though she knew that the occupants would not be able to hear her – logic and reasoning had taken a back seat.

The car didn't start to slow down until after it had sent her flying into the air, somersaulting over the bonnet and landing limply in the middle of the road with a sickening crunch. Angela lay there. It had happened so fast, but she still remembered every detail: the feeling of her legs and pelvis breaking as the front of the car hit them, the dizzying sensation of being thrown into the air and the force of the ground as she smashed helplessly into it. From her position on the tarmac, she could see the man in the dark jacket running. The driver of the car got out and hurried to the rear of his vehicle, where she was joined by her passenger.

"Fuck, you hit her."

"She just ran out, I couldn't help it."

"Is she dead?"

"No, come on, nobody saw, let's get out of here."

"What about her?"

"Somebody'll help her, I'll go to jail if we hang around here."

"But she's hurt."

"She'll be okay, come on, before anybody comes."

"Help me, please," Angela managed to get the words out, but only to the backs of the departing driver and her passenger. Her phone was still in her hand, undamaged and still shining. As the pain started to well up through her body, she managed to open the lock screen, and as her eyes started to lose focus, she was able to call the first number that came onto her screen – David.

*

Angela had once read somewhere that people who had been in induced comas often had no memory of the events that led to their hospital stay. No such luck for her though, she had replayed the scenario more times than anybody could count, every detail of that evening was etched stubbornly into her brain.

She looked down at the painting in her hand; it showed Elsie laughing as she was surrounded by a mob of ducks. Angela had an appointment with some banana bread, and she was determined that nothing was going to stop her. Not the road, not the passing cars or any strangers that happened to be nearby, she was bloody well going to do this. Because if she didn't, she was going to be stuck in this house for the rest of her life.

CHAPTER TWENTY - EIGHT

The visit to the gallery was a washout. David Hacer had been happy to meet with them; he had made them drinks and invited them to join him in his small studio at the rear of the gallery. He had been convivial and polite, talking about his paintings and discussing the techniques and materials he used. He had happily posed for some photos that Steph took with a camera she had borrowed from her dad, and invited them to come back whenever they wanted. The only awkward moment came when Steph looked in her notebook and casually asked,

"Did your sister's accident influence your work at all?"

The brief silence that followed gave no clues to any possible answer. David looked down at the floor and said,

"I'd really rather not talk about that, thank you."

He then changed the subject, talking about a recent trip to the coast where he had put together a portfolio of sketches and photographs that he was using to produce a series of seascapes. He quickly regained his composure, and Joe and Steph did not raise the subject again.

They thanked him before they left and promised to send him a copy of their essay once it was finished.

"It was all landscapes," Joe said, once they were a respectable distance from the gallery.

"I saw, and he wasn't working on any of the other paintings."

"He changed the subject pretty quickly when we asked about them."

"And when we asked about his sister. Come on, let's get a drink and something to eat. I'm hungry."

They went into the first café they passed, ordered something to eat and sat at a quiet corner table.

"So what do we do now?" Joe asked.

"I don't know, it's a bit of a dead end, isn't it?" was Steph's reply.

There was a pause while their food was delivered to the table. Joe took a bite of his sandwich and watched Steph carefully pick through her salad to remove any visible traces of cucumber before picking up her fork.

"Do you think it was just a passing phase? Something he tried for a while?"

"I don't know, he's still selling them. And what about the books?"

"I don't know either. Can I have your cucumber?"

"Eugh, help yourself. I don't know why you would, though."

She looked out of the window at the people passing by.

"Do you ever wonder where everyone else is going?"

"I don't know, I didn't used to think much about anyone else. I guess I was just too wrapped up in my own problems to be bothered about other people's lives."

"Do you ever wonder what I'm thinking?"

"Sometimes, why?"

"I'm thinking that my parents have gone out for the day; they won't be back for hours yet."

Joe crunched the last piece of cucumber and looked at her, trying to decide if she was suggesting what he thought she was.

"So, drink up, let's go and make the most of it."

He still wasn't certain that she was proposing what he thought she was, but he was willing to find out. He drank his Coke, and they left for the bus stop, hoping to make the most of the time they had available.

CHAPTER TWENTY - NINE

The banana bread was delicious, warm and rich with sultanas, which David had always hated, but she thought any self-respecting cake was not worth its name unless it had some. Elsie was excited to have a visitor, bringing a selection of her favourite toys from upstairs to show Angela. A pink plastic pony with a rainbow mane, a teddy bear similar to the one Angela and every other kid had when they were small, and a painted box filled with shiny pebbles and marbles. She marvelled over them and agreed that it would be fair to swap the duck picture for a piece of green sea glass that Elsie had found at the beach the previous summer.

Elsie carried the picture carefully upstairs to put on her chest of drawers where she could see it from her bed. During this lull, Deb asked Angela if she was okay now.

"I'm fine, I'm sorry about earlier – it's just hard sometimes."

"I can see that, but you did well. You know you're welcome here anytime, don't you? Elsie likes having someone new to talk to. I think she's ready to start school."

"I think she'll love it, and thank you. You've been so kind, so has Elsie."

"Not at all; like I said, Elsie loves you. She's always pestering me to see if you want to come out with us. To be honest, I think she may be starting to get bored with just me for company."

She laughed as she said this.

"You know she calls you Angel when she's talking about you, don't you?"

Angela hadn't picked up on this; it would have been hard to notice amongst the stream of information that poured from the little girl when they met. She smiled.

"It's as good a name as any. I like our walks, I'm building up to visiting my brother's gallery in town. I still think I'm a little way off that, though."

"The man in the suit who calls round?"

"Yes, David. He opened a shop while I was recovering; I got hit by a car a few years ago. I've never seen it, but I will."

"That's terrible. The getting run over, not the gallery. We can help if you want. Fancy having two famous artists in the family."

"Oh, David's the famous one, not me. I think getting to the gallery is something I've got to do by myself, really, but thank you."

"I understand, but the offer's there."

Elsie came back into the room, carrying Misty. The cat was hanging from her arms like a rag doll.

"Misty wants to know if you're staying for tea?"

Angela and Deb exchanged smiles,

"No, I'd better not. I'm still full of delicious banana bread, but thank Misty for asking me. Maybe another time."

Elsie dutifully relayed the message to Misty, and Angela got up to leave.

"You should ask your brother to put some of your pictures in his gallery, you know. I'm sure people would like them."

Angela shook her head,

"I don't think so, I only do it for fun."

"Well, me and Elsie think they're wonderful; all the colours and patterns are beautiful. Maybe you could show Elsie how you do them sometime? I know she'd enjoy that; I would love it."

Angela looked over at Elsie, who was now dangling a piece of ribbon in front of Misty, who was dutifully trying to catch it as it was repeatedly pulled out of reach. 'Why not?' she thought to herself, it might be fun.

"Okay," she answered, "shall we say the day after tomorrow? It'll give me time to tidy up."

Deb smiled,

"That would be lovely, thank you. Usual time?"

'Usual time' had become just after lunch when Elsie needed some form of diversion. Now that Angela had agreed, she felt nervous. It felt like a lot was happening very quickly after so many years of solitude. There wasn't much to tidy in her house, but she wanted to look around and check that it was kid-safe before Elsie came in. Apart from David, they would be the first visitors she had had since the nurses and carers stopped coming to check on her recovery. She couldn't remember for sure when she had finally regained her mobility and independence, but she knew it was at least two years ago.

The moment she got back indoors, she put down the piece of banana bread that Deb had wrapped in foil and given her on the way out. She looked around, trying to decide what tidying would need to take place to prepare for the impending visit.

CHAPTER THIRTY

Deb stood in the doorway and watched as Angela stood on the kerb waiting to cross the road. There was no traffic coming from either direction, but still Angela hesitated, looking from one end of the road to another and seeming to take an age before finally summoning the courage to traverse the short distance. When she eventually did, she scurried quickly over, making her limp more pronounced, she didn't slow down until she had reached the other side. This level of caution made more sense to Deb now that she knew a little more about what had happened to Angela, although she suspected that there was more to the story. She was sure Angela would tell her in her own good time, when she was ready.

They had moved into the house two months after Elsie had been born. The timing couldn't have been worse, but house sales take as long as they take, and her desire to be in before the baby was born was not part of the deliberations and machinations of the Land Registry, the bank or the estate agent. Everybody she spoke to was sympathetic but ultimately powerless to do anything about it. The chaos of moving and looking after a baby at the same time was every bit as bad as she had thought it would be; the only saving grace was that she was at least back with Gareth, who worked for an engineering company that had relocated to the town shortly after she found out she was pregnant. He had very nearly quit, not wanting to be separated from Deb before the baby was born, but Deb had persuaded him that it would be okay, which it mostly was, even though there were times she had not been so sure it was a good idea.

There were weekends together, house hunting, packing, planning and preparing, and Gareth's company had been understanding about giving him time off for antenatal appointments and scans. But ultimately, Deb had been by herself a lot of the time. It was made worse by knowing that Gareth was missing out on big chunks of what was one of the most exciting and important events in his life to date. She didn't like to tell him on their evening calls if she was tired or hurting, as she didn't want to worry him. Similarly, she didn't tell him the first time she felt that slightly surreal moment when the baby first started to kick, waiting instead for it to happen at the weekend and acting as surprised as him.

He had, of course, been there at the birth and had taken leave to be with her and Elsie for as long as he could. But by the time they had to move house, he had used up all the days off he could. The removal guys were great, and Gareth spent two straight nights at the new house getting it as move-in ready as he could. Even so, a lot of the nitty-gritty had fallen to her, which only added to his guilt. It felt like unpacking had taken an eternity; reclaiming all their belongings and finding places for them while feeding, changing and caring for Elsie had been tough. It had taken a full six months before she managed to locate her precious album of family photos. Gareth eventually found them after he came home to find her crying after another unsuccessful search one evening. They had been tucked inside some folded-up curtains they had bought with them from the old house and had not needed.

Finding herself in a new and unfamiliar town, with a two-month-old Elsie to look after and all their possessions in boxes, had been hard. There had been a lot of late nights, some arguments and a great deal of stress. Eventually, they found their equilibrium and started to enjoy parenthood together as Elsie grew into and then out of her terrible twos.

At first, Deb had paid little attention to the apparently unoccupied house across the street from them. But sitting up at night, feeding and soothing Elsie, she looked across to see lights on in the upstairs window and the occasional shadow of someone moving around the rooms. She would notice the man in the suit visiting occasionally with bags of shopping and other parcels, and her curiosity was piqued. Several times, she had considered going over and introducing herself, but decided that would be rude and intrusive, as it would mostly be to satisfy her curiosity.

Over the course of time, she continued to watch the house, noticing any comings and goings. She had glimpsed once or twice the woman that she now knew lived there as she opened the door to the man in the suit. Occasionally, she would see her looking out of her window, watching the comings and goings in the street, but until recently, she had never seen her leave the house.

All of that changed a few weeks ago when Deb got up in the night to get a glass of water. Wide awake in the silent house, she had stood in the front room looking out of the window as she sipped from her glass. She had seen the lady from across the road come out of her house, draped in her dark coloured dressing gown. She went out of her gate and walked the short distance to the lamppost. Her steps were tentative and cautious on the way there, scurrying and hasty on the way back. And then she was gone, back inside her house with the door firmly closed behind her. It was the first time Deb had seen her neighbour properly since they had moved into the house.

The next time she saw her was the day that she and Elsie found her crouched by a wall up the road. Recognising her, she offered to help. Everything about her told Deb that she was frightened to death; she knew she couldn't have left her like that. She was relieved when the neighbour started to calm down as quickly as she did. Later, Gareth told her that she should have left her; what if she'd scared Elsie? He'd asked.

She told him then that he was wrong, and all her subsequent meetings with Angela had confirmed this. She felt like she was doing a good thing for someone, of course, but she also knew that she and Elsie had started to enjoy the company of their newly found friend. Since she had left her job before Elsie was born and then moved to a new town, adult companionship had been in short supply. She was already looking forward to visiting her with Elsie in a couple of days.

CHAPTER THIRTY - ONE

It was Janet who got things moving again. Joe had been filling her in on all the latest developments as they unpacked and priced up bags of donations in the back room. He had been keeping her updated on their progress regularly, as she was as curious as everyone else about the mysterious books that had come from her shop. He told her about the visit to the gallery and how it had left him and Steph feeling they had hit a brick wall. He didn't tell her about what happened after the trip to see David Hacer; that was personal, but he did say that things were going well between them. "Hmm," she mused as she lifted a fresh bag of oddments, books and clothes onto the sorting table. "Sounds to me like he doesn't want to talk about them. Maybe it was just a passing phase."

"That's what we thought, but Steph doesn't understand why he would do that and then go back to doing exactly what he was doing before."

Janet shook out a shirt and put it on a hanger, ready to steam.

"Maybe he didn't."

"Eh? Didn't what?"

"Maybe he didn't go back to the landscapes, maybe he never stopped."

"What? He did them at the same time?"

"No. Maybe the other paintings were done by someone else."

"But they've got his name on them."

Janet waved her hand in a dismissive gesture,

"So? Look."

She took a pen from the pot on the table and wrote her name on an awful print of an angry-looking dog with a broken frame that had been leaning against the bin. She held it up to show him, in case she hadn't made her point.

"This has my name on it, but I'm glad to say it isn't mine."

"I suppose. But why? Why would he do that?"

"I don't know, maybe whoever painted them wanted to stay anonymous. Or maybe they did them for him, like some of the Renaissance artists used to get their apprentices to do bits for them."

"Well, it's weird, but I guess it kind of makes sense."

"Thank you for your vote of confidence," Janet replied through a plume of steam.

The front door opened, and Joe went through to the shop. A pair of customers browsed the shelves before selecting some books and a couple of DVDs. Sometimes the customers in the shop asked him for his advice or opinion on a prospective purchase, others just seemed to want to have a chat. When this happened, he remembered watching the video of the old lady who had inadvertently got him into trouble in his old job. He recalled how embarrassed he felt for having been so short with her, and he tried harder. This couple were busy talking to each other, leaving Joe free to think while he waited at the counter. He hurried back once he had finished serving them.

"So, who do you think painted them then?"

"Beats me, it's only a thought. It's just so unlike his other paintings, and you said he didn't even seem to know what they were about."

"I'm seeing Steph later, I'll see what she thinks about that. I'm just going to put out these CDs, then I'm about done."

"Me too. You can get going once you've done that. Have a good weekend."

" You too."

*

Mike was already at home when Joe got back. He was sitting on the sofa with a tin of cola and a doughnut. He pointed at the kitchen counter as Joe came through the door,

"Eat one of those before I finish the lot."

Joe saw the open packet on the counter. There were only two doughnuts left, so Mike must have been on his second one already. Joe helped himself and joined Mike.

"How's it going?" he asked.

"Yeah, all good," replied Mike. "How about you?"

I'm great, work is good, and I'll get paid next week. I'll be able to give you some towards rent."

"Nah, don't worry, it's all good."

"I want to, though. Don't make me feel bad."

"Okay, if you insist. It's good having you staying here."

"I'm really grateful, though, you got me out of a tight spot."

"Like I said, stay as long as you want. It's no problem."

"It'll take me a couple of months to get a deposit together, I'll probably start looking for somewhere else then."

"Fair enough," he licked the sugar from his fingers and wiped them on his work shirt. "I'm going away this weekend, we're playing some team up near Liverpool. Tiny's brother lives up there, so we're going for a night out after the game."

Joe knew Tiny from school, he was one of Mike's football supporting friends who went to as many matches as he could, like Mike.

"Anyway, you're welcome to use my room if you want. I already tidied it up for you, just in case. Steph's welcome too."

Joe considered waving the suggestion away, but the thought of sleeping in an actual bed - and being able to invite Steph to stay over - was not to be dismissed so easily.

"Really? Thanks, mate, you're a real friend."

"No worries. How's it going with Steph anyway?"

"It's going really well, I really like her. I think she likes me too."

"Course she does dumbass, anyone can see that. Just nobody understands why."

"Piss off."

Mike grinned,

"So have you two….you know?"

Joe thought of the afternoon at Steph's house, then tried to change the subject,

"Janet reckons that someone else might have painted the pictures."

The grin grew even broader,

"You have, haven't you? You dog, you don't hang about, do you?"

Joe felt his face getting hot.

"Ah, sorry mate, it's none of my business, is it? But good on you, I'm glad you two are an item; you suit each other. Anyway, what is it with you and those pictures? You can't let them go, can you?"

"I guess not. I just want to know that's all; they've got under my skin. I want to find out more about them, but the more I find, the less sense it all makes." He looked at the framed photocopies on the wall and was quiet for a moment.

"Did I tell you about work?"

"What about work?"

"I've got a meeting with the boss next week."

"Steph's dad?"

"Yeah, but he's the boss at work."

"What about?"

"I've got this idea for using their archives to make posters and prints, there's some really good stuff there just sitting around in drawers. I thought it might make a bit more profit for the business. I don't know really, but Steph thinks it's worth a try."

"I reckon if Steph's given it the thumbs up, it's probably worth a go. It sounds like a good idea to me. I hope her dad goes for it."

"I don't know, it was only a thought at first. But the more I've been thinking about it, the more it makes sense, the artists would all earn more too, from the royalties."

"Sounds like you've got too much on to go looking for new flats then."

"I'll get round to it. So what time are you going tomorrow?"

CHAPTER THIRTY - TWO

The art session with Deb and Elsie had gone well. All three of them had enjoyed it, and Elsie had taken home several pictures she had created of herself, Deb and Angela. She had also left one behind for Angela to keep; it was a charming depiction of the three of them in the park. Nothing was to scale, and there was very little detail, but it was clear what it was, and Angela had put it up on her mantelpiece, then taken it down again and tucked it away. She wasn't sure why, but she didn't feel ready to share this new part of her life with David just yet.

She had invited them back for another afternoon, and Deb had insisted that she should come over for a cup of tea and to meet Gareth. They had agreed on a day, and Angela had not been put off by the thought of the trip across the road, which she was starting to feel a bit more confident about now that she had done it a few times.

Meeting Gareth hadn't been as bad as Angela had thought it would be. He was introduced by Elsie, who had proudly proclaimed,

"This is my dad, he's like a giant – but nice."

Angela had laughed at this; Gareth was indeed tall. She already knew that, having seen him from her window many times before. What she had not known from her observations was that he was softly spoken with a faint Scottish accent. He repeatedly pushed his fringe up and away from his eyes and adjusted his glasses; his fair complexion and clear skin made him look very young. Although Angela was finding that an increasing number of the people she saw walking up and down the road looked young nowadays.

Gareth the Giant had invited her in, and Angela saw that Deb and Elsie had been busy preparing for the occasion. A plate of fairy cakes was set on the kitchen table, each one decorated with pink icing and a scattering of sugar sprinkles. There were cups and saucers, a milk jug and a steaming teapot ready and waiting, along with a small glass with a picture on the side of the brightly coloured pony that Angela had been introduced to on her earlier visit.

This was the largest social event that Angela had attended since the leaving do on that fateful evening. Elsie, who had instigated the tea party, was the one who was responsible for putting her at ease. She had walked over to meet her, under Deb's supervision, and escorted her to the house with the instruction not to be scared because Daddy's funny, even though he does get cross sometimes. Similarly, Gareth had been well-briefed by Elsie not to make Angela afraid. He didn't. The conversation was easier than she had imagined it was going to be; she had been worried that she would have another panic attack or simply lose the ability to speak. Neither of those things happened.

*

After her accident, she had spent two months in the hospital, mostly in excruciating pain, after she had come out of her coma. David had spent countless hours sitting at the side of her bed, only absenting himself when her discharge was imminent and he needed to sort out their parents' house and make it ready for her to live in while she finished her recovery. Once she was back at the house, he arranged for carers to come in and help, but he was still a semi-permanent fixture for a long time. It felt like an eternity; the pain of her rehabilitation exercises was enormous, and the frustration of not being able to complete even the most mundane of tasks was enraging. But worst of all were the nightmares.

She would wake up in the early hours of the morning, bathed in sweat. She imagined she could feel the broken ends of her bones knitting themselves slowly back together as her pain meds wore off and every detail of the night of the accident refreshed as she relived that awful sequence of events in her sleep. The faint wisps of fog, the darkened road, the smoking man, the sound of his breathing and the dazzling headlights speeding towards her. By day, she was tired and irritable; by night, she was awake and scared, trembling in her bed, too afraid to close her eyes and be transported back to the night of the accident.

Slowly, her body started to repair itself; she became more mobile, her appetite started to return, and she stopped getting headaches. But the dreams continued unabated. If she dozed off in the afternoon, the sequence of events would start to replay itself. At random times during the day, the memories would arrive, uninvited and unwelcome, in her mind. Doctor Parnell, who David had arranged to come and talk to her about it, gave her some tablets and assured her the flashbacks would become less frequent. They didn't, and the medication reduced her to a zombie-like state for most of her waking hours, unable to focus on anything for long or engage with anything meaningful. And still, the nightmares came.

It was quite by accident that she discovered a way of making the thoughts stop. During one particularly lucid dream, she fell out of her bed, landing on her hip. It did not cause further damage to her now-mended pelvis, but the pain was excruciating; it flared across her lower back and all the way down her leg, and in that instance, she forgot everything. The visions and memories that had been filling her head were gone, driven away by the intense flash of pain.

Over the next few weeks, she experimented. When she was having intrusive thoughts and flashbacks to that night, she would pinch herself or prick her arm with a pin she had started to keep near to hand for that very purpose. And to an extent, it worked. But it didn't do what Angela most wanted it to do, which was to stop the thoughts from arriving in the first place. She couldn't say when it started to happen, but she started to pre-empt the negative thoughts, jabbing herself occasionally or punching herself on the thigh over the damaged bones and ligaments. The pain became a release, a way to escape from the demoralising and exhausting life that she had been living.

David didn't realise what was happening until Angela had progressed to scraping her arms and thighs with a blade she had taken from a craft knife. He walked into the kitchen and found her sitting with her arm held out in front of her, watching the blood well from a fresh cut in amongst a latticework of older scars and welts. Horrified, he asked her,

"How long?"

She couldn't look him in the eye as he helped her clean and dress the wound, and then went to look for Doctor Parnell's phone number to ask what he should do. Angela grudgingly agreed to see him; as far as she was concerned, she had already achieved what he hadn't. Even though she knew what she was doing wasn't right, she thought it was better than the alternative.

Predictably, Doctor Parnell offered some kind words and another, different batch of pharmaceuticals. Angela agreed, mostly to please David. But she had no intention of reducing herself to the semi-comatose shadow of herself she had been the last time. She decided that it would be easier all around if she paid lip service to the treatment while working on being more discreet and secretive about what she was doing.

David began spending more time at the house again; he had been visiting less frequently when he thought she was on the road to recovery. The next couple of months were tense, a game of cat and mouse with Angela pretending to take the tablets and carrying on hurting herself while David tried to monitor her to achieve the opposite. He had brought his work with him, setting up a temporary studio in the spare room upstairs. An easel, a stack of canvases and a table of neatly arranged paints and brushes next to pots of turps and linseed oil. Everything was in its correct place and set in neat rows, ready to be used.

Angela had wandered into the spare room one afternoon. The sun came through the window, lighting one side of her brother as he studied the photos and sketches pinned to the side of his easel before leaning forward and adding more detail to the rolling hills, trees and sky that was currently taking shape on his canvas. She remembered how the paintings she had used to do had spread themselves across the surface and everything surrounding it when she had been at school. That was before she had chosen to go and study maths at university, which had left little time for artistic pursuits. Her subsequent job with an insurance company, which was only meant as a stopgap, had also eaten into her leisure time. Now, she felt an urge to paint again.

She didn't want to wait for David to leave the house, not knowing when that might be or how long he would be out. So she just came right out with it and asked him,

"Can I use some of your paints and a canvas?"

If David was surprised, he didn't show it.

"Sure, have this one."

He handed her a clean white canvas and a selection of paints and brushes, which she took downstairs to the kitchen and spread out on the table. She then spent the next thirty minutes staring at the blank space in front of her, not knowing what she wanted to put on it. David came down to make a drink.

"Still deciding what to do?" he asked.

"Yes, it seems a shame to mess up such a perfect thing."

"You won't mess it up, you were always good at painting."

"Well, it's been a long time. What should I do?"

"Just paint what you see out of the window."

"Yeah, maybe. I'm going to leave it here for a bit and think about it."

"Okay, let me know if you want more paint or different brushes."

The canvas stayed propped up on the table for the rest of that day without being touched. It was still there in the evening; David had worked around it when he was preparing their meal, and they had sat in the front room to eat.

"I've got to go to the gallery tomorrow morning," he told her. "Will you be alright while I'm gone?"

"Of course I will. I'll be fine." She smiled at him to demonstrate how fine she was.

"Okay, if you're sure. But give me a ring if you want me to come back, won't you?"

"Of course I will, I'll be okay, stop being such a worrier."

"Well, you know I worry about you; I can't help it."

By the time he left the following day, Angela had spent hours thinking about what she would do once he was gone. Recently, the occasions when he had left the house, she would wait for the door to close and listen for his car engine. Then she would take her shirt off and add to the growing numbers of nicks and scabs on her abdomen, ones that he wouldn't see. But as the door closed behind him today, something made her change her mind, as the memories of the accident, which now accompanied the pain she inflicted upon herself, started to well up, she went to the canvas in the kitchen instead.

It was like turning on a tap. Once she had started, her anger, pain, and humiliation poured themselves onto the space, filling it with colour and shape. The lines and curves came from somewhere deep inside her, manifesting her feelings and filling every corner until finally she stopped, exhausted. She stepped back and looked at the empty tubes of paint, the scatter of brushes and the painting. The picture was as visceral as it had been cathartic, a chaos of every feeling that she had been denying or suppressing.

She was fast asleep in the armchair by the time David got back. His only comment had been to ask her if he wanted him to get her some more art materials.

*

Now, sitting with Elsie, Deb and Gareth, she knew what she needed. She knew it as instinctively as she had known how to paint her pictures. She needed to start talking to people, to take the leap of faith and start to reintegrate with society. To meet people and remind herself that even though bad things had happened, there was still good in the world. This thought brought a tear to her eye.

"Are you okay? Do you need to go home?" asked Deb.

Angela wiped her cheek with her sleeve,

"No, I need to stay here. Gareth was going to tell me about Elsie's first swimming lesson, and I'd like to spend a few more minutes with you and your lovely family if that's okay."

"I'll put the kettle on," answered Deb.

CHAPTER THIRTY - THREE

"It was kind of Mike to let us have his room," Steph said.

"It was," Joe answered. "he's a nice bloke."

"Not as nice as you, though. That was good."

Joe felt that familiar warm tinge to his cheeks; he wasn't sure how to reply to that. He didn't have the experience to know what the correct response was in this situation. Steph saved him by leaning across and kissing him.

They were sitting in Mike's bed with toast and tea, enjoying the morning and not in a rush to do anything after what had been a busy night. Joe had done his best to cook a meal for Steph, following the instructions from a recipe on his phone. It hadn't turned out too badly, although he had needed to improvise one or two things. He had chosen a bottle of wine to go with it, mostly based on it being not the cheapest, but not the most expensive. It was only after they had opened it that he realised that Mike didn't have any wine glasses.

"It doesn't really surprise me," Steph had said.

"Me neither. He's got these." Joe held up two half-pint glasses.

"That'll do nicely; fill it to the top."

Steph got up to go to the bathroom, crossing the room in nothing but one of Joe's baggy shirts. He watched her as she went, feeling like he was the cat that got the cream. He resolved to start looking for a place of his own as soon as he could. It would be good to have a proper bed to sleep in, and he wanted to be able to invite Steph to stay again. He cringed slightly now as he remembered asking her if she wanted to stay the night. He had been flustered and not sure what her answer was going to be. He had asked her if she wanted to come for a sleepover, immediately wondering how he could unsay the words that had just come out of his mouth.

"Only if we can have a midnight snack and watch cartoons," she had answered.

He was glad they were on the phone so she couldn't see the colour of his cheeks.

"I thought maybe playing Pokémon, actually," he answered. They both laughed, and she told him she would be there later. He had hurried out to buy some food and hoped that he didn't make any more of a fool of himself. He didn't.

Steph came back into the room.

"You know what we were talking about? What Janet said about the paintings."

"Yes."

"What if she's right? You know how it goes, once you eliminate the impossible…"

Joe looked blank.

"It's from Sherlock Holmes: 'once you eliminate the impossible, whatever remains must be the truth' – or something like that. Anyway, nothing else makes sense. I just don't know why someone else would let him put his name on their work. I wish we could figure it out, it's driving me mad."

"He doesn't."

"What?"

"He doesn't put his name on the work."

"Yes, he does."

"No, he just puts 'Hacer. ' It never says D.Hacer or David."

Steph looked at him,

"Are you sure?"

"Yep. I've spent long enough looking at them. He always signs the landscapes with his full name. It's weird, isn't it?"

Steph didn't say anything at first; she just looked at him. Finally, she broke the silence,

"Run that conversation back to yourself."

Joe stared at her, unsure what she was getting at.

"Yeah, he only puts Hacer on the big pictures, not his full name."

Steph waited. She saw the expression on Joe's face change when the penny finally dropped.

"There's another Hacer, isn't there? His sister."

"Yes, the one who was in the accident. What if it's her who did the paintings?"

"But why would he pretend they were his?"

"I don't know, but it makes sense. Look…"

She got up again and went to the other room to collect Joe's laptop. She started it up and found the news article again.

"Look, some of the things that are in the paintings; the cars, the hospital, the ambulance, they're all in the paintings, aren't they? We thought it was David who was painting scenes from the accident because he's the artist. What if it's her?"

There was a long pause while they both reread the article. Joe checked the pictures on his phone.

"They're telling the story," he said, "there are lots of other things, too, all the later ones don't make sense."

"Not yet, that's true. But come on, it's got to be worth checking out, hasn't it?"

"I suppose. It makes sense."

Steph put the laptop to one side and smiled as she wriggled over towards him.

"I love how you always seem to have the answer to things, but don't realise it."

"Do I?"

"Yes, let's celebrate, make the most of Mike's bed while he's away."

Joe didn't need to be asked twice; he pulled Steph towards him and helped her out of the shirt.

*

When they restarted their day, it was with the intimate touches and closeness of new young lovers. Watching each other when they were apart, pulling towards each other like magnets and smiling knowingly at one another as each privately recalled the moments of intimacy they had so recently shared. They were sitting together in the café in the arcade, side by side, looking at the laptop which was open in front of them.

Angela Hacer had a frustratingly small online presence, almost to the point of being non-existent. There was certainly nothing from the last few years since the accident, apart from an occasional news report about the driver of the car that hit her losing their license for eighteen months and a couple of brief mentions in articles that were otherwise about David.

"How are we going to find her then?" asked Steph, a note of exasperation starting to creep into her voice.

"We're going to have to trawl through all of her brother's interviews; there's bound to be a clue in there somewhere."

"I suppose. That's going to take forever, though."

"Well, we're not in a rush, are we? It means we'll get to spend more time together."

"I was planning on spending time with you anyway, but it's still frustrating."

"Maybe Tom would know," suggested Joe.

"How would he…" Steph started, then her expression changed to one that Joe was starting to recognise; she'd thought of something. "Pass me the laptop."

He slid it across to her and watched as she searched for the Desidero gallery. She didn't open the gallery webpage, as Joe expected, but carried on scrolling through the results. Finally, she stopped and clicked on the link for Companies House.

"Dad has to have all this bumph for his business. You have to have named directors, and their details are on here. Maybe his sister is one of the directors for Desidero. It's a long shot, but we've got nothing else to try right now."

There was some scrolling and clicking, which Joe watched, although mostly, the words on the screen flickered past too quickly for him to read. Finally, Steph stopped.

"Here, Angela Hacer. She is one of the directors, and there's her address." She pointed at the screen, with a huge smile stretched across her face. Joe peered at it,

"So what do we do now?"

"We visit her," Steph answered, "see if it was her who did the paintings."

"What, just go to her house and knock on the door?"

"That's how you usually visit people, yes."

"But won't that be a bit weird?"

Steph thought for a moment,

"Maybe, if we just arrive unannounced. Perhaps we should drop her a note first, to ask if she'd mind."

"It still feels a bit…I don't know, odd."

"Well, help me word it, we'll try and make ourselves sound as normal as possible."

They spent a large part of the afternoon attempting to draft a letter to Angela. Not too creepy, not too familiar and hopefully, nothing that would result in a restraining order. Steph suggested they use the same approach as they had with David, to say that they were writing an essay about David and wanted to gather some background. Joe agreed; they couldn't just come straight out and ask if she'd done the paintings. If she had, and he believed that she did, there must be a reason why she was staying under the radar. He wondered if they were poking around in things that had nothing to do with them, but they were too far in now to give up.

Steph agreed, and the letter was drafted after numerous rewrites and start-overs. She included both of their phone numbers and was going to post it from work tomorrow. Hand-delivering it might seem a little bit stalker-ish. They had implied that it was David who had suggested they talk to her when they had met with him. Of course, if she were to ask him, then they may have blown any chance they had of meeting her. It was a chance they would have to take if they wanted to find out about the mysterious artwork.

CHAPTER THIRTY - FOUR

Unknown to Joe and Steph, it was highly unlikely that Angela would show the letter to David. She had been cutting his visits short and trying to make sure that they didn't clash with her liaisons with her neighbours. This wasn't too complicated, as he usually came after work, when Deb would be busy settling Elsie for the evening. She still held on to the idea that she was going to surprise him, walking unannounced into the gallery and asking to speak to the owner. It was silly, she knew. But what had been a fantasy was beginning to seem like it could be a possibility at some point. Only two days ago, she had walked to the park by herself. She had been terrified and exhilarated in equal measures, unsure what she would do if something unexpected happened, if she had another panic attack.

But nothing happened. She came back home safely and sat in the kitchen, feeling smug. Her next ambition was to go further afield, maybe take a taxi to another part of town. Nowhere too populous, of course; it would be about the journey, not the destination. She wondered if she could ask Deb to drive her somewhere, but was loath to do so. Deb had already done so much for her, and she didn't want to impose. She decided there was still more to think about, and she wouldn't rush it. Although she knew that this was just more procrastination, she made her peace with it.

The letter that arrived that morning was unexpected. Apart from circulars that she put in the bin and bills that she gave to David to sort out, she didn't get much mail. All her friendships had dwindled and then disappeared in the years following her accident. She wasn't surprised; she hadn't wanted to see or speak to anybody, and she never replied to the various cards and messages that her friends had sent to her. Even the most determined of them had stopped sending her birthday and Christmas cards after a couple of years. She did feel slightly guilty that she had not responded to their genuine concern and care, and a little rueful that she had lost her entire social circle.

But it was what it was. She had been in a dark place and frequently still was. Many of her memories of that time were fuzzy, half-remembered dreams. Others were vivid, lucid nightmares. Her mind could not process what had happened to her, the meaningless destruction of her body by indifferent strangers. She had been naturally timid and a bit shy even before the accident; afterwards, she had become a full-blown recluse. Now, when she looked back, she could see that her brain had rewired itself in that instant on the darkened street. It had gone into survival mode, then stayed there as her body recovered and long after.

She read and then reread the letter and didn't know what to make of it. Why did these people want to talk to her about her brother? What did they think she would add to the sum of what they already knew if they'd met him? Her instinct was to throw it in the bin, forget about it and carry on as she had been. But she didn't, she left it on the table, where she stopped and read it back through each time she came into the kitchen.

What could it hurt? Two young people coming to the house would hardly be any different from having Deb and Elsie round – would it? It could be another part of her rehabilitation, another step on the path towards her planned visit to David's gallery. It bothered her that she could be so conflicted about something that she should have just ignored. Eventually, she reached a decision: she would ask Deb what she thought she should do. Although she already knew what the answer would be, it would be good to hear Deb confirm it. She was seeing her later, for a coffee and a chat, so she would ask about both things, the car ride and the letter. She hoped that she wasn't beginning to rely on Deb too much, but for now, who else could she turn to?

*

Elsie was waiting outside the front door as Angela carefully crossed the road. She was waving a piece of paper excitedly in her hand. As Angela approached, she could see that it was a drawing. Elsie couldn't wait for her to get to the house; she ran down the path and presented her with it.

"It's a drawing of Misty. I did it by myself, and it's for you. Look, I wrote her name on it as well."

Angela looked; it was indeed a drawing of Misty, slightly out of proportion and possibly carrying an additional limb. Nevertheless, it was a good likeness of her pet, which now appeared as if on cue and started winding around their legs and demanding to be made a fuss of. The writing was similarly accomplished, aside from the s being reversed.

"It's terrific, I love it. When I get home, I'm going to put that on the wall. Thank you, Elsie."

Deb was now at the front door, holding it open for them.

"She's been so enthusiastic about using her art box since she started coming to your house; you've really got her fired up. Come on in; the kettle's boiling."

The two women and the little girl sat at the kitchen table, two mugs of coffee and a glass of milk resting in front of them. Elsie was telling them how much she liked being artistic, only she had trouble getting her tiny mouth around the word, so it came out as 'artisic'. It didn't matter as both the women knew what she was talking about and were able to engage. In due course, Elsie decided that she needed to go upstairs and find her favourite cuddly toy.

As soon as Elsie had gulped down the last of her milk and left the room, Angela pulled the letter from her pocket.

"This came today. I'm not sure what to do about it." She passed the letter to Deb, who read it in silence while Angela waited for her response. Deb put the letter down on the table between them and asked,

"Do you want to see them or not?"

"I'm not sure. I'd like to help David out, but I don't know if I'm up to meeting new people."

"You've done brilliantly so far. Remember how nervous you were about meeting Gareth?"

"Well, yes. But that was different."

"I know, but you get my point. If you do want to see them, I'll come over and sit with you, if you'd like that."

"That's very kind of you, thank you. I actually wanted to ask you for another favour as well. You've been so patient already, and I don't want to be a nuisance."

"Well, now I'm intrigued. Honestly, it's been no trouble at all. Elsie adores you, and I'm glad of the company. So what's the other favour?"

"Can I go for a ride in your car? Please."

Deb's answer was nonchalant,

"Sure, where do you want to go?"

Angela hadn't fully thought through her idea beyond asking to go out in the car.

"Umh, I'm not sure. I just thought maybe we could go for a drive and see somewhere that isn't our road or the park."

It suddenly dawned on Deb what it was that Angela was asking. It wasn't about going somewhere, it was about the journey itself.

"Oh, I see. Sorry, I get it. How about we take Elsie down to the river? She likes it there. We can always stay in the car if you want."

"What, now?"

She hadn't been prepared for such a swift turnaround for her suggestion.

"Yes, why not? It's not raining. Els would like a little runabout."

"Okay, just let me go to the loo first."

"Sure, you do that, and I'll get Elsie's boots on her."

As she walked towards the car, Angela teetered on the brink of panic. With every step she took, she wanted to change direction and run back inside her own house where she could stay safe and secure. The feel of a gentle guiding hand on her elbow was enough to keep her moving in the right direction. Deb knew what a big deal this was for Angela; their previous conversations had gone some way to helping her understand why she would be so nervous, terrified even, of going in the car. She held the door open, waiting for her skittish friend to summon up the courage to sit in the passenger seat. Elsie, seeming to sense that something was up in the way that small children 'just know,' waited next to Deb, holding the hem of her mother's jacket.

Once everybody was in the car and all the seatbelts were fastened, Deb turned to look at Angela. A film of sweat was visible on her forehead, and her fists were tightly clenched.

"We don't have to go anywhere, we can just sit here for a bit if you want."

Angela nodded, then turned her head slightly to the right,

"Are you ready to go for a walk, Elsie?" Her voice was strained, as if she was forcing the words out.

"Yes, please," came the answer from the back of the car.

"Well, let's go then," said Angela, nodding at Deb.

Deb started the engine and slowly pulled away from the house in the direction of the river.

The drive was uneventful; the traffic was light on the short journey, and they arrived in the small, mud-packed car park without incident. The car came to a stop facing the wooden fence that separated it from the riverbank. The three of them sat quietly for a moment before Deb turned to Angela and asked,

"Do you want to come for a little walk with us? Or are you okay just sitting here for a while?"

Angela would have been happy to just sit and watch the river as it swept by, the undulating surface catching an occasional sparkle of light and reflecting it into the air. She could see the foliage at the river's edge, dense with colour and every shade of green there had ever been, and two swans affecting lofty disdain for one another while neither let the other out of its sight. She thought that might be enough, but now that she was here, she wanted to hear and smell it properly. To feel the damp air on her skin and run her hands across the leaves and grasses. She got out of the car.

Deb unfastened the buckle on Elsie's car seat and lifted her out, all the while watching as Angela walked to the gate and onto the footpath. She knew that at that moment, she and Elsie had been forgotten, that Angela had been consumed by the beauty and wonder of the dirty river edged with weeds under a sky that couldn't quite decide how dark and grey it wanted to be. She waited with Elsie for a moment before joining Angela on the riverbank.

The walk was short, just up to the bridge and back. Elsie asked the standard one hundred and one questions that she managed to fit into any length of walk, while being reminded at intervals not to go too close to the edge. Angela walked as if in a dream, answering questions distractedly and pointing out everything and anything that caught her eye. The most mundane and insignificant details were as much a source of wonder as anything else along their walk. Deb tried to look at it through Angela's eyes, curious as to how it must look to someone who has been trapped in their own home for several years. She hoped this was another small step that would help her rediscover the world.

On the journey back, Deb could see that Angela was crying. Not the scared, frightened tears that she had seen before; these were silent and private. The short journey home was as uneventful as the one there. As she parked outside the house, Angela spoke,

"Thank you."

"You're welcome, we had a nice walk."

"Me too, I don't think I'd be doing any of this without you two. You're saints."

"No, we're not. We're neighbours – and that's what neighbours do."

"Well, thank you anyway."

They all got out of the car, and Angela started to walk back to her own house. She paused at the side of the road and turned back to Deb.

"You know, I think I may give those kids a ring. If it helps David, I'll try."

"Good for you. If you want me to be with you, just ask."

"I will, and thank you again."

With that, they all returned to their respective houses. Elsie to take off her boots and coat and have a nap, Deb to start getting the evening meal ready, and Angela to make a phone call before going to her little back bedroom studio.

CHAPTER THIRTY - FIVE

Mike and Steph were squashed together on the settee. They each had a game controller in their hands while the TV screen in front of them pitted their two digital football teams against one another. Joe watched them from the kitchen as he cooked the pasta and sauce that was going to be their dinner. It cheered him to see the two most important people in his life having fun together, especially when Steph went two-nil up and Mike went into full-on mock tantrum mode. They were interrupted when Steph's phone rang. She paused the game so she could answer it, but Mike was still griping about the scoreline.

Holding the phone to her ear and putting her finger to her lips to shush Mike, she backed into the bedroom from where Joe could hear her voice but not make out what she was saying. She wasn't out of sight for long, she bounced back into the room with a smile.

"She said she'd see us," she announced.

"Who?" asked Mike.

"Great," said Joe at the same time. He realised that they had not yet given Mike an update.

"It's about the paintings," he said. "I'll just dish this up and we'll explain while we eat."

Once the eating and the explaining were done, the three of them sat in the lounge with their empty bowls beside them.

"We need to decide what we're going to say to her," Steph said, "we can't just ask if David's passing her paintings off as his own."

"You're right, how should we bring it up?"

They sat in silent thought for a moment, then Mike spoke up.

"You should just talk about her brother, don't bring up the other pictures unless she does. You can always ask her if David ever experimented with any other styles of painting."

"You're not as daft as you look, are you?" Joe replied.

Steph pretended to hit his leg,

"Don't be rude, Joe, he's right, that's exactly what we should do."

"I'd be more worried about being as daft as you look," Mike retorted.

Joe got up and started to collect the dirty dishes.

"Go and finish being beaten at football, I'll do the dishes, then we can all go to the pub."

"Don't you need to get anything ready for your meeting with Tom tomorrow?" Steph asked.

"Already done, I've made a PowerPoint and everything. Besides, I'm going out with his daughter, it'll be a breeze."

"I don't think that'll help much if he doesn't like your idea. I think he will, though. It's a great idea. Can we see the PowerPoint?"

"I'll bring the laptop to the pub, you can see it there."

"Multitasking, I like your style," Mike said. "C'mon Steph, I've got a two-goal deficit to make up."

*

The meeting with Tom was tougher than Joe had expected. Although he had joked about it yesterday, he still went in nervously and got confused about what he had intended to say. The PowerPoint, which Steph and Mike had helped him refine in the pub the night before, had been the only thing that stopped him from talking nonsense.

Tom had listened attentively. He had made notes while Joe spoke and had a seemingly endless stream of questions at the end. He'd finished by thanking Joe and telling him that he was going to give the idea his serious consideration.

Joe went back to the reception desk, where he had been helping Steph organise the filing system into a database to make it easier for everybody to track. It was time-consuming and monotonous, but ultimately would make things quicker and easier for everybody. With two of them working on it, the interruptions of phone calls and requests meant that they could keep adding to the system for the majority of the time.

"How did it go?" Steph asked.

"I don't know. He didn't say yes, so I'm guessing not that well."

"Did he say no?"

"No, he said he was going to think about it."

"That means it went well. If he didn't like the idea, he would have said so straight away."

Joe thought that if anybody knew what Tom was thinking, it would probably be Steph. But he still wasn't convinced that he was going to run with his idea. It had only been a suggestion anyway, not a fully formed business idea. He tried not to be too disappointed.

"Well, I'm proud of you for doing that," she gave him a quick peck on the cheek. " Forget it for now, we're going to see Angela Hacer after work. Are we all agreed about our questions?"

"Yes, I'm going to let you do most of the talking anyway. Otherwise, it will feel more like an interrogation. I'll just waft the camera around and be the eye candy."

"Fair enough, although I think you'll find that I'm the eye candy."

"You wish," responded Joe. "No, actually, I think you're right. I'll just be there for moral support."

Steph laughed. Joe had a way of making her smile that she liked. Dad had noticed it too, telling her that she seemed to be much happier than she had been before Joe had arrived, dishevelled and nervous-looking, at the office. He was right. She had started working at the office as a temporary thing. They had needed a receptionist, and she had nothing to do, having just finished her college course and not quite started applying for jobs yet.

Temporary had extended from a week or two to what had now been over six months. Once she had started, she found she enjoyed the work. They had interviewed for the post several times, but they hadn't been able to find a suitable candidate. Her misgivings about working for her dad had quickly been laid to rest; she got on well with everyone else in the office, and she could do the work. So she had just carried on. Joe's arrival had been the icing on the cake of what had been a good year for her.

It was not that the other years had been bad necessarily, but a string of failed relationships with various narcissists and egotists had left her feeling deflated. The last partner, Dan, had veered dangerously close to being controlling and coercive before she realised what was happening and dumped him. But the time she had spent with him had made a serious dent in her friendship group. He hadn't liked her going out without him, but didn't want to socialise with her friends. He had made his disapproval of some of them clear, and like a fool, she had stopped seeing them, so she didn't upset him.

His attention had been flattering and made her feel special, like she was the most important person in his life. She had finally recognised what was happening when she thought her friend Kaz had not invited her to her birthday party. She had been quite offhand about it when Steph had asked her.

"I just thought that you didn't want to come, you don't come out with us very often nowadays, and you never replied to my texts."

"What texts?" Steph had asked.

Kaz had shown her the messages she had sent in the days leading up to the party.

"Well, I never got them," she had answered before stalking off home.

When she got back, she checked back on her phone and could find no trace of them. She then searched through her deleted messages folder, and there they were, along with dozens of other invites, requests and engagements that she had never seen.

When she confronted Dan, he casually admitted that he had been checking her phone regularly and getting rid of any messages that he didn't think she needed to see. She was shocked and upset, but it was the wake-up call she needed to pull the plug on the relationship. She had gone back to her parents' house, where Tom had done his best impression of a nightclub bouncer when Dan had come knocking on the door. Her mum had welcomed her back, and she had gradually started to get back to a sort of normal.

She had tried to get back into her previous social circle, but it was hard. Her feeling of being judged by them, along with her embarrassment about what had happened when she had started to cut them off one by one, despite their unheeded warnings, had made it hard. Now she had cautiously started to reconnect with them again, but she knew it would never be the same as it had been.

She hadn't talked to Joe about this; he seemed to have enough baggage of his own for now. But everything she had found out about him so far had reassured her that he would understand. For now, she felt like they were partners in adversity, giving one another the strength and courage they needed to be resilient. After her experience with Dan, Joe was a breath of fresh air.

Their quest for the mystery artist had been what had drawn them together initially, and she was determined now to unravel the rest of the story.

CHAPTER THIRTY - SIX

Angela had spent most of the afternoon pacing around the downstairs, frequently stopping to look out of the window, on the off chance that they would come early. The girl that she had spoken to on the phone, Steph, had sounded nice. Well-spoken and polite, and extremely understanding when she told her that she didn't normally have visitors. She had assured her that it was no problem, that they already had enough information, and they wouldn't trouble her. Then she thanked Angela for taking the time and trouble to call her and let her know. It was her insistence that they didn't need to meet with her that had finally made her mind up. What could it hurt? A couple of students who wanted to ask some questions about what her brother was like when he was growing up, it couldn't be that bad, could it?

Now her nerves were frayed. The anticipation of waiting for them to call was torturous. When Deb had rung the bell earlier, she had nearly jumped out of her skin. She had popped over the road with some biscuits and cold drinks for her visitors. She didn't know if Angela would have anything to offer them and just wanted to make sure. She had stopped and drunk tea for a while, until it was time for her to go and collect Elsie from the nursery that she went to a couple of mornings a week.

It had calmed Angela, and they'd dipped into some of the home-baked biscuits as they sat talking. But that had been hours ago, and now she was teetering on the edge of panic again. She was taking deep breaths and slowly exhaling, as Dr. Parnell had shown her how to do when she was anxious. It wasn't helping that much today, though. She paced the kitchen a bit more and then went back to the front room to take another peek through the front window.

The window was directly next to the door, and at the very moment she pulled the curtain to one side, the doorbell rang. She dropped the curtain and stepped quickly backwards as she came face to face with a young man with a bird's nest of hair. He was wearing a black anorak and had a camera slung around his neck. He had looked as surprised as she had been to be looking straight at her, she didn't have time to catch more than a glance of the other visitor. She stood motionless, knowing what she needed to do next, but finding herself unable to move from where she was standing.

She breathed in, then slowly out three times, then made her way to the front door and opened it with a slightly trembling hand. In front of her stood the man she had seen through the window, and a young woman with short brown hair, wearing a leather jacket and sporting one of the most charming smiles Angela had seen for a long time. Behind them, on the far side of the road, she saw Deb deadheading flowers outside the front of her house. Deb was looking across at her, she smiled and raised both thumbs before returning to her gardening. It was all the motivation that Angela needed.

"Hello, you must be the young people who wrote to me. I'm Angela, come on in."

"Thank you so much, I'm Steph, and this is Joe, we promise not to take too much of your time. We're so glad you agreed to talk to us," Steph answered as they were led towards the sitting room. There was a brief moment of awkwardness as they each waited for one another to take a seat. No sooner had they sat down than Angela was back on her feet,

"My goodness, where are my manners? Who would like a drink?"

Joe and Steph both answered that they were fine, but Angela was already at the door,

"Oh no, I insist. I'll make a pot of tea."

And with that, she was gone, leaving Steph and Joe alone in the room. They looked around at the slightly dated décor, some photos that were younger versions of David and Angela and an older couple that they assumed were their parents. There was a selection of ornaments, shelves filled to overflowing with books and, in pride of place on the wall, a painting of a beach with grassy dunes to one side and a tranquil ocean on the other. The sky was dotted with clouds, but the picture was awash with the bright colours and shadows of a summer's day. Joe picked up one of the books and flicked through it, looking at Steph and shaking his head as he replaced it. Steph pointed at the painting and whispered,

"That's one of David's. I recognise the style."

"Yeah, I thought so," replied Joe, getting up to have a closer look.

In the kitchen, Angela gripped the edge of the counter as she waited for the kettle to boil. Everything else was laid out ready on a tray, it had been for over an hour. She adjusted the cups slightly and then poured the boiling water into the teapot. Again, she took three deep breaths, letting each one out slowly, and then carried the tray into the front room where she set it on the coffee table. The young man, Joe, was standing looking at the picture. He turned to her, and she looked at his face properly for the first time. He looked so young, and his smile as he spoke was enough to calm her nerves.

"This is one of David's paintings, isn't it?"

"Yes," she answered as she arranged the cups and gave the teapot a stir. "It's the beach we used to go to for our holidays when we were children. He painted it for my birthday a few years ago."

"It looks beautiful," he told her, "it makes me feel like I'd like to be there."

Angela often had the same thought herself, to be transported back to a happier, safer time and to be in a place she loved. She decided that it would be one of the places she would visit when she was able to.

"There are biscuits too," she told them, "help yourself."

"They look delicious," Steph said, "did you make them yourself?"

"No, my neighbour did … well, my friend actually."

She smiled at her correction, at the fact that Deb was more than just somebody who lived nearby. The two youngsters were charming and polite, and she started to feel more comfortable with this alien situation as she poured the tea.

Once they were settled with tea and biscuits organised, Steph produced a notebook and flipped it open.

"I wrote down some questions, if that's okay. I can already cross one of them off, now I've seen where you went for your holidays. They're all just about what David was like when he was younger, the sort of things you both liked doing and when he started drawing and painting, things like that."

"Oh, that's fine. He was – is – a great big brother."

Steph smiled and glanced down at her notebook,

"I'm sure, he was nice to us when we met him at the gallery. Do you want to get started?"

Angela nodded,

"Yes, but first tell me, what's the gallery like?"

"It's beautiful, haven't you been?"

"No, I don't go out much. I'm planning to soon, though."

"That'll be great, you'll love it."

Angela seemed to be satisfied with her answer. Steph continued to ask her a series of questions, all of them innocuous and innocent. Angela answered them, her answers became more fluid the more she started to talk about her and David's childhoods, turning the interview into more of a conversation. After forty-five minutes or so, Angela even seemed to be enjoying herself.

"So," Steph asked, looking up from her notebook, "did David ever experiment with any different styles of painting?"

"I'm not sure what you mean. He's always concentrated on natural landscapes."

"So he never tried anything different? He wasn't tempted to have a go at any other ways of representing things on his canvases?"

"Oh lord no, I love David, and I love his paintings. But he isn't the most imaginative person; he paints what he can see. I don't think it would occur to him to do anything else."

Joe looked across at Steph and raised an eyebrow. She ignored it and closed up her book, which she had been scribbling notes in.

"Okay, thank you, Angela. I think we've got everything we need now. It was really lovely to meet you. It sounded like you and David had a great time growing up. You almost made me wish that I had a brother."

It was easy for Steph to sound genuine when she said this; she had enjoyed meeting Angela. She could have happily stayed talking to her for the rest of the evening.

"We've already taken up so much of your time, could I use your loo before we go?"

"Of course, dear, it's upstairs on the right."

Steph went upstairs, and Joe, who had mostly stayed quiet, offered to help Angela tidy up the tea things. She waved him off, taking the tray away to the kitchen herself. She arrived back at the same time as Steph and saw them both to the front door. There was a lot of thanking each other on the doorstep before Joe and Steph walked off hand in hand into the dimming light of the early evening.

Angela stood in the doorway, waiting. She knew that Deb would appear in a moment and beckon her over. She was dying to tell her what a good time she had had meeting the two charming and inquisitive young people. On cue, Deb's door opened, and Deb stepped out. She waved to her, and Angela smiled and started to carefully cross the road.

Steph and Joe didn't speak to one another until they were safely around the corner and out of sight.

"What did you think?" asked Joe, stopping and facing Steph.

"She was lovely, I liked her."

"Me too, but what about the paintings?"

"They're definitely not David's."

"Well, we already kind of knew that, didn't we?"

"Yes, but I think I might know who did paint them."

"Who?"

"She did, I'm certain of it."

"How can you be so sure?"

"Because when I went up to the loo, I looked in the other upstairs rooms. She's got a little studio up there. It's full of paintings, just like the ones David is selling as his own."

There was a brief moment of silence between them.

"You looked in her rooms? Joe asked.

"It's private detective 101, anyway, the door was open, I only peeped in."

"So what do we do now?"

"I don't know. I mean, I guess we've answered the question. We found out who did the pictures."

"I know, but it doesn't feel like a proper answer, does it? She didn't say they were hers."

"We didn't ask her that."

"Maybe we should have."

"It's too late now. We need to think about it. I'm not sure if there's anything else we can do."

On the way back to Mike's, Steph described what she had seen in the studio. Joe was jealous, wishing he had been able to see them too. They talked about why they thought David might be selling the paintings as his own, but couldn't come up with an explanation that made sense. After eating at Mike's flat and filling their friend in with all the details of the meeting, Joe walked Steph to the bus stop. They wrapped their arms around one another as they waited and kissed goodnight as the bus arrived to take Steph home.

"I wish we had our own place," he said as they parted.

She thought about it on the way back. Had Joe just invited her to live with him? Even if it was in his non-existent flat, the Intention was clear from what he had said. She didn't have to make any decisions now, of course, but what would she do when the time came? She didn't know if she was ready for a commitment like that, but how would she know when she was? It was all too much for one day; she went straight up to bed when she got home, with only a passing hello and goodbye to her parents as she passed the blue light flickering out of the open sitting room door.

CHAPTER THIRTY - SEVEN

Tom had already left early for work when she got up the following morning. She made some toast for Mum and sat at the kitchen counter with her as they drank their tea. Casually, Steph asked her how long she'd known Dad when they moved in together. Her mum raised her eyebrows and smiled,
"Popped the question, has he?"

"No, not exactly. He's still homeless, technically. It's just something he said."

"Well, you need to do what you think is right when the time comes – if it does. Whatever you decide, you know this is always your home, and you can come back whenever you need to. We'll always be here for you. And for what it's worth, we both like Joe, Dad's got a lot of time for him."

"I know, thanks Mum." Steph put her mug on the edge by the sink and gave her Mum a kiss on the cheek.

"Good, now go to work or you'll be late and Dad will give you the sack. He said he wanted to see you this morning."

"What about?"

"He didn't say. He wanted to talk to you last night, but you didn't get back in time."

"Okay, I wonder what that's about? I guess I'll find out when I get there. See you later. Love you."

"Love you too, have a good day."

She arrived at the office at the same time as Joe, both of them were there with plenty of time to spare. They were getting their drinks from the coffee machine and talking to a couple of the designers about how to access their files when Tom came over. He addressed Steph and Joe,

"Morning you two, I need to see both of you this morning. Can you set up the reception, then leave the phone with Gary and come to the meeting room, please?"

He didn't wait for an answer. Gary pulled a comical face as the meeting room door closed,

"Better give me the phone then, it's about time you two slackers got what's coming to you."

"Shut up, Gary," Steph smiled. At the same time, she wondered what it was that Dad needed to speak to the two of them about so urgently, if it was to do with Joe's idea, why did he want to see her too? Whatever it was, she would know soon.

"Come on, Joe, let's go and find out what it is."

"Are we in trouble?"

"He wouldn't have asked us to see him in front of everyone if we were, he's not like that. Take no notice of Gary."

The two of them went into the meeting room and closed the door behind them. On the large screen was Joe's PowerPoint from the day before. Tom invited them to take a seat.

"Relax, both of you, I've just got some questions, is all. I asked Steph to join us because I know she's been working with you on this."

"Only a bit," Steph protested, "it's Joe's idea."

"Okay, noted. I'll get straight to the point, I like the idea of this. I think it could be a good extension of our current business. I'm sure the designers will be happy to be getting some extra royalties, too. It would work for all of us. Joe, you did a great job of convincing me that this would work yesterday, but I still have some reservations."

"Okay, I get it if we can't do it. It was only a suggestion."

"I'm not saying we can't do it, I'm saying there's a lot to sort out first. There's all the legal stuff, contracts, copyright, and payments. There's also the practicality of how we would fit the extra operation into our existing space. I'm not moving offices again, not after last time. There's also the question of who's going to head the project up. It'll need at least two people to manage it and deal with the day-to-day running, as well as the archive work and distribution. There'll be setting up a sales portal and organising packaging and postage as well. It's a lot to take on, especially as we've just expanded and taken on a lot of extra clients."

Steph looked across at Joe and gave him a small 'sorry' shrug. She turned to her dad,

"We get it, Dad, it's going on the back burner until you can find someone to manage it. Joe could help with the archive work when it's ready to start; he knows it better than any of us already. Mostly because he had to pick it all up off the floor, I guess."

Tom laughed,

"He did, I couldn't believe you did all that in the time you did, Joe. Lesser mortals would have despaired and given up, I already had, I was just going to leave it like that and pretend it wasn't there. You've made yourself indispensable here. No, Steph, I don't want to put this on the back burner; I want to move ahead with it. I was just giving you an idea of some of the things that I'm going to have to do before that can happen."

Joe relaxed and smiled at last,

"Thank you, I'm glad I managed to explain it properly." He started to get up from his seat.

"Hold on, I'm not done yet. Like I said, once it's ready to go, it'll need someone to manage it. Do you think you two would be up to it?"

"Eh?" Steph looked at Joe. They both looked at Tom.

"I get it if you need to talk about it or some time to think, I'll go and get a coffee while you have a chat."

Steph and Joe just looked at each other.

"Is he serious?" asked Joe as Tom left the room.

"I don't think he'd joke about something like this," Steph replied.

"Could we do it?"

"I think so, yes. Do you want to?"

"I'm not sure, it's quite a big thing. I didn't even have a job a few months ago."

"But you do now, and you're good at it. You organise and arrange things better than anyone; you're a natural. You've got a good eye for the art part of it, too. I can do all the people skills and office stuff, we'd have it all covered between us."

Joe shrugged,

"Why not? I've got nothing to lose."

Steph got up and kissed him. They were just separating when Tom came back in.

"I'm going to guess that's a yes, then. Good. Steph, can you arrange some refreshments for Friday afternoon, please? We'll have a staff meeting, and you can let everybody know what the plan is."

"What, you mean…?"

"Yes, if you're going to manage the project, it's all on you." He smiled at the stricken look on Joe's face,

"Don't worry, I'll be right beside you. Just go through the PowerPoint exactly like you did for me. I'll have some bits to add on the end, and we can answer the questions together. Trust me, if we feed them first, they'll be too full of sandwiches and cakes to ask too much."

"Is that our first lesson in management?" Steph asked.

"I guess it is, yes. I'm going to leave you two in here for a moment, I'm sure you'll need a few minutes to take it in. I should say, of course, that it will be a pay rise. And if you know any good receptionists, I guess I'll be looking for one soon."

"What just happened?" asked Joe when Tom had left.

"We both got promoted, I think. It's great, Joe, you'll have enough money coming in that we'll be able to start looking for a flat together."

The surprised look on his face told her that she may have misjudged this.

"I'm sorry, is that not what you meant yesterday? I just thought…" Steph didn't know what to say or do next, she looked away and felt a small tear of either embarrassment or humiliation start to well in her eye. Then she felt Joe's hand reach out to hers, and she took it and looked at him.

"Yes," he said, "yes, we can. Sorry, you caught me a bit by surprise then. What with the job thing and the staff meeting, I wasn't expecting it. I'd love for us to have a place together. I can't think of anything I'd like more. I just hope you'll be able to put up with my moods."

"I think we'll probably be a good match in terms of moodiness. We've been together a lot recently, and you haven't annoyed me yet. You haven't had any angry moments for ages."

Joe thought for a moment,

"I haven't, have I?"

"No, because I'm a good influence on you. You do need to know that I can't cook to save my life, though. Also, I'm not good at putting my laundry in the basket, and I leave the bathroom in a mess."

"Well, I'll just have to learn to live with that, won't I? Or get you housetrained. You can't be any worse than Mike."

"Does he leave women's underwear on the bedroom floor?"

"Dunno, I'll ask him."

"Come on, we'd better go and rescue the phone from Gary. We'll talk about it later."

CHAPTER THIRTY - EIGHT

Angela and Deb were sitting at a table outside a coffee shop on a small row of out-of-town shops. It was a big outing for Angela, they had come in the car, and walked past some busy shops to get here. The thought of it had been worse than actually doing it; she was finding it easier and easier each time they tried something new. There had, of course, been small setbacks, moments when she panicked or became anxious. Deb knew her well enough now to watch for the warning signs. If Angela started looking around, hunting for an exit, she needed to be guided gently to an area where she felt safer. If she started absently rubbing the scars on the backs of her hands, she needed to talk to her and offer the distraction of conversation. Together, they had started to rediscover Angela's place in the community she had been hiding from for so long.

They'd had the excitement of a supermarket outing, the joy of drinking Coke outside a pub, and eaten some chips on a bench in the last couple of weeks. Deb had enjoyed their outings; it was fun thinking of small things they could do, then seeing Angela's delight when she found that they were not only achievable but also very enjoyable.

Deb finished her hot chocolate, leaving a small brown moustache on her upper lip. Angela pointed to her own top lip and passed Deb a napkin.

"Thank you," she said as she dabbed the offending chocolate mark until it disappeared. "Where do you want to go next? Or are we finished for today?"

Angela was thoughtful for a moment.

"I know," she announced, "can you drive into town?"

"Into town? Which bit?"

"Don't worry if we haven't got time, it was just a thought."

"It's okay, I've got plenty of time. Gareth's picking up Elsie today. Whereabouts in town do you want to go?"

"Oh, it's just a silly idea. It doesn't matter."

"It mattered enough for you to ask. Come on, spill the beans, what are we doing?"

"I thought we could drive past the gallery, so I can see where it is. I don't want to go in today, but I might soon. It's a daft idea, let's go home."

"Nonsense, we can drive round that way and then go home. I don't even have to drive right into the town centre for that, it's just a detour."

"Are you sure you don't mind?"

"Get in the car, let's do this before you change your mind."

Every trip in the car had been a revelation for Angela. When you see a place every day, the changes that happen are gradual, imperceptible. The names of shops are altered, along with whatever it was they were selling. New landmarks are erected, like street signs, flower beds, and benches. Sometimes entire buildings appear, disappear or are replaced. Angela was seeing five years' worth of changes all in one car ride, which made it hard to recognise the town she grew up in at times.

But the layout of the town and the enormous statue of the philanthropist slave trader that dominated the roundabout that led there remained the same. Even the road works on the approach to the junction appeared to be the same ones she remembered from her previous life. Although she had never been to the gallery, she knew exactly where it was. As they got closer, she asked Deb if she could slow down, so she could have a good look.

"Are you sure you don't want me to stop? It looks like there are a couple of parking spaces. I can pull over."

"No, not today. Just go as slowly as you can without pissing off the cars behind, that'll be fine, thank you, Deb."

"Sure thing, here we are now."

The car slowed to walking pace, cruising past the brightly lit gallery window. The name 'Desidero' was emblazoned across the fascia in gold writing on a dark blue background. Angela wriggled closer to the car window to get the best view she could.

"Ooh, here it is now, look."

This was followed by a moment of complete silence as they drew alongside the large plate glass window and Angela got her first proper view of the main display.

"What…?"

The surprised tone of her voice was enough to make Deb take her eyes off the road for a moment and look across. She saw the shop front and the beautiful canvas that took pride of place in the centre, a swirl of multi-coloured lines and colours standing on a large easel just behind the glass. She looked back in the direction they were travelling, aware of the car behind edging closer as she slowly crawled past the gallery.

"What's up? Do you need me to go back around the block for another look?"

The gallery was now disappearing behind them, and Deb was starting to pick up speed again.

"No. Take me home, please."

She looked around at Angela and saw her slumped down in her seat with her eyes pointed at the floor of the car.

"What's up? Are you okay?"

"Yes, I just need to go home, that's all. We shouldn't have come this far into town, I'm sorry."

"It's not a problem. Come on, let's get you safely back to the suburbs."

She took the next left turn and started to navigate her way back to their quiet road. The silence inside the car was disconcerting. Deb had no idea if Angela was having another panic attack, and if she was, what had triggered it. As they got closer to home, she asked again,

"Are you sure you're okay? You seem very quiet."

For a moment, she thought she wasn't going to get an answer. Then, as she turned onto their road, Angela replied,

"It was my painting."

"Huh? What was?"

"In the gallery window, it was my painting."

Deb had only glanced at the gallery, but she remembered the glimpse she had caught of that large colourful picture on an easel.

"Are you sure?"

"I'm sure, why was my picture in the window?"

Deb didn't have an answer to Angela's question. She parked the car and turned to face Angela.

"Why don't you ask David?"

Of course, that would be the sensible thing to do, only she couldn't. Telling David that she had been to see the gallery would spoil the surprise she intended for him; she would have to tell him about her new friends, her outings, and her newfound freedom. She didn't know why, but she wasn't ready to share those things with him yet. This was 'her thing'; she had been reliant on David for so long, now she wanted to show him that she could do something for herself, that she was finally getting her independence back. But she didn't want to say anything until she was absolutely certain that she could do it; she didn't want to get his hopes up just for them to be dashed when she found out it was beyond her.

And none of that explained what she had seen when Deb had driven her into town. To see her painting displayed so publicly, baring her soul to anyone and everyone who was walking by, was shocking. The picture was private and intimate, part of a document of what had been the worst time of her life. She had asked David to destroy them once they were completed. For her, the act of creation was the catharsis she needed. She had no wish or desire to have a visual reminder of what had happened, god knows she relived it enough times in her nightmares to not need to.

She had no idea how to explain any of this to Deb. Instead, she just thanked her for taking her into town and said that maybe she would ask David next time he came round. Making her excuses, she went inside where she sat in the darkness, trying to work out what was going on.

CHAPTER THIRTY - NINE

"Well, that went okay," Steph reassured Joe as the staff of Griffin Graphics collected their belongings and said their goodbyes for the weekend.

"Did it really, though?" Joe answered, "I think they were all just waiting to go home."

At this moment, some of the designers walked past, and there was a flurry of 'good idea Joe' and 'let me know if you need a hand' comments as they left.

"Well, they seemed to think so," Steph said.

Joe had been just as nervous as he had been when he made his pitch to Tom, maybe even more so. Steph had suggested the previous evening that he should imagine that everyone was naked, to make him less scared of speaking to them. Halfway through his PowerPoint, the advice had resurfaced; it was such a horrific thought that he almost found himself unable to continue.

"I don't know…" he answered.

He looked over Steph's shoulder to see Tom walking towards them. Tom stopped behind Steph. He put his hands on her shoulders and spoke,

"Well done, Joe, you did fantastically."

"Thanks," he mumbled, "I think they were mostly happy because you said I could tell them they could knock off early today."

Tom laughed,

"That didn't hurt, did it? I've just had people coming up and congratulating me on my good idea. I told them that I'd love to take the credit, but it's all on you two. Have a good weekend, we've got a lot of planning to do next week if we want this to work, and I'm going to be putting quite a lot of it on you two."

He smiled, kissed the top of Steph's head and left them together.

"I think I'll be sleeping all weekend. I didn't get a wink last night."

"Well, we'd better go for a drink now, then, while you're still awake."

Joe agreed; he knew his mind was going to be racing with all the things he knew they would need to do. And worrying about all the things he didn't know yet. It seemed like a daunting task, making him wonder why he had suggested it. Of course, he hadn't realised that it would be him who was implementing it. Well, him and Steph. Which was a blessing as she seemed to have a better idea of what to do than him.

The project dominated the pub conversation. Joe wasn't in the least surprised when Steph produced an A4 notebook from her bag, setting it on the table amongst the glasses and empty plates. She went through the notes she had already started making about what they needed to do next. Joe's main task for now was trawling the archives and noting possible pieces they could use. He knew what was there better than anybody, so it was the perfect job for him. Also, he'd already started doing it, so he was ahead of the curve.

"What about all the other stuff that Tom said? The legal stuff and the contracts and…" he started.

Steph stopped him,

"Do you know how we're going to do this?" she asked.

He looked at her.

"One thing at a time. See what needs doing now, then make sure that's done properly. If we're always worrying about what we've got to do next, we're going to lose focus on the things we're doing and make mistakes. We're better than that."

Joe relaxed a little. It was clear that he had the right partner, both at work and in his private life. Things were going well for him.

"Bugger, look at the time, I need to get to the shop now. It's Friday, Janet will be expecting me. Do you want to come? We can go back to Mike's afterwards."

Steph agreed, she liked meeting up with her Dad's old friend, the one who had sent Joe in her direction. She collected her things and they got up to leave. The pub had got busier as the afternoon moved along, still not crowded but heading towards the start of the weekend.

As they passed a group of drinkers, middle-aged men in their 'going out' shirts, one of them turned around, took hold of her arm and spoke to her. Joe didn't hear what it was the man said; from the look on Steph's face, he knew it was something inappropriate. He looked at the group of men. There were five or six of them, all with carefully curated hair arranged over varying degrees of baldness and an invisible cloud of aftershave hanging over them. Amongst the faces he saw one he recognised - Trevor.

For a moment, he froze, then their eyes locked, and Trevor spoke to him,

"Look who it fucking isn't, the fucking car wrecker."

Joe broke his gaze and started to walk away with Steph, who had now changed from being angry to confused. A barrage of abuse from the group of men followed them as they left the pub, and Joe took long, quick strides as Steph hurried to keep up with him. Eventually, she caught up with him, putting her hand on his arm to slow him down until he stopped. He continued to look nervously back at the pub as she asked him what that was about.

"It was Trevor, my Mum's new husband. The one whose car I smashed up. I thought he was going to follow us."

"Oh my god," Steph turned and looked at the pub door, "is that the sort of thing he'd do? Should we run?"

"No, I don't think he's coming. I don't know if it's the kind of thing he'd do."

He looked back over his shoulder to check, then carried on,

"He was alright at first, you know. Tried to act nice. But once he moved in, he changed; he started taking over Mum's life. He was the one who wanted me to move out. He could be pretty nasty sometimes, when Mum wasn't around. He wanted Mum to look after his kids, and me out of the way."

"That's awful. His friend was pretty creepy."

"I think that about sums him up, too. Pretty creepy. Come on, let's get to the shop. Janet will be waiting."

They made it in plenty of time. Janet and Steph, who had already met several times before, went straight to the small kitchen area to make drinks and catch up. They came back with a mug for Joe, who had started organising the clothes rail in his vintage section.

"I hear congratulations are in order," Janet said as she passed it to him.

Realising Steph must have already told him about the work project, he thanked her and took his drink.

"Any new books in?" he asked.

Since he had brought the books with the drawings in the margins, he had been reading far more than he ever had before. Janet had been curating his reading list for him, putting back books that she thought he might enjoy. Steph had eagerly joined in with this informal book club, they had all recently read The Catcher in the Rye, which Janet had managed to get hold of two copies of. Joe had enjoyed the book, but thought Holden Caulfield was a bit of a dick, a summary that had made both Janet and Steph laugh; although they couldn't disagree with the sentiment.

By the time they left, it was well past the time that the shop would normally close. Joe and Steph said goodnight to Janet and walked back to Mike's flat together. Mike was already there, ironing a shirt in the living room, which was a surprise to Joe as he didn't know they had an iron, or that Mike had a shirt that wasn't a work polo or a football shirt.

"Going somewhere?" he asked.

Mike grinned,

"Yeah, I've got a date."

"Who with?" asked Joe.

"Where are you going?" Steph added, almost simultaneously.

Mike answered them both,

"A girl I met in the café where me and the lads get lunch sometimes. She works there."

"You pulled the waitress?" Joe asked. Steph hit his shoulder,

"Shut up, you. So, where are you taking her then?"

"We're going to the cinema to see the new Tom Cruise movie, then out for a curry afterwards."

"Sounds great, so you won't want to be eating with us tonight then?"

"No, but I do want to know how your work thing went. Did they like the idea?"

"I think so," Joe replied.

"Don't be modest," Steph said, "they loved it. I think we can really make a go of it."

"I think you'll do brilliantly, you two are a real double act. Hey, I don't want to get all ahead of myself, but if it goes well tonight and Tanya wants to come back here, are you okay with that?"

"You don't have to ask me that, mate, it's your flat."

"I know, but I didn't want to, you know? Embarrass you or anything. Anyway, I'm putting this on and getting going, I don't want to be late."

He took the crisp, clean shirt into the bathroom and emerged a couple of minutes later looking smart in it, with his hair brushed. He grabbed his jacket, checked his pockets and smiled,

"Wish me luck. At least I'll get to see a film, and not get dragged into a church group bible study meeting like last time."

He smiled, and Joe laughed at the memory of Mike's last, unsuccessful date, which had turned more into an attempt to save his eternal soul. Mike left, and Steph turned to Joe,

"We need to start looking for a flat."

"I know, we can look, but have you seen how much deposit you need for anywhere decent? I've got nowhere near that."

"It's 'we'. I've got some money, all we need to do is find a place."

"I'm not a charity case, I'll pay my own way."

"Too right you will, you can pay me back."

He smiled,

"I'm being a dick aren't I?"

"No, you're just being you; independent and proud. It's why I want to be with you."

"Come on then, let's eat, then we can hit the laptop."

"Or we could make the most of having the flat to ourselves."

Joe smiled and wrapped his arms around her,

"I wasn't hungry anyway," he told her as she stepped back, kicked off her shoes and started to unbutton her shirt.

CHAPTER FORTY

It had been three days since Deb had driven Angela into town, and she hadn't seen her since then. Two days wouldn't have been so unusual, but not three. Today, she hadn't turned up for their regular trip to the park with Elsie. Deb had taken Elsie over the road and knocked on the door, but there had been no reply.

"I bet she's busy doing some more beautiful paintings," she had told Elsie. She had used language her daughter would understand, but she was worried. As they walked around the pond, she got lost in thought about what she could or should do about it. She felt Elsie's hand slip into hers,

"It's not as good without her, is it?"

"No, it's not."

"Is Angela okay?"

"I'm sure she's fine. I'll talk to her later."

This seemed to satisfy Elsie, who let go of her hand and went to investigate some daisies that were growing in a snow-like clump on the grass. Deb watched her while she thought. She would go back to the house again later, but if Angela still didn't answer, she had no idea what to try next. She knew that Angela had kept their friendship a secret from her brother because she wanted to surprise him; she didn't relish the thought of a complicated discussion about the secrets they had been keeping. She was also acutely aware that Angela's change of mood had occurred when she had seen her paintings in David's gallery.

On the walk back, Elsie followed her in silence. They both looked across at Angela's house as they neared it, but Deb saw no signs of life from behind the blank screen of the windows. She glanced again as she closed her front door, but still nothing moved. They went inside for Elsie's snack and Deb's cup of tea and to finish their afternoon.

Later that evening, once Elsie was in bed, Deb went over and knocked on Angela's door again. There was still no answer, so she posted a note she had written through the letterbox, asking if Angela was okay, and to give her a call and let her know if there was anything she could do. Back in her own house, she kept thinking of reasons to go into the front room so she could look across and see if any lights came on in Angela's house as it got darker.

She was finally rewarded late in the evening when an upstairs light shone out. Not one from the rooms directly overlooking the road, but the filtered, wan light of a back room that had found its way through. It was either from the bathroom or Angela's art room, but whichever it was, it helped Deb's anxiety levels when she saw it blink on.

Despite this, she was still worried. She was a mum, and it was part of her job description to make things better, to fix things. When Elsie was sad, she cheered her up, and when Elsie was sick or hurt herself, she was the one who would magically produce whatever was needed to remedy the situation. Now she wanted to do the same for Angela, but she didn't know how when she was so firmly shut out.

She tried talking to Gareth about it as they sat in bed with their mugs of tea, watching the late news. She got irritated with him when he suggested that she should just give Angela some time, and maybe wait for her to get back in touch. She took her drink to the kitchen and sat at the table, gazing absently at the pictures on the fridge. They were some of the drawings that Elsie had produced, with Angela's help, the last time they had been to visit. They had been drawing on pieces of paper that Angela had collected from around the room, old envelopes, post-it notes, and scrap paper. Angela had a habit of drawing on anything that came to hand. Deb remembered the first time she had seen Angela open a book, which had been the closest thing to hand, and do a quick sketch in the blank area at the bottom of a page. She hadn't said anything, but had been a little shocked as it had been deeply ingrained in her to treat her books as precious objects.

One of Elsie's pictures, a clumsily drawn flower next to a beautifully rendered sketch of the same object, was on an A4 sheet with two neat folds across it; the back of a letter. Deb got up and took it from the fridge. Turning it over, she saw that it was the one from the two young people who had come to visit. It had their names and phone numbers printed at the bottom, beneath their polite request to come and talk to Angela. She was looking at it and thinking that maybe it had been an odd request; why did they need to talk to Angela if the article they were writing was about her brother?

Gareth came into the kitchen,

"Sorry, darling, I didn't mean to upset you. The truth is, I don't know what else you can do. Come on back up to bed and we'll think about it tomorrow when we're less tired."

He kissed her. She folded the letter and put it in her dressing gown pocket before kissing him back.

"Good idea," she said, "I think I need a good night's sleep."

"That's good," he replied, "I hope she's okay, I'm worried too. And Elsie's missing her already."

"I know, and you're right, she probably does just need a little more time. It was a shock for her."

Deb did sleep better that night, now she had at least the kernel of a plan for what she should do next. She was going to call the girl, Steph, and see what she could tell her, after all, they had met David too. It wouldn't hurt to try.

CHAPTER FORTY - ONE

The following week, Tom told Steph that he had some face-to-face client meetings. He wanted her to come along with him so she could start getting some first-hand experience of that side of the business. It was, he told her, something that she would need to get used to doing when the new enterprise got underway. It was also something that he felt would be suited to her skill set, she was good with meeting people and making a good first impression. He was at pains to tell Joe that he would be involved in this side of things too, once he was feeling comfortable in his new role. Joe was secretly relieved about this.

The days had been interesting, watching how her dad listened carefully to what the clients wanted, reassured them that it was possible and negotiated mutually agreeable conditions. He was so different from the way he was at home or around the office, and she realised immediately why he had wanted her to come along with him. She still had a lot to learn, and she was going to need to be fully up to speed if she and Joe were going to make a go of the new venture.

In the car, between meetings, Tom reverted to his normal self, joking, singing along with the radio and chatting with Steph.

"How's the flat hunting going?" he asked.

Steph's mum had told him that she and Joe had talked about getting a flat together after they had discussed it. Dad had said that he would be glad to have her out from under his feet, then gave her a big hug and told her that he was happy that she had found someone nice.

Mum had also hugged her and said she would miss having her around, and reiterated that this would always be her home when she needed it.

The short answer was that the flat hunting was going terribly. They had spent a lot of time looking at flats to rent at the weekend and in the evenings. Scrolling through endless paragraphs describing well-appointed studio flats and one-bedroom apartments with good décor throughout. The only thing that they all had in common, apart from the florid estate agent speak descriptions, was the exorbitant amount of money you needed for the deposit. Even though Joe had told her this, she didn't quite believe it until she saw it for herself. She did have a little money in savings, but that would be wiped out by even the meanest of the living accommodation on offer.

"Joe could move in with us," he suggested.

The subtle nuance of the tone of his voice was enough to convince her that it was not his preferred option.

"How awkward would that be?" she answered. "Especially for Joe."

"Fair point, how about if I paid the deposit for you? When you find a place you can afford."

"Really? That would be… Hold on, I see what you just did there. You only said about Joe moving into our house so that I would go for the deposit thing, didn't you?"

"You got it, it's all in the negotiation. You're learning. Anyway, seriously, I can help with the deposit if you want."

"Thanks, Dad, we'll pay you back."

"Of course you will, otherwise I'll take it out of your wages, or make you Gary's PA."

"I'm sure he thinks I already am," she answered.

They both laughed at this as they headed on to their next appointment. Steph's day considerably brightened; she couldn't wait to get back and tell Joe. Then they could start flat hunting in earnest.

Around mid-afternoon, as they were on their way back to the office, Steph got a call from an unknown number. Her phone had been on mute for most of the day, rule number one when meeting a client – they are the most important person. Normally, she wouldn't take a call if she didn't know who it was from; there were so many creeps, weirdos and scammers out there. She pressed the red button and put her phone back in her lap. Before they got back to the office, the same number had called again. Whoever it was, they must really want to sell her something. She pressed the red button again.

"Not answering it?" Tom asked.

"Unknown number, life's too short."

"Fair enough. It might be important, though."

"Also, it might not be. I'll take the risk."

They were getting out of the car when a message came through with a loud ping. She stood by the car and read it. Tom started walking in,

"I'll see you inside, love."

She gave him a thumbs-up as she read the text.

'Hi, my name is Deb, I'm a friend of Angela Hacer. I'm sorry I tried calling you earlier, but something has happened and I don't know what else to do. I think you might be able to help, please can you call me back.'

Intrigued, she called the number, it was answered immediately.

"Hi, is that Steph?"

"Yes, sorry I didn't answer earlier. I don't like unknown numbers."

"I get that, it's okay, I'm sorry to bother you, but I don't know what else to do. I thought maybe you could help."

"I've only met Angela once, I don't know if I'd be much help."

"I know that, she said she enjoyed it, being interviewed. She was ever so nervous about it, you know?"

"Are you the friend from over the road? The one who made the biscuits?"

"Yes."

"They were delicious. Listen, I'm at work right now. Can we meet somewhere later? I'll bring Joe along too if that's okay?"

"That would be fine, where shall we meet?"

They agreed on a coffee shop near Deb's house, Steph knew where it was.

"How will I know who you are?" she asked.

"I'll be with a small girl, probably answering a hundred and one questions. It's okay, I know what you look like. I saw you when you visited Angela."

They thanked each other, and Steph rang off and followed Tom into the office. She was eager to tell Joe about this latest, mysterious development, and intrigued about what Angela's neighbour thought she might be able to help with.

CHAPTER FORTY - TWO

Deb's note sat on the table. She knew she should call her, but couldn't quite bring herself to. She added guilt to her raft of conflicting emotions, knowing how much Elsie enjoyed park walk day. So did she, but she wasn't in the right frame of mind for it today. They would probably go without her and have a good time anyway.

She sank back into the armchair and turned her mind back to the question at hand. Why was her painting in the gallery window? Why on earth would David do that in his gallery? The painting was private and personal, not something that she wanted every passer-by on the high street to stop and look at. It didn't make any sense to her.

When she painted the canvases, it had been cathartic, a small step on her long road to recovery. They had quickly amassed in the house, and she found that once they were complete, it was hard to look at them. It was as if the experience had been transferred from her to the picture, expunged from her memory. Of course, they came back again eventually, and then she had to pour them onto another canvas. But as long as she kept doing that, she could keep her demons at bay. Recently, they had been receding, fading away as more pleasant events started to come back into her life. Now she was drawing and painting to remember things, not to forget them.

She didn't know what she was going to say to David when he came to visit, how she would broach the subject or get to the bottom of it. Her instinct was to avoid him, to stay in bed and refuse to talk. He had got used to that over the last few years. But although that would avoid a confrontation, it would not get any of the answers that she badly wanted now.

She stayed in the chair, staring at the painting of the beach in front of her, paralysed by her indecision and fear.

CHAPTER FORTY - THREE

The coffee shop wasn't busy, Joe guessed it was because most people were heading home for their tea at this time of day. The warm smell of the coffee greeted them as they came through the door, the way coffee can only smell in the right environment. It was never as good at home or work.

He saw the lady with the little girl as soon as he walked in, sitting at a table to one side of the room. She had been watching the door and recognised them too, waving to get their attention and clearing some space in front of the two free chairs. They crossed to the table, littered with pieces of paper and a handful of felt-tip pens, and joined them. Joe offered to get coffee for everyone. The woman thanked him, her cup was empty already, and she had evidently been waiting for them for a while.

He had been intrigued when Steph told him about the phone call. She said that Deb had been so oblique, she couldn't figure out what had happened, or how they might be able to help. Neither of them could imagine what use they would be, but they both wanted to find out. Another piece of the puzzle that had been perplexing them for so long now.

Once they were all sitting down with drinks in front of them, Deb started to explain what had happened. It was a long and convoluted explanation, but the end of the story was succinct and Deb started picking distractedly at her fingernails as she told it. They had driven past the gallery, Angela's painting was in the window, she was upset, and I haven't seen her since then.

"So, as you interviewed David recently, I wondered if you knew why it had upset her so much."

"We thought that he was passing off someone else's work as his own. We only suspected it before, but now you've told us that, it confirms it," Steph answered.

She gave a brief recap of how they'd come to be searching for the mystery artist whose doodlings they'd found in the pages of a book.

"Oh, the books are so Angela, she draws everywhere. Sometimes I'm not even sure she knows that she's doing it."

"Well, that's how it started. I feel a bit bad that we pretended to be something we're not so we could talk to David and Angela," Joe said, "but I'm glad we've found out who it is. I'm not sure what else we can do to help, though."

"Yeah," Steph added, "I don't know if it's a criminal thing, I'm not sure the police would be interested."

"No, me neither," replied Deb, "but what if we went to see David together? We need to let him know that his sister is upset; she may need his help. I don't want to go by myself, but Angela's my friend. I feel like I should at least try."

"We'll go with you," answered Joe, surprising himself and Steph with this decisive response.

"Sure, we will," Steph added, "when do you want to go?"

"It has to be tomorrow, it needs to be before his next visit."

"I'll ring the gallery and find out if he'll be there," said Steph. "I'm not sure what we'll do if he's not."

Deb waited, and Joe started talking to Elsie, who was beginning to get restless.

"Are you Angela's friends too?" she asked.

"I kind of guess we are," answered Joe, "although we only met her once."

"She's nice, she draws pictures for me."

She pulled a notebook out of her backpack and offered it to Joe, who took it and looked inside. Once he had opened it, he couldn't tear his eyes away. He spoke to the little girl without looking at her,

"Did Angela do all these?"

"No, I did some, look."

She took the book from his hands and turned to the middle of the book where her own compositions were. They were very competent for a four-year-old. But Angela's pictures were revelatory; he had been enamoured enough with the first pictures he saw to track her down, with the help of his friends. But these drawings, created for the entertainment of a small girl, were fantastic. The colours, lines and shapes spread easily across the pages, creating a series of beautiful images. These were more figurative than some of her other work, but small details and concealed images still hid within the entrancing pictures.

"They are beautiful, you should look after that book, it's really special."

"I will," she answered, tucking it back inside her floral backpack and zipping it shut.

He rejoined the conversation with Deb and Steph in time to find out that they'd booked an appointment with David Hacer at 9.30 the following morning.

"How did you get him to agree to that?" he asked Steph.

"Because I want to commission some of his landscapes for the hotel I own in the Lake District," she told him.

"You are awful, what about work?"

"I'll explain it to Dad tonight, he'll understand. Anyway, we are allowed to take time off when we need to."

"Are we?"

"Yes, we get paid holiday leave."

"But it's not ..." he paused, thought, then continued, "it's not like school holidays, is it?"

"No, welcome to the world of work, Joe." She smiled, then turned to Deb, "Will you meet us there?"

"Yes, I'll come straight after I've dropped Elsie off at nursery. I have to go now, but I'll see you tomorrow. Thank you so much for doing this, I'm so worried about her, you know."

"I know, we only met her once, but she was completely charming. See you in the morning."

Deb and Elsie collected up their belongings and left, Elsie giving Joe a small wave and a beaming smile on her way past.

"I think you've made a new friend," said Steph.

"I think I have, did you see the pictures in the book?"

"Not properly, I was on the phone."

"They are fantastic, I wanted to steal it."

"Well, run after her now and grab her bag. I'm going home to talk to Dad about tomorrow morning. I'll meet you in town in the morning."

"Okay, let me walk you to the bus stop."

The early evening was just starting to get chilly, he wrapped his arms around Steph. Ostensibly to keep her warm, but in reality, he was sharing her warmth as much as she was his. As the bus pulled up and Steph got ready to get on, she turned to Joe,

"Oh, what with everything else going on, I nearly forgot to tell you, Dad's going to lend us the deposit for a flat, so get looking."

"What?"

"I said, find us a flat, see you tomorrow."

She kissed him and got on the bus, showing her pass to the driver and finding a seat. Joe stood and watched as the bus pulled away, trying to make sense of what she had just said. Then, when he had started to process it, he hurried back to the flat to fill Mike in on the events of the day.

In the end, he had to wait until gone eleven to share anything. Mike had gone out to meet Tanya again, just for a quick drink this time.

Joe looked around the clean, tidy flat and decided he wanted to meet the woman who could spur Mike into this level of domesticity. While he waited, he opened his laptop and scoured the local estate agents, making a note of any properties that might be suitable. He was both nervous and excited about the prospect, but having the deposit made a huge difference to what they could look for.

CHAPTER FORTY - FOUR

David was in early the next morning, excited at the prospect of a potential new client. He'd never considered the idea of producing bespoke works for hotels in select areas before, but now that it had been suggested to him, he could see the potential in the idea. He was hopeful that if this commission went well, it could lead to others in the future. His mind had been buzzing all night with ideas for how he could build on this, if today's meeting was successful.

The coffee pot was on, and Courtney had gone to get some fresh pastries from the bakery a few shops down. He checked once more that everything in the gallery was in order, with some of what he felt were his best pieces prominently displayed on easels. He had briefly considered wearing something that gave the image of an artist, not quite a smock or dungarees, but something slightly shabby, covered with brightly coloured smudges. He had quickly abandoned the idea, though, opting instead for his usual suit and tie. This was a business meeting after all.

He checked his watch and then took himself into his small studio area, where he sat down and opened his laptop. He flicked through the stored images, making a note of which ones had lakes and hills, that might help to seal the deal with the woman from the hotel.

On the corner of the street, Steph and Joe waited for Deb to arrive. They hadn't argued, but they had disagreed on what they expected to happen when David realised it was them again. Joe thought they would be shown the door, but Steph was adamant that they would have a chance to ask him about his sister's paintings. They stood slightly apart from one another, each quietly considering the points that the other had made. Whatever the outcome was going to be, they had both agreed that they at least had to give it a try.

"Here she comes now," Joe pointed down the road at Deb, who was hurrying towards them.

Steph greeted her as she joined them, and together they started to walk the short distance to the gallery.

"Do you think he's going to be angry?" asked Deb.

"I don't know," Steph replied, "Joe thinks he's going to throw us out."

"Well, ask us to leave, maybe," Joe answered. "He's not going to like it."

"Probably not, but we have to do it, for Angela's sake," Deb said.

"Have you still not seen her?" asked Steph.

"No, I'm still worried about her."

With that, they arrived at the gallery, the receptionist smiled and greeted them as they walked in, and Steph introduced herself using the name she had given when she booked the appointment. If the receptionist was surprised, she didn't let it show.

"Come on in this way," she indicated the small studio area, " would you like tea or coffee?"

"No, thank you," Joe answered as he followed the two women into David's studio.

The receptionist's composure was better than David's. As they walked in, his eyes moved rapidly across each of them, and the expression on his face was a mixture of confusion and irritation.

"I'm sorry," he told them, "I can't see you now, I'm expecting a visitor."

"No," Steph answered him, "I'm sorry it was me who made the appointment. We just really needed to speak with you."

"So you're not writing an article? Or are you? And who's this?" He pointed to Deb.

Deb took the initiative, speaking quickly to make sure she said what she needed to,

"Hello, David, I'm Deb. I'm Angela's neighbour. I didn't know how to contact you. I'm just really worried, I haven't seen her for days now."

"Well, that's not unusual, she doesn't leave the house."

"Actually, she has been recently," Deb said. "She's been going out regularly; she didn't want you to know until she was sure she was confident she could do it."

She went on to explain how she and Elsie had become friends with Angela, quickly telling David about the trips to the park, drives in the car and visits to one another's houses. David's face was a picture of incredulity as Deb explained his sister's friendship. He didn't say anything for a moment, when he did, it was a single word,

"What?"

Deb started to repeat it, but he waved his hand at her,

"Are you sure you've got the right person? My sister doesn't go out, she's very vulnerable."

"I know, that's why I'm worried about her. She planned to come and visit you here, to surprise you. It was what was driving her. Then, the other afternoon, in the car, she asked me to come past the gallery, just so that she could see it."

David blanched, as if he knew what was coming next.

"She saw her painting in the window, and she got upset and asked me to take her home, and I haven't seen her since. Now she won't answer the door or return my calls, and I'm worried."

There was a hush in the room. David opened his mouth and then closed it again wordlessly. Joe wondered if this was the moment that he would ask them to leave, or get angry and demand to know who they thought they were. Steph broke the silence,

"Deb asked us to come because she knew that we'd met you before; she was nervous."

"How did..." he started. "I mean, you knew, didn't you? You asked me about her paintings."

"We thought we did, yes. That's why we went to see Angela, we didn't say anything, though. We were just trying to figure it out."

Joe had anticipated several possible ways that David might react, but not what happened next. David's face went slack, and he started to cry. He slumped back in his chair and put his hands over his face, loud sobs and tears that shook his body, bringing the receptionist in to see what was going on. While Steph, Joe, and the receptionist stood around not knowing what to do, Deb hurried over and put her arm around David's shoulder.

"It's okay," she told him, "Angela's safe, I think she's just confused. We are, too. We hoped you could help us to help her."

For Deb, this was a natural reaction; she was doing the same as she would have done for Elsie if it had been her who was upset. It seemed to do the trick, and David started to calm down. He took his face out of his hands and looked at Deb,

"I'm sorry," he said. "I'm so, so sorry. Just give me a minute. Courtney, can you close up the gallery, please, and pour some coffee for everyone. If you all want to go out to the seating area, I'll join you in a moment. I just want to freshen up first." He stood up and went into the bathroom, closing the door behind him. As they went back into the gallery, Courtney turned around from where she had been flipping the sign on the door to indicate they were closed.

"What's going on?" she asked.

"To be honest, we're not really sure," Joe told her.

"I think we're going to find out in a minute," Steph told her, "do you want a hand with the drinks?"

Courtney still looked concerned, but she took up Steph's offer of assistance. They were passing out the cups when David reappeared. His eyes were red and bloodshot, and even though he had washed his face, it was still red and blotchy. His first few steps attempted to regain some of his composure and dignity, which evaporated as he approached the group. He dropped onto a chair, and Courtney passed him a drink.

"Do you want me to take a break while you talk to these people, David?" she asked.

"No, Courtney, stick around. You need to hear what I'm going to tell them, too. Did you get those pastries?"

"Yes, shall I get them?" She didn't wait for an answer, but collected a bag of Danish buns and croissants from behind her desk and put them on a plate that she had prepared earlier. She placed them on the little coffee table they were clustered around before picking up her drink.

"Please, everyone, do help yourselves. I don't think my guest from the Lake District is coming." He managed a half smile in Steph's direction as he said this. He continued,

"I think I need to explain myself, and I will. But first, you kind of ambushed me this morning. Can I just ask," He turned to Deb, "Did you say Angela had been out of the house?"

"Yes, she's been all over the place; mostly the park, though. She comes with me and Elsie, my daughter."

"And she let you into her house?"

"We've been lots of times, she comes over to ours regularly as well. She wanted it to be a big surprise for you. She's been so determined to push herself, she's done ever so well."

"I can't tell you how pleased I am," David said. "After she got run over, she was ill for so long. It was nearly a year before she started to get anything like enough mobility to get around. It was so long that she had enough time to convince herself that the outside was too dangerous for her. She hasn't left that house for years."

"I know," Deb replied, "She told me that. She was still ever so nervous when we first met her. She's tried so hard, she wants to make you proud of her."

David started to cry again. Not the dramatic sobs of earlier, but a stream of silent tears running down his cheeks. He wiped them away with a tissue he was still clutching, then took a large swallow of his coffee, not seeming to care how hot it was. He put his cup down and ran his eyes across the group.

"I guess I owe you all an explanation," he said. "I'll try to explain it as best as I can."

"Are you sure you don't want me to step outside for a bit?" Courtney asked.

"No, I want you to stay; this affects you too. All I ask is that you don't judge me too harshly. I thought I was doing the right thing, but I think I knew it would all come out eventually. I always had Angela's best interests at heart, even if it doesn't look like it. She's my baby sister, and I love her to pieces, and the accident was partly… well, mostly, my fault. I was supposed to give her a lift home, you see, but I got too drunk to go and pick her up. That's why she was walking home on her own, late at night; it was because of me."

More tears followed. Courtney collected the box of tissues from the reception desk, David took a fresh one, dried his eyes, then started to speak again. The others stayed quiet, nobody wanted to interrupt or ask questions, they were all too intent on finding out the truth.

"When she started to get a bit better, she began to paint. The doctor said it would be good for her, that it would help her to release her inner feelings, so I got her all the stuff she needed. All she did was churn out those great big abstract pieces. I didn't stop her, but I couldn't see how they were helping, other than she seemed to enjoy it."

"Did you not see the pictures in the patterns?" Joe asked.

"What pictures?" David answered.

"The… no, it's alright, I'll show you another time. Sorry, I didn't mean to interrupt."

"That's okay, where was I? Oh yes, well, the house started to fill up, and I bought some of them here. I was going to paint over them and reuse the canvases. Angela said she didn't want them anymore, that they were too painful and that I should take them."

"I had a pile of them in the corner. I was going to move them into the studio, but I got sidetracked by something else. The next thing I knew, a customer was looking through them and asking if he could buy one. I was just going to tell him they weren't for sale, I still don't know why I didn't, I just told him it was two thousand pounds, expecting him to put it back. But he didn't; he got his credit card out and took the painting away with him. I left some of them out to see what happened, and a week later, I sold another. You can't look a gift horse in the mouth, especially when sales had been slow for my own work."

He took another drink of coffee, seeming calmer now, and continued,

"I didn't tell people they were mine because I wanted the credit; it was because I wanted to keep Angela's name out of it. It was just easier that way, there was no way that she would have been able to do photo shoots or interviews. She would have been horrified. So I just kept it like that, and people kept on buying them. They're very popular."

"It's because they're beautiful," Steph informed him.

"But," added Joe, "They're so personal. They tell the story of what happened to her, all of it."

David looked at him, puzzled.

"Look," said Joe. He went over to one of the paintings on the wall and started to describe what he could see. Steph was now used to looking at the pictures in Joe's way, but for the others, it was a surprise. A gradual dawning of realisation for David, which led to him starting to cry again. Joe showed them the doctor and the ambulance, and the trays of medical instruments in the operating theatre. Once you had seen it, you couldn't unsee it.

"I didn't know," David whispered, "I didn't realise. I would never have... I would never. Oh, Angela, I'm so sorry."

This time it was Steph who went and comforted him, with an arm on his shoulder, she quietly said,

"You can fix it. You need to tell Angela what you just told us. You need to do it now. Deb is worried about your sister, and I expect you are too. You've got a key to the house, why not go and talk to her?"

David looked stricken,

"What will I tell her?" he asked, his voice almost childlike.

"What you told us, how her paintings came to be on sale. And that you're sorry."

"I'll come with you," Deb offered. "I can help explain things. At the very least, I can make drinks for you both."

David looked surprised,

"You really are her friend, aren't you. Thank you for helping her."

"It's more her helping me. Have you ever tried keeping a four-year-old occupied all day? Come on, I'm parked around the corner."

David did as he was told, and he turned to Courtney,

"Sorry you got caught up in all this, can you lock up for me, please? Take the day off."

"I will lock up, but not until 5. I'm staying right here. You go and look after your sister, and tell her that when she's ready to come and visit the gallery, I'll put on a party for her. Go on, go."

David thanked her and followed Deb out onto the street. Steph and Joe helped Courtney tidy up the space.

"Wow, that was intense. I never knew. I should have though, they're nothing like his normal paintings. He's not a bad man, you know," she told them, "He's a good boss, and a very talented artist. I hope he's going to be okay."

"He'll be fine," Joe mumbled through a mouthful of pastry, "Angela will understand."

"I guess you haven't met her, have you?" asked Steph.

"No, not yet."

"Well, she's lovely. I'm sure they'll work it out."

On that note of optimism, they all went back to work, all anxiously wondering what would happen next, and waiting to hear.

CHAPTER FORTY - FIVE

The sound of the front door opening was audible even through the closed bedroom door and the duvet, which was pulled up over her head. She knew it was David, as he was the only other person who had a key. She wondered what he was doing here, she wasn't expecting him until tomorrow. Or maybe it was tomorrow already. She had spent so much time in bed that she really couldn't be certain that she hadn't got her days muddled up.
Whatever day it was, she didn't want to talk to him. She wrapped the duvet tighter around herself as she heard the footsteps on the stairs, and turned her back to the bedroom door when she heard it opening. Staying very still, she waited for him to go away, hoping he would think she was asleep and not speak to her. She was almost surprised enough to turn around and look when it was Deb's voice she heard.

"Angela, are you okay? I've been worried about you."

She tried to make herself even smaller, to disappear inside the material that was wrapped around her.

"I understand why you're so upset. It must have been an awful shock seeing your pictures in the gallery."

The mound of duvet on the bed did not stir.

"You can talk to me if you want, I'll listen. Or you can talk to David, he's downstairs. He's really upset too; he wants to explain what happened."

There was still no response. Deb came into the room and knelt by the bed. She put one hand gently in the place that she estimated Angela's shoulder to be.

"If you come down, I'll make a pot of tea, then we can talk. He wants to tell you what happened, you'll need to do this eventually. I'll sit with you if you want, we all want what's best for you."

There was still no movement or sound from the bed. Deb was uncertain about what she should do or say next. She couldn't force Angela to talk to her brother, and she didn't blame her for not wanting to. But she had seen such a change in her since they had first met, it hurt her to see Angela in such a bad space.

"Me and Elsie missed you at the park. She kept asking if you were okay. You've become quite a fixture for her. She told me the other day that you were like her other mummy. She's been drawing pictures for you all week. There's one of her with me, Gareth and you, she said it was her family. She also wants you to know that you are formally invited to her fifth birthday party next month."

Angela shifted slightly, she pulled the duvet away from her face so it didn't muffle her voice.

"I don't want to talk to him."

Deb persisted,

"You'll have to eventually. He wants to talk to you, but he's scared."

It had never occurred to Angela that her big brother would be scared of anything. Her face appeared through a gap in the bedclothes, an unkempt fringe of hair surrounded her bloodshot eyes.

"Scared of what?"

"He's scared that you're going to go back to how you were before. He couldn't believe that you've been leaving the house; he was so surprised. He thinks he's hurt you. In fact, he knows he has, he wants to apologise and to explain himself. He said he'd go away if you wanted him to, but I think you should hear him out, Angela, at least give him a chance."

"Why should I, after what he's done?"

She turned around and started to sit up and face Deb. There was no bitterness or anger in her voice, just a resigned sadness.

"Because he's family, because he's sorry, and because you need to hear what he has to say. I'm sure he wouldn't do anything to intentionally hurt you."

Angela sighed because she knew that, too. Deb was right, and he was family. She pushed the duvet to one side, revealing a baggy shirt and crumpled joggers, and swung her legs over the side as Deb moved out of her way.

"Will you stay?" she asked.

"Of course I will, if that's what you want."

"Thank you," she took her tatty dressing gown from the back of the door and wrapped it around herself, then started to walk downstairs.

David was sitting on the sofa, waiting. He started to stand up, almost smiled and generally got flustered when Angela walked into the room. He sat back down as she walked across the room and took the armchair opposite him. It would have been hard to say whose expression was the sorriest-looking. David spoke first,

"I'm sorry, Angela, I can explain."

"It had better be good," she answered, leaning back into the chair.

"I'm going to make tea for everyone," Deb informed them before moving into the kitchen.

As she stood by the counter, waiting for the kettle to boil and sorting out the mugs, milk and tea bags, she could hear only David's voice. He was explaining to Angela how her paintings had come to be on sale in the gallery. She could hear some of what he was saying, enough to work out that it was the same story he had told her, Joe and Steph, only this interspersed with numerous profuse apologies.

She carried the tray of drinks into the room just as he had finished speaking. For a moment, the only sound was the clinking of the cups as Deb set the tray on the coffee table. She looked at David, who gave the impression that he might be about to cry at any moment, then turned to Angela as she started to speak,

"Even when we were kids, you managed to do stupid things all the time. You just don't think about other people, do you? They were my pictures, and they are so personal. You've been selling my deepest secrets to anybody with a bank card. How could you?"

"I didn't know, I thought it was just patterns." Now he did start to cry again, "It was only when I was shown what was in them that I realised."

"What do you mean, you didn't know?"

"I mean, they aren't obvious – you have to look at them in just the right way. I still can't see half the things that Joe told me were in it."

The mood in the room shifted, and Angela looked slightly perplexed.

"But it's all there, the accident and everything."

"I know, but not everybody can see it. You've hidden it all."

Deb interjected,

"It's true, Angela, I didn't realise at first. They're very beautiful, but also mysterious. I think most people just see the surface. Some of the pictures you did for Elsie have things hidden in them, too. She saw them straight away. I can see some of them now. I don't know how you do it, but it's wonderful."

Angela looked at Deb, then her brother, with a slightly puzzled look on her face.

"What do you mean, you can't see them?"

"Well, I can now, some of them anyway. It was that lad, Joe, who could see them. He worked out how to do it after he found some of your doodles in some books," David told her.

"What, Joe, the photographer who came with that girl who was writing the article about you? Steph wasn't it?"

"Yes, but they weren't writing an article, it's complicated."

Between them, Deb and David explained to Angela what had happened, retelling the story that they had been told. When they were done, Angela sat quietly for a moment before drinking her now tepid tea in several long swallows. Once she was done, she spoke to David.

"You really didn't know what was in the pictures?"

"No."

"Those young people liked them enough to go to the trouble of tracking me down?"

"Yes."

"People pay a lot of money for them?"

"They're happy to, everybody loves your paintings. Much more than mine."

Angela looked guiltily at the beach scene on the wall.

"They're just different," she told him.

"Anyway," David said, "I hear you have secrets of your own."

"What do you mean?"

He looked meaningfully at Deb.

"You never told me you had friends, or that you'd been going out exploring."

"It was meant to be a surprise."

"Well, it was certainly that. Tell me what you've been up to."

"I'll go and make some more tea, then I'll have to get going." Deb said, "I think you two have some catching up to do. Angela, I don't want to hassle you right now, but Elsie wants to know if you're coming to the park tomorrow."

"Well, you tell Elsie that I'll see her at the usual time. David's going to take me to the gallery before that."

David looked surprised, but didn't dare contradict his sister.

CHAPTER FORTY - SIX

The aftermath of David's revelation felt anticlimactic to Joe. Not so much a criminal mastermind, more of a foolish error of judgement. He and Steph both agreed that, whatever happened next, it wasn't their business. They decided that they should forget about it for now, except Joe couldn't. He'd had the beautiful, mysterious pictures on his mind for so long that it was hard to just switch them off. For a start, there was his curiosity about how David and Angela would resolve the issue. Then he wanted to know where all the missing paintings from the series were. David never said that he had got round to painting over any of them, so where were they? Although they had done as much as they could, it still felt like unfinished business.

At work, things began to get busy, very busy. Although Tom was guiding them, he wanted Steph and him to do as much of the preparation work as they could by themselves. For both of them, this meant a steep learning curve that they were still near the bottom of. They needed to know about copyright law, licensing, royalty payments, printing costs, printing techniques, costings, distribution, marketing and a host of other things that would take a lifetime to fully understand. Tom helped them make contact with experts in all of these fields, but strongly advised them both to gain as much knowledge as they could so they would be able to approach the project in an informed manner.

The office had been reorganised to create space for them, with a pair of desks in a corner of the room. It was good to still be amongst the designers and artists, who showed a keen interest in how things were going, as well as offering practical help and support when they could.

They both worked hard, putting in long hours and attempting to get samples ready for the following month, when they would give Tom a full progress report and update. Although the work was hard, it was stimulating and varied enough for Joe not to mind. Also, Steph was easy to work with. They complemented one another, both finding different aspects of the work came more naturally to one or another of them, they had become a team.

Leaving work late and tired, left little time for flat hunting. Flats went quickly when they became available, and the ones they had been to see had been entirely unsuitable. They had left their numbers with several estate agents, with a request for them to call if anything became available. Although their situation wasn't desperate, they wanted to spend more time together, to get to know one another better, to start building a life together. Also, things had started to get more serious with Mike and his girlfriend, Tanya. He hadn't said as much, he never would, but Joe knew that he was in the way.

The wait was frustrating. Tom had invited Joe to stay with them temporarily, until they found somewhere of their own. Although he stayed over occasionally, he was loath to move in with the boss; he just wasn't comfortable with the idea. Steph was understanding about this, but as time wore on, it was beginning to look like it would be his only option.

Whatever was happening at work, he still went to help in the shop every Friday afternoon. Most weeks, Steph came along too, or, if she couldn't, she met him there later. Their informal book group was still going strong, Janet still managing to surprise them both with books they might not have considered reading previously. There were some weeks when the three of them would still be inside the shop over an hour after it had closed, drinking tea from mugs with cartoon pictures, and sitting on a collection of mismatched chairs, talking. The longest they had stayed was the week after they had finally tracked down Angela, and Janet had wanted to know every detail of what had happened.

It was a grim evening outside, with the light a heavy, dark orange colour, heralding the potential arrival of rain. The wind had been rattling the door as if it was trying to open it and let in the pile of leaves that had blown against the front of the shop. Janet sipped her freshly made tea and asked,

"How's the flat hunting going?"

Steph sighed,

"It's hopeless, anything we can afford seems to get snapped up before we even have a chance to view it. The only places we're seeing are studio apartments, and I think I'd go nuts living in a single room."

"I think we're going to have to start looking at places further out of town," Joe added, "it'd be a pain. Steph hasn't passed her driving test yet, and there's no way we can afford a car right now anyway."

"My friend Carol has a colleague, Simon, who lets out his basement flat. His tenants are moving out soon because they're expecting a baby. Do you want me to ask for you? It's in Minster Road."

Joe didn't know Carol or Simon. He had no idea where Minster Road was or if Steph wanted to live in a cellar; nevertheless, he said yes immediately. Slightly more pragmatic, Steph asked if Janet knew how much it would cost.

"Carol says he likes to keep the rent down, it encourages good tenants to stay. He won't go through a letting agency, so there are no extra fees there. It's just him making some income from a part of his house he doesn't use. I'll call Carol and ask her to pass on your number, you never know."

With this agreed, they finished up for the evening, tidying the shop and leaving it ready for the Saturday rush, then heading out into the ominous yellow twilight and swirling wind.

By the end of that weekend, Joe knew who Simon was and where Minster Road was. He was a very nice man whose kids had all left his large family-sized home, which was walking distance from town and on the right side to be able to get to work easily. Steph had joked about them becoming moles, but the basement was well lit from ground-level windows. On the day they visited, the sun poured through them, bathing the flat in a golden glow. It had a good-sized kitchen, a small lounge and a double bedroom. She fell in love with it immediately, and arrangements were made for the following month, when the couple who currently occupied it were due to move out. Joe had no idea what Simon had been told about them, but everything was agreed quickly; he guessed Janet had given them some sort of glowing recommendation, and he made a mental note to buy her a bottle of wine to thank her.

Back at Mike's, he broke the news. To his surprise, Mike looked disappointed.

"I thought you'd have had enough of me by now."

"I've got used to having you around. Who's going to keep the place tidy now?"

Joe laughed, then said,

"To be honest, I'm quite nervous about it."

"Why?"

"Well, what if it doesn't work out?"

"You won't know until you try it. Why wouldn't it? You and Steph are great together."

"I know, it's just…you know? It didn't work out so well for my parents, did it?"

"You can't think like that, you're not your dad. You're nothing like him - or Trevor. Did you tell your mum yet?"

"No, she stopped replying to my messages ages ago. I haven't spoken to her for months."

There was nothing Mike could say to that, so he changed the subject.

"Let me know if you and Steph need a hand moving in, I'll ask the boss if I can borrow a van."

"Cheers mate, I'll probably be able to carry my stuff on the bus though."

Mike laughed,

"Okay, I think you might be surprised, though."

He was right, Joe had never really thought about all the things that they would need to kit out the flat. Steph had. With her mum and dad, she had been busily assembling everything they would need: crockery, cutlery, pans, microwaves, TVs, a table, chairs, a sofa, and chests of drawers. They had been storing it in the garage, when Steph opened the door to show Joe what they had accumulated, he was taken aback.

"I guess we will be taking Mike up on his offer then," he laughed.

Moving day was busy, from first thing in the morning, when Mike turned up in the van. He'd brought along a colleague who said he was willing to work for beer; between them, they managed all the packing and lifting in the expert and efficient way that you would expect from men who did it for a living. Joe was impressed, seeing Mike in work mode, cast him in a whole new light. By the time he and Steph were sitting at their new table with a takeaway, it was starting to get dark outside.

"What are we unpacking next?" Joe asked.

"Nothing, I've already unpacked the bedroom and made the bed up."

"But what about…" Joe started, then realised what was being implied. "The rest of it can wait until tomorrow, can't it?"

"I knew you'd get the idea," Steph smiled. She picked up the half-empty bottle of wine, and Joe followed her into the bedroom.

CHAPTER FORTY - SEVEN

The plan to visit the gallery after David and Angela's conversation went ahead, but with some revisions. Angela had got used to going out, but with Deb as her crutch. She had crossed the road to ask her if she would come. Deb was happy to go along with Angela. She offered to drive her there and stay with her.
"But Elsie will want to come too," she told her.

"Elsie is my rock," Angela replied, "I would love for her to come. We can go straight to the park afterwards. It'll be a proper day out."

They arrived at the gallery the next morning, Deb and Elsie holding one of her hands each. Courtney greeted them at the door, putting up a sign reading 'closed for private viewing' on the door after they had all come in. David appeared nervous. Angela had asked him not to change anything, and he had left all her paintings on display. The two women and the little girl spent some time looking around, Angela taking it all in.

"These are your paintings, aren't they, Auntie Angela?" Elsie asked, pointing at some of Angela's work.

"Yes, yes, they are. Do you like them?"

"I like all your drawings," the girl answered. "I like the others too, are they your brothers?"

"They are, and I like them as well." She turned to David, "I never could draw like you, David, you have such a good eye for detail, and you catch the atmosphere of places so well. I'm glad the gallery is doing well. But do people really pay that much for my paintings?"

"To be honest, I think they'd pay more than that. People adore them. Quite rightly, they're very good."

"Well, isn't that something. I have to admit, it's good to see them again. I didn't look at them properly at the time, it was all about the doing."

"We need to sort out how we're going to display them now. I need to make sure people know they're yours. I can't keep passing them off as my own."

"No, I guess not. It's going to take some getting used to, being a famous artist."

"Do you think you'll be up to the publicity? I can arrange a press release if you are."

Angela looked at Deb and Elsie.

"What do you two think? Will you help me with this?"

"Yes," said Elsie, without pause.

"I will," Deb answered, "but why stop at a press release? Why not get someone to write an actual article about it, like Joe and Steph had said they were going to? I think it would make a great story."

Angela smiled.

"I like that idea, we could get them involved too, it was their detective work that unravelled things first. Also, I quite liked them, they were nice."

"I'll get Courtney to give them a call, shall I?" David asked.

"No, it's okay, I've got their number. I think I'd like to see them again, to thank them."

"Okay, I'll start asking around some of my contacts to see if anybody is interested in writing the story. I know quite a few of the art critics on various newspapers, if they're not up for it, I'm sure they'll know someone who is."

With that settled, they sat together and had tea (and orange juice) with biscuits. Courtney was invited to join them as David explained how he intended to rearrange the gallery into two distinct parts, one for each of the Hacers. He wanted Angela to be involved, if she felt up to it, and to add some of the new pieces she'd been working on recently.

She was hesitant until Deb gave her hand a gentle squeeze. In that moment, she knew she could do it. There would be difficult days and setbacks, of course, because life was like that. But this was what she had been building up to, and now that David had put it into words, she knew it was what she wanted. She got up and hugged her brother.

"I'm sorry it's taken so long, thank you for being there for me."

"No, I'm sorry. Sorry that I wasn't there when you needed me most. I'm glad you're back now."

They both looked as if they were on the verge of tears. The tension of the moment was broken when Elsie asked,

"Are we going to the park now? I've finished my juice."

CHAPTER FORTY - EIGHT

One of the first things Joe and Steph did, once they were unpacked and settled in, was to invite Mike and Tanya over for a meal. Neither of them had much experience of cooking for other people, but with Steph's parents on the end of the phone to offer assistance, they managed to put together a fine spread. Joe only had to run back out to the shops twice for ingredients that they didn't have.

Mike arrived with a housewarming present. A bottle of wine and a large rectangular parcel, neatly wrapped in a way that suggested that Tanya had been in charge of that department. Mike had chosen the card, a sombre-looking bunch of flowers and the message 'please pass on our sincere condolences to your new neighbours'. Joe supposed it could have been worse when he recalled some of the cards Mike had given him in the past.

Steph unwrapped the gift to reveal a beautifully framed colour enlargement of one of Angela's paintings.

"Oh, it's beautiful, thank you both. That's going on the wall in here, I love it."

"I'm just returning the favour, you did the same for me, Joe, for my housewarming."

Joe recalled that he had indeed done that, although it hadn't been entirely altruistic; he had been living there after all.

"You can keep that there until you two highfliers have saved up enough to buy an original."

They laughed, the evening went well, and after everyone had eaten a bit too much and drunk a little more than they should have, Joe and Steph were left sitting on their sofa together.

"That was a good night, your friend Mike really is the best, isn't he?"

"He's a good mate, I literally don't know what I would have done without him."

"I like the picture."

"Me too, I wish we had enough to buy an original, though. I can't believe how much they cost."

"Well, who knows? One day, when the prints are going well."

Their new enterprise at Griffin Graphics had reached the stage of producing prototypes of some of the prints they had chosen. It helped with the final costings and quality checks. Soon, it would be all hands on deck with getting the marketing and sales sorted. Hopefully, they would be able to piggyback on Griffin's existing marketing campaign while they developed their own. Everything was on track, and Tom was pleased with the progress they had made.

"Anyway, I'm going to turn in. Coming?"

"We haven't finished tidying yet."

"It's okay, we can do it tomorrow."

Joe was beginning to realise that this was the kind of compromise you had to make when you were in a relationship, just like the way he was having to ignore the shelves full of unknown and unknowable lotions, unguents and ointments in the bathroom. He frowned at the empty glasses and bowls of nibbles, then followed Steph into the bedroom.

CHAPTER FORTY - NINE

Angela arranged to meet Joe and Steph at her house. They had been surprised to hear from her, thinking that their part in unravelling the mystery of the painting had come to an end. They had agreed on a time and turned up bearing a gift of cookies.
"I don't think they'll be as nice as the ones your friend Deb made," Steph told her, "but my baking skills aren't up to much, I'm afraid."

"Nonsense," Angela retorted, "They'll be perfect. I'll go and put the kettle on, you two take a seat, you know where you're going."

They did as they were told and waited for Angela to join them, which she did, carrying a tray with the tea and the cookies arranged on a plate. She set them down, sat across from them and was about to speak when Joe beat her to it.

"I'm sorry if we caused any bother, it wasn't what we meant to do, it just sort of happened."

"You didn't, it would have all come out eventually. You may have hurried things up slightly, but you also helped a great deal. Anyway, now that I know you're not writing an article about David, I want to know who you are."

Between them, they gave their potted histories and told her about their current venture. Angela listened without interruption until they got to this point.

"So you're setting up your own printing business?"

"Umh, well, not exactly. My dad owns the company, we'll be doing business under the umbrella of Griffin Graphics. We're lucky to get a chance to do this; it's only happening because of Joe."

She looked at him, certain that he was going to blush. He didn't.

"Yeah, I kind of got the idea because of you really."

"Because of me?"

"When we first found your pictures in the book, my friend Mike liked them so much that I made photocopies of them and put them in a frame for him. I kind of owed him one; he was putting me up while I had nowhere to live. Sorry, I know that's not ethical – or legal, I didn't do it to make money."

"Don't be silly, I'm flattered. Hold on a minute."

She got up and left the room, returning moments later with a sketchbook that she started to flick through.

"Which one do you think your friend would like?"

"I couldn't, that would be too much."

"Nonsense, here, this is a good one."

She carefully pulled a page from the book, then took a pen from the small table beside her chair.

"Mike, wasn't it?"

"Yes, but that's too much. It's worth hundreds of pounds."

"It's worth what someone can pay for it. Is your friend Mike rich?"

"No, he's a removal man."

"Is he a good friend?"

"Yes, he looked after me when I had nowhere else to go."

"Then he's a good friend, and he deserves it."

She wrote 'To Mike – a good friend' in the space at the bottom of the page and signed it before passing it to Joe.

"Thank you, he'll love it. I'll get it framed for him."

"Good. Now, tell me more about your printing business. Tell me everything."

CHAPTER FIFTY

Deb and Angela were back in the gallery. Elsie was playing in the corner with a selection of toys that she had brought from home. Courtney was supervising her, which mostly seemed to involve her forgetting she was in her business clothes and crawling on the carpet, joining in with Elsie's games.

"I'll miss having her around when she starts school." She told Angela.

"Me too, although I'm sure it will make the weekends and holidays even more special. Are you going to go back to work?"

"Probably, hopefully. I don't want to go back to my old job, though. I never got passed being a junior, even after six years working for them. They kept saying it would be next year, but it never was."

"So what did you used to do?" Angela asked. She couldn't think why she'd never asked this before, probably because she'd only ever seen Deb being a mum.

"I was an assistant project manager, although it was actually me who did all the work; my boss just put his name to it and took the credit. It took me years to figure out what was going on."

Angela summoned David over to join them.

"Deb used to be - sorry, is- a project manager when she's not busy being a fantastic mum."

David nodded, unsure of what response was required of him after this statement. Angela sighed and rolled her eyes.

"We have a project that needs managing. It's not your speciality, nor mine. I think we could use some help from her, don't you?"

David had no intention of contradicting his sister, so he agreed before asking,

"Yes. What project?"

"Well, my exhibition, of course. All the publicity that goes with that, plus the press release about how you've been pretending my paintings are yours, to protect me while I was ill. It's a lot of work, and it's keeping you from your new project."

David's new project had been inspired by recent events. He had been contacting hotels set in picturesque localities and offering to work on commissions for them. It was the cover that Steph had used to book her meeting with him; it had struck him as a good idea, and he already had some interested responses.

"Okay, what else will she do? Sorry, Deb, I don't mean to be rude, I'm just getting my head around the idea."

"Me too," she replied. Angela took no notice.

"She'll be liaising with Steph and Joe. If my pictures have to be out in the wild, I want anyone who likes them to be able to get a copy without taking out a bank loan. Steph and Joe are in the middle of setting up a fine art printing company as part of Griffin Graphics. I'm sure they'll want to be involved with this, being superfans and everything."

She continued,

"Also, I want some of the profits to go to charity, to support other women who were in my position. Victims of violence and abuse. That will need to be managed too."

She looked across at Courtney, who was now sitting with Elsie on her lap, reading her a story from a picture book.

"Do you think you'd be able to work with Courtney, Deb? I'm sure she could do a lot more than David currently lets her. Then you wouldn't need to be around in the holidays or after school."

"I think she already has the seal of approval from my boss," answered Deb.

"Good, I think we're going to smash this."

"So, are you running the gallery now?" asked David.

"I used to run a whole accountancy department. I think between us, we can make this into something even bigger and better than what you've already done. I also think we could help a lot of people at the same time. I'm quite excited about it now that I'm here."

"So, I get to spend more time painting?" asked David. There was relief in his voice.

"Yes, but you'll be the public face of the gallery. I'm not ready for that yet."

"I'll talk to Gareth about it," said Deb. "It seems like too good an opportunity to miss, though."

"So this is all agreed then?" Angela asked.

"Well, we haven't asked Courtney yet," David pointed out.

"I was listening," she called from the floor where a rabbit drawing competition was now in progress. "It's fine with me, I'd like to have a bit more to do."

"Okay," Angela clapped her hands together excitedly, "let's get started. I'll ring Joe and Steph."

CHAPTER FIFTY - ONE

It was the first time Joe had been to anything as well-heeled as a launch party. Tom had given them some money to get new outfits. "You've got to look your best if you're representing Griffin," he told them.

Steph had chosen a blue, sparkly cocktail dress for herself. Joe thought she looked super sexy in it, but he was worried that he would embarrass her by looking like a toddler who had tried to dress itself for the first time. He shouldn't have worried, Steph helped him pick out a suit, his first suit. With her help, he managed to get something that didn't look like he was recycling his old school uniform or dressed like a used car salesman. A dark blue, well-fitted, casual-looking ensemble that he thought he looked pretty good in.

They arrived early, as Angela had requested. She greeted them like old friends, which wasn't entirely wrong, as they had seen a lot of her recently. Joe had been helping her select which of her works should be made into limited edition prints. There were far more pictures to choose from than Joe or Steph had anticipated. He had loved having the opportunity to go through them, knowing that he was the first person to see some of them, apart from the artist herself. They had started to produce some of them alongside the pictures from Griffin's archive, and had been regular visitors to Angela's house with samples and test runs.

During these meetings, they got to know more about each other, and Deb, who was frequently there with her daughter when they called. Angela was delighted when they told her about their informal book club, the one that had only happened because of the drawings they had found inside one of her old books. The following week, Angela and Deb had turned up unannounced at the shop on Friday afternoon to meet Janet. Angela appeared to be revelling in her new social life. From the moment she met Janet, it was as if they had been friends for years. Joe wasn't sure, but he thought that their book club may have just increased its membership.

As a direct result of this, Janet was at the party. She was wearing a black dress that someone had donated to the shop. Joe didn't know much about dresses, but it was from a famous fashion house, apparently, and it looked fantastic. She was standing, talking to Tom, who had become reacquainted with his old college friend David Hacer as a result of Steph and Joe's venture. As Joe looked around the crowded room, he realised that everybody important in his life was in this room. Tanya had even got Mike to wear a jacket and tie for the evening, although the tie was already half undone and would undoubtedly be in his pocket within the next half hour.

The paintings lining the wall were exclusively Angela's, not a landscape in sight. It was a beautiful sight, a huge mess of colour and pattern, and hidden pictures. There were also signed, framed prints of the work on sale, fresh from Griffin Prints (as Joe and Steph's sideline was now officially titled). Steph took his hand in hers.

"Isn't it wonderful?" she said.

Joe agreed,

"It's fantastic, I'm glad Angela came. I wasn't sure that she would."

They had both seen how nervous Angela had been about the event beforehand. But now she was here, she was mingling with the various guests and looking entirely at ease with the situation. Before the doors officially opened, a small group of journalists had been given a preview and an interview with David and Angela. The siblings had related the story of how David had initially sold the paintings as his own to protect his sister. But now she was ready to take ownership; she had joined in with some hesitation at first, but with increasing enthusiasm as the event went on. Photos were taken and follow-up interviews were arranged by one writer, who wanted to write an extended piece for a national paper.

Steph stayed by his side. They both tried to play down any part they may have had in the story, but the other people involved all kept directing questions towards them and insisting that they had solved the riddle. Joe supposed that they had, in a way. But he also knew that all the courage and skill and determination belonged to other people.

"How many glasses of fizz have you had now?" Steph asked him.

"Umh, not sure. This may be my fourth. Is that bad?"

"No, but you may want to slow down a bit, there's still a little while to go."

"I know, but I'm just so happy. All my favourite people in the whole world are here, and I love you." He reached out to put his arm around her waist, meaning to kiss her, but somehow he missed. He half fell and wine slopped out of the top of his glass, splashing onto the floor.

"Oops, you're right, maybe I have had enough. I think I might need some fresh air."

"Come on," Steph guided him gently through the groups of guests and out of the front door. "Just take a few deep breaths, I'll pop back in and get you some water."

"Don't go, I'll miss you."

"I'll be right back, just lean against the wall," Steph laughed. "Honestly, I can't take you anywhere."

"You can, you just have to remember to take me back the next day, to apologise."

"Ha ha, wait there, I'm coming back."

Steph went back in and grabbed one of the small bottles of water from the table next to the reception desk. Janet saw her.

"Is Joe okay? She asked.

"Just a little bit tipsy. He didn't have anything to eat before we came out, the bubbles have gone to his head."

"Do you need a hand?"

"No, not unless you want him to start telling you how much he loves you, too."

Janet smiled.

"Happy drunk then? You'd better get back to him before he decides to go off looking for a puppy to adopt."

"That sounds like him. See you later."

She went back outside and looked over to where she'd left Joe. He was leaning against the wall with his head tipped back, his eyes closed, and a smile on his face. A woman in her forties with shoulder-length dark hair and a long brown coat was walking towards him from the opposite direction. They both reached him at the same time, and Steph stepped aside, expecting her to walk on past. She didn't; she stopped and looked at Steph's slightly drunk boyfriend, who opened his eyes and looked at her. He took a brief moment to register who it was, then spoke a single word,

"Mum."

What happened next was a little confusing. Joe started looking around for Steph, who came and took his hand. The woman, Joe's mum, started to talk to him. But she was talking too quickly, trying to get all the words she wanted to say out at once and ending up with an unintelligible gabble. Steph looked hopefully around to see if anybody else might come to the rescue, but they didn't. Then Joe tensed up; she could see it in his face and feel it in the grip he had on her hand. He stood upright and demanded,

"What are you doing here?"

There was nothing friendly or curious in the way he asked it. His mum started to answer, but before she could get more than a few words out, Joe turned abruptly to Steph.

"Take me home," he said, "now, please."

He started to walk away, and Steph went with him, leaving the woman standing alone. Steph looked back and saw the look on her face, crumpled and defeated.

"Joe, slow down. What's up?"

He paused and looked at her.

"She doesn't want me to have anything nice or good. I expect Trevor sent her to ruin this evening." He turned to his mum, "Happy? Tell him it worked, let him know he spoiled it. Oh, and tell him he's a dick."

"Joe, it's not that…" his mum started. But before she could say anything else, Joe had started to walk again, taking Steph with him in the direction of the bus stop. They didn't even make it that far. Joe flagged down a passing taxi.

"Don't you want to go back in and say goodbye to everyone?" asked Steph.

"No, I don't want them to see me like this," Joe answered. He turned, and Steph saw that his cheeks were wet with tears. She made sure he didn't bump his head on the taxi roof as he climbed in, then gave the driver directions as she got in beside him. Joe's mum stood and watched as the taxi drove along the road and disappeared around the corner.

When Joe woke up, Steph was already sitting in the kitchen with a steaming mug in front of her. He shuffled to the counter, where there was a drink waiting for him. He picked it up and turned to look at her.

"Sorry," he said.

When they had got home, he'd gone for a walk to clear his head. He'd come back nearly an hour later, thrown his shoes and jacket in the corner, and got the blankets to cover himself with before curling up on the settee. Each time Steph had tried to talk to him, he had pulled the blankets tighter and ignored her, stewing in his anger. Eventually, she had given up and gone to bed.

Now she was on the other side of the table, looking at him. Not with the reproach that he had expected, but with concern.

"Are you okay? You were quite cross last night."

"No, I wasn't, I was bloody furious. It was the best night of my life, and she came just to spoil it."

"I'm sure she didn't, but I'm sorry it made you feel that way; it must have been awful."

"I'm sure she did, and yes, it was." He could still feel the anger and resentment rising inside him, just from thinking about it.

"Okay, do you want some toast?"

"I may have some paracetamol first," he touched his head gingerly and started to get up.

"No, stay there, I'll get them for you." She went to the kitchen drawer that had been designated as the place to keep the medicines.

"Why are you being so nice to me? I was horrible last night."

"Because we're a couple, we support each other. And you weren't horrible, you were upset, and I understand why. So that's what we do." She put the box of tablets in his hand and bent down to kiss him.

She had been fielding messages all morning asking about their sudden departure and if Joe was okay. She'd told everyone he'd just had a bit too much to drink and needed to lie down. Except Mike, because he knew what had happened. He'd told her on the phone earlier that he had followed her outside to check that Joe was okay; he'd witnessed the altercation, although they hadn't seen him as they hurried past.

A day or two earlier, Joe's mum had recognised Mike in the supermarket and stopped to say hello. He'd always liked her when they were kids, so he didn't mind stopping for a chat. She'd known that Joe had been staying with him, and had assumed he still was. Mike had corrected this misapprehension, telling her about Joe's job, his new flat and the launch party. She had been pleased to hear all about it and had asked lots of questions. Mike was pretty sure he would be standing there talking to her still if he hadn't politely made his excuses; he had no idea that she was going to turn up at the gallery. He'd apologised profusely to Steph on the phone, and she had assured him it wasn't his fault.

Joe swallowed down two of the painkillers with his tea. He looked sheepishly at Steph.

"I don't support you much, though, do I?"

"You do, by being you. You are kind and thoughtful, you let me be who I want to be, and you don't treat me like I'm stupid or inferior."

It had never occurred to Joe that there would be any other way to treat someone, especially someone you loved. Then he thought of Trevor and the way he had been with Mum.

"What was it my mum was trying to say last night anyway?"

"I don't know, you never gave her a chance to say whatever it was."

Joe looked down at the table.

"Was I awful to her?"

"You weren't nice, but I get it, they did throw you out."

"I know, but even so…"

"Do you want me to talk to her? Find out what she wanted."

"I ought to, I don't know her number though."

"Don't know her number? How can you not know your mum's number?"

"It was on my old phone, I don't remember it. I didn't put it on the new phone because she never used to answer it anyway."

"So she doesn't have your number either?"

"I guess not, no."

"So it's no wonder she came to find you. I'll give Mike a call and see if he has her number."

"Eh? Why would Mike have my mum's number?"

"Never mind, I'll explain later. Go and have a shower."

Joe finished his tea and went to stand in the shower for twenty minutes or so. By the time he got back, there was a fresh cup of tea, toast in the toaster and a phone number written on a piece of paper on the table.

"I'll leave you in peace for a bit if you want to call her."

"I suppose I'd better, hadn't I?"

He looked as if he would rather be doing anything but.

"You could. Once you find out what she wanted, you can always block her number afterwards if you want."

Steph left the room, and Joe reluctantly picked up his phone and started to enter the number.

CHAPTER FIFTY - TWO

The launch had been a great success, even though Angela had been nervous about it beforehand. But once it had got underway, she had been swept up by it, her caution and reticence being forgotten after the first half hour. Having her friends and family around her had been the key to the success of the evening, although she hadn't had a chance to say goodnight to Steph and Joe, who had disappeared halfway through the evening.
David had stayed with her for the first part of the evening, being his usual protective brother self. Deb and Gareth took over later, no Elsie though. She had been disappointed when she found out it was an adults-only event, but cheered up when Angela promised to take her for an ice cream the next day and tell her all about it. By the end, after a couple of glasses of wine, she found she was perfectly comfortable in the group of people. She knew it wouldn't always be like this, that there would be bad days, but for now, it was enough.

Her paintings had been well received, many had been purchased, and the prints had almost sold out. The journalists and critics who had attended had been more than complimentary, and the back story had caused a lot of excitement. There were promises of extended articles and full colour spreads in numerous papers and magazines, which she was both excited and nervous about.

Now, sitting in her kitchen, she was able to look back on the past few months. She knew it had been a team effort and was grateful for the support and love that she had had from everyone. But she was also proud of herself for finally managing to put the traumatic events of her past behind her, relegating them to the 'awful things that happened' box in the back of her mind.

She was expecting David to come around later. Ostensibly to check how she was doing, but actually wanting to talk about the evening and how well it had gone. He'd bustle in enthusiastically, talking excitedly about how great everything was, barely giving Angela time to answer. Today, she decided, she wouldn't mind.

She subconsciously traced the tip of her index finger along the lines of scars on her left arm and thought, for the first time since she could remember, about the future.

CHAPTER FIFTY - THREE

It wasn't easy, but then, nothing that's worthwhile is. Griffin Prints managed to break even in its first year. Tom assured Steph and Joe that this was normal, good even. When he started the company, he told them he ran at a loss for two years. They put in the hours and worked hard to show a profit in the second year, much of this thanks to the relationship with Angela and the exclusive rights she had given them to reproduce her work. As her popularity grew, so did the business.

There was also the not inconsiderable rewards from a distribution deal with a national charity. They had been so thrilled with the publicity from the Angela Hacer story and how one of their shops had been the centre of the mystery, that they were happy to stock posters in their network of shops. They had even approached Angela to help redesign their shop logo in her distinctive and colourful way.

With all this going on, Joe and Steph's flat became their subterranean sanctuary. The place where they could be themselves and recharge their batteries. The place where they grew to know one another and cement their relationship. It was difficult for both of them sometimes, knowing when to make compromises, finding the best way to resolve arguments, and discovering the beautiful things about one another that you only find out in the fullness of time.

Over this period, Joe managed a reconciliation with his mum. It was rocky at first, with Joe finding his anger frequently threatening to rear its ugly head. But Trevor was no longer in the picture, which paved the way for a fresh start. There was a lot to put right, and nothing that wasn't going to take time. But for now, their fractured relationship was beginning to mend.

It was a miserable evening in November, and Joe and Steph were nestled in the warmth and safety of their underground flat, with rain lashing against the window and the distant sound of the wind making its presence known outside. Joe looked up from his book and asked,

"Should we get married?"

Steph looked up from her own book,

"What?"

"Well, you know, it's what people do, isn't it?"

"Yes, people do. Do you want to?"

"I don't know, I just thought…well, we're living together, and we love each other…"

He tailed off as Steph continued to look at him over the top of her book.

"Are you proposing to me?" she asked.

"What? No, well, I don't know, am I?"

"Oh God, I love it when you go that colour."

Joe felt himself blush even more.

"The answer is yes, by the way," Steph told him.

CHAPTER FIFTY - FOUR

The new picture took pride of place in the sitting room. The canvas was a mass of colour, different bands of various hues forming concentric circles that merged and mixed at seemingly random intervals across the surface, creating a kaleidoscopic effect. At a glance, you could easily mistake it for a piece of tie-dye material or maybe an exotic batik.

But if you looked at it closely, and in just the right way, you could make out other images hiding in its midst. Familiar figures and places, all sitting within the swirls and patterns that enveloped them. The outlines and contours of the secret parts of the painting are not clearly defined, blending, as they do, with the colours and shapes that surround them. Lines and curves are carved, chiselled, scratched and scored into the thick layers of paint, creating tiny reflections and subtle shadows among the undulating contours.

Look in the centre of the picture and you can find a house. Not just any house, but the exact house that the painting now resides in. A small end-of-terrace home with a blue door (see how the blue covers the whole of the centre, but seems somehow more vital and energetic at this point).

In the top right corner, a girl in a bridesmaid's dress smiles out of the green mist that surrounds her. She is standing with her mum, who is also smiling. Although it is not shown in the painting, it is somehow evident that it is a bright June afternoon. The two of them are almost angelic, with halos of sunlight seeming to appear from behind their heads.

In the bottom left, there is the suggestion of a group of people. They are standing near but not close to one another, friends, but not family. One has long, red hair, and another sports a beard that almost, but not quite, hides his beaming smile as he leans towards his partner. There is a younger man with tousled hair and his arm around a young woman.

Lastly, in the bottom right corner are a couple. They are as close together as they can get, arms around one another, expressions of joy on their faces. Because of the colours of the painting, her dress appears purple. Despite this, it is obviously a wedding dress, flowing and falling around her. Examine her more carefully, and you can see that the dress has a rounded bulge at the front. It could be the way the pattern of the painting distorts the image, or a slip of the brush. But it's not.

This painting is the newest addition to this house. There are many new additions to the house, the home that was only moved into a few months ago. The home that is at the centre of the universe for the people that live there, the couple in the bottom corner of the painting. Under their almost invisible feet are the words 'Angela Hacer'.

Steve Beed was born in 1964. He has three adult children and a beautiful wife. He lives in a small coastal town in the southwest of England and has published five novels and one novella:

Nothing Happened in 1986

Nothing Else Happened in 2011

Bloglin

Smartphone

King of the Car Park

The Stupid Things We Did When We Were Kids

These can all be found via his author page on Amazon.

You are welcome to write and let him know if you enjoyed this book at:

Stevebeed64@gmail.com

In return, I will add you to my mailing list and let you know about any forthcoming releases.

You can follow his blog at:

https://steevbeed.wordpress.com

Printed in Dunstable, United Kingdom